she

was going to say something. Then changed her mind. I hated that. It was like knowing a secret was there. And the secret was about you. Knowing it was there, well, it hurt. "You're nice," she finally said. Nice, I thought. There were better compliments. She smiled. "Someone's gonna hurt you. And you're gonna wish you never had a heart."

sammy

and

juliana

in

hollywood

benjamin alire sáenz

rayo

HARPERTEMPEST

An Imprint of HarperCollinsPublishers

Rayo is an imprint of HarperCollins Publishers.

HarperTempest is an imprint of HarperCollins Publishers.

Sammy and Juliana in Hollywood.
Copyright © 2004 by Benjamin Alire Sáenz.

Library of Congress Cataloging-in-Publication Data
Sáenz, Benjamin Alire.
Sammy and Juliana in Hollywood / Benjamin Alire Sáenz.— 1st
HarperTempest pbk. ed.
p.   cm.
Summary: As a Chicano boy living in the unglamorous town of Hollywood,
New Mexico, and a member of the graduating class of 1969, Sammy Santos faces
the challenges of "gringo" racism, unpopular dress codes, the Vietnam War, barrio
violence, and poverty.
ISBN-10: 0-06-084374-8 (pbk.) — ISBN-13: 978-0-06-084374-8 (pbk.)
[1. Death—Fiction. 2. Grief—Fiction. 3. Violence—Fiction. 4. Mexican
Americans—Fiction.] I. Title.
PZ7.S1273Sam 2006   2005028688
[Fic]—dc22

Typography by Sa
First HarperTempe
Published by arrangement with Cin

For Amanda, Roberto, John,
Cynthia, Mark, Isel, Nana
and in memory of Amy

Every generation has to
find its own way.
Embrace the journey.

contents

"**The**

first thing the dead do is lose their voices. But they have their ways of making us listen. Maybe the dead need those of us who made it out alive to go out into the streets and tell everyone what happened. Maybe they want us to do more than tell. Maybe they want us to shout. Maybe they want us to point fingers. Maybe they want us to tell anyone who'll stop and listen that once, the world was theirs, too. Maybe they won't leave us alone until we say their names out loud again and again and again."

—Sammy Santos

the way she looked at me

"If you just talk, Juliana,
you can talk yourself into being alive."

"Let's not say anything, Sammy.
Let's not say anything at all."

one

I remember her eyes, the gray of a sky about to let loose a storm. I remember the way she placed her finger on her bottom lip when she was lost in thoughts as dark as her eyes. I'd have given anything to live that close to her lips.

I used to picture her eyes as I was lying in bed. Her eyes and that finger touching her bottom lip. I'd lie there and listen to the radio on my favorite station, K-O-M-A in Oklahoma City. It reached me all the way to where I lived in southern New Mexico. But it could only reach me at night. Just at night. I used to wait and hope they'd play that song by Frankie Valle *You're just too good* . . . Even if I was half asleep, if I heard the song, I'd suddenly be awake. I'd hum along and put together a scene: a girl dressed up for me and a dance floor shiny as glass. Even the ice cubes in our drinks sparkled in the light. That girl was Juliana. And the whole damned world was mine. *I need you ba-a-by* . . . And then, after the song was over, I'd fall asleep exhausted from trying to keep the two of us together. Being obsessed with Juliana was hard work. The word obsession came into my vocabulary the second I met Juliana.

It was the way she looked at me that kept me coming back. Just as I was about to give up on her, just as I was about to tell her, "Look, screw it all. I don't need to suffer like this. Just can't take it." Every time I was about to tell her something like that, she stretched out her arm and made a fist. She'd tap her fist with her other hand, until I nodded and pried it open. I would stare at her open palm, and she would ask: "Do you see?"

And I would nod and say, "I see."

"You see everything now, don't you?"

"Yes, everything," I'd say.

"You see everything."

"Yes. Todo, todo, todo."

Now, when I think of her open, outstretched hand, I have to admit I didn't see a thing. I see my lips moving, "Yes, todo, todo." I wonder why I lied to her. Maybe it wasn't a bad lie. Maybe it was. Maybe there aren't any good lies. I don't know. I still don't know. And I didn't know anything about reading palms either. I've never known anything about that. Not then. Not now. One thing I did know—no matter how many times she let me pry her hand open, her fists were still clenched. They'd stay that way forever.

Juliana letting me pry open her fist. That was a lie. Maybe it was a good lie. I think it was.

I told her once that she collected secrets like some people collected stamps.

"You're full of shit," she said. "Where do you get that crap? You're so full of shit."

"No, I'm not," I said.

"Well," she said, "everyone needs to collect something."

"Collect something else," I said.

"Like what?"

"Books."

"No, I don't like them. That's *your* thing, Sammy. Did you know everyone calls you 'the Librarian'?" She looked at me. I pretended I knew. I didn't. But I pretended. And she let me. "And besides," she said, "only gringos can afford books. But secrets don't cost a damn thing."

She was wrong about that. Secrets cost plenty.

I used to write her notes in class that said, "Stop collecting."

"Not yet," she'd write back.

"Then tell me one. Just one secret." What did I think she was going to tell me?

The first time she told me what she was thinking, I found myself trembling. "I've always wanted to smoke a cigarette." That's what she whispered. I pictured her wearing a backless dress in some smoky bar with a cigarette between her lips. A drink in her hand. I pictured my hand on her bare back—

that's what made me tremble. And that song came into my head *you'd be like*…I almost offered to buy her a pack, buy her two packs, buy her a carton. But I was sixteen and could never talk when I needed to—and my pockets were empty. So I just stood there trying to figure out what to do with my hands. I wanted to die.

That night, I decided to be a man. I was tired of sitting there like a chair. That was me. Sammy Santos. A chair. Sitting there. Thinking. As if thinking ever did any good. To hell with everything. After dinner, I walked out of the house, borrowed Paco's bike and stole two cases of Dr Pepper bottles from Mrs. Franco. She had a nice house. She didn't live in Hollywood. She didn't need the bottles. I cashed them in at the Pic Quick on Solano—and bought my first pack of cigarettes. My dad wanted to know where I was. "Just taking a walk," I said.

Dad's smile almost broke me. "You're like your mom," he said. "She'd walk and think. You take after her." He looked so happy. If you can be happy and sad at the same time. That's how he looked when he talked about her.

I hated to lie to him. But I couldn't tell him I was stealing Dr Pepper bottles from Mrs. Franco. I couldn't. He thought I was some kind of altar boy. He never went a week without telling me I was good. Good? What's that? Sometimes I wanted to yell, "You don't know, Dad. You don't know these things." I wanted to yell that. It would have broken his heart.

Later, in bed, I held the red pack of Marlboros and studied

it like I was going to be tested on what it looked like. I smelled the cigarettes through the cellophane—and it was then that I fell in love with the smell of tobacco. The next day, during lunch, I offered Juliana the pack of cigarettes. She stared at my hand, that trembling hand of mine, holding out the pack of cigarettes. She took them. Real casual. But there was something in her eyes. Something. She put them in her purse. Then she stared into my palm. "You work," she said. It was true. I got up at four to clean seedy bars for Speed Sweep Janitor Service. "We can sweep anything you can own." That was our motto. Every day from 4:30 to 7:00, I worked. Worked, came home, showered—then fixed breakfast for me and my sister. "Everyone works," I said.

She was going to say something. Then changed her mind. I hated that. It was like knowing a secret was there. And the secret was about you. Knowing it was there, well, it hurt. "You're nice," she finally said. Nice, I thought. There were better compliments. She smiled. "Someone's gonna hurt you. And you're gonna wish you never had a heart."

I wanted to tell her that my mom had died, and that I already knew about hurt. I didn't say that, didn't say anything. Nothing. I just watched her walk away, my eyes following her until she disappeared like a sun taking a slow dive into the earth.

Everything was darker when she was gone.

She knew something about hurt, too. But she knew how to

fight back, and she could scare you into silence with just a look. It wasn't that she was ugly or mean—it's just that she'd learned certain ways. The world wasn't all that good to her, and she wanted to remind everyone around her—but mostly herself, I think—that she was worth something. That the air was hers, too. That the ground she walked on was as much hers as it was anybody else's. She was so afraid of being beaten down. I think that came from having a father who wanted to crush her until she turned into powder. So the wind could blow her away. Then she'd be nothing.

I remember what she told me. I remember exactly. "When I was four, I fell off a swing at a park. I dirtied my dress. My father just kinda looked at me. Like I was dirty. And I knew right then he didn't care if I sat in that dirt for the rest of my life. I think he was disappointed when I didn't cry. I got up, dusted myself off and got back on the swing. But I never forgot that look. He hated me. And there was nothing I could do about it. I tried to make him change his mind about me, but nothing worked. I served him tea, I shined his shoes, I cooked meals for him. Once, I ironed his favorite shirt, and it was perfect. He grabbed it from my hands and wadded it up like a piece of paper. So I just gave up. I was twelve. When I was in the eighth grade, I read a story. The teacher made us look up words we didn't know. The word I was looking up was 'disdain.' And when I read the definition, I said to myself, 'Yeah, I know that word.'" That night, when she was telling me these things, we were smoking cigarettes in my dad's Chevy Impala. We were at the Aggie Drive-In Theater off Valley Drive. We'd turned down the speakers because we'd both already seen *The Odd Couple*. There was nothing real or interesting about that movie—watching it made us tired. It was supposed to be funny. I guess so. But it wasn't. Not to Juliana. Not to me. And Juliana said it was weird, the kind of movies gringos went mad for. "But you can't do anything about gringos," she said, "just like you can't do anything about fathers." And then she kept talking about her dad, and how he made sure he put everyone down. "If I'd have been born a bird, he'd have cut off my wings."

I wanted to tell her that I would kill myself if my father hated me. Every day, when my father came home from work, the first thing he did was rub my hair and tell me supper smelled good. I tried to cook like Mom. I did okay. And Dad always thanked me. That's the way he was, a thanker, always thanking people for the things they did. And damnit, I hated Juliana's father. I did. For not being like my father. For not knowing what he had. I did hate him. And finally, that's what I told her. "I hate him. I really hate him." That's what I said. And that was the first time she kissed me. She tasted like cotton candy. Not sticky, but sweet, as if something inside her was making up for the something she didn't have in the house where she lived.

"You're nice," she said. "Someone's gonna hurt you."

"Yeah. You've said that before."

"It's true." She kissed me again.

I kissed her back, hard as I could, and when she stopped she looked at me. "You were born to get hurt."

"Nope," I said. And then we just went back to kissing. We sat on the hood of the car and smoked all night. And kissed some more. I still remember her smell. She didn't wear perfume or jewelry like all the other girls. I liked that about her. She talked about how her mother would sometimes leave, but always come back, and she wondered why her mother wouldn't take them all with her when she left. "She just leaves us there—with him." I listened. I liked listening to her. I didn't care if the stories she told weren't soft or beautiful or nice. The barrio we lived in wasn't soft or beautiful or nice. It didn't matter that someone had named the barrio where we lived "Hollywood." Maybe it was a joke. Maybe it was a prayer. Didn't matter. Nice stories were hard to come by in Hollywood. So I just listened. Juliana said her aunt told her that she didn't have to worry about anything because she was born beautiful. But another aunt told her that she had to pay for her looks because nothing was free—not even good looks.

"Someday," Juliana said, "I swear I'm gonna kill my father. I'm gonna watch him bleed like he's a dog someone ran over in the middle of a busy street." It scared me to hear her talk like that. I knew she was picturing the scene in her mind.

And then, after she said that, it was me who kissed her. I

wanted to make her forget. I thought that a guy's kisses could make a girl forget all the bad stuff. Sixteen-year-old boys don't know shit. How could a tongue down a girl's throat make her forget?

Her eyes were always half on fire, lightning about to strike—and beautiful in the way that fires and lightning are beautiful, a kind of natural and graceful rage that made all living things stand back in awe. Or maybe just fear. Sometimes, she could look at you and you could see what she was trying to tell you *don't screw with me because I've been through things, and you don't know a damn thing about what it's cost me to be here, right here, right here on this worthless piece of ground, so don't treat me like I'm some crack on a sidewalk because if you step on me, you'll never take another step without thinking of me. I swear to God you won't.* I saw that look a hundred times. I took that look home with me. I studied it. I never understood. Not back then. How is that we can look at something every day, and still not know what we're looking at?

One time, she was walking out of the gym door and some guy looked at her and said, "Ayyyyy muñeca!" And then he made this motion thing with both his arms and body as if he was having sex with her against a wall. She walked up to him, got real close, then kneed him right in the place that made him a man. He bent down in pain, screaming like a boy. She stood there. Watched. When he was breathing right again, she smiled at him. "Now you can tell everyone what it was like to be with a girl from Hollywood."

Another time, this guy asked her out. It wasn't as if she belonged to me. It wasn't that way. Boyfriend, girlfriend, that kind of thing didn't mean that much. Not to her. It meant more to me, I think, but I was always a little soft, like my father. Manzito, my father used to say about himself. Tame. As in the opposite of wild. As in a dog that would never bite.

Sometimes, I wanted to tell Juliana that I was hers. She would've laughed.

So this guy asks her out, this good lookin' gringo basketball player who always walked around Las Cruces High like he'd bought and paid for the gym and the parking lot. He just walked up to Juliana in the hallway and said, "So what time should I pick you up on Friday?"

Juliana looked at him. "You asking me out?"

"Guess so," he said.

She looked at him. "What's your name?"

"Everybody knows my name," he said.

"I don't." Then she walked away from him.

"Where you going?" he yelled.

"To class," she said. "It's a school, you know."

He ran after her and grabbed her arm. "I asked you what time I should pick you up?"

All she did was look at him. She stared into his blue eyes, wanting him to see. She could be that way. When she wanted you to, she could make you see everything she felt. I saw the way she looked at him, and I knew what she was telling him, and I knew that she wanted him to remember what she was telling him for the rest of his worthless life: *You think I should be grateful because you'd drive into Hollywood to pick me up for a night, spread my legs for you, that's what you think, that's what you've made up in your head—and if you don't take your hand off me, I'll break it clean off your arm and feed it to the pit bull that lives next door to me —and I won't feel a thing, not for you, not for your worthless hand, are you getting all this?* She said all those things in the look she gave him—and I swear his jaw dropped. For the first time in his entitled life that son-ofabitch understood that the world was a helluva lot bigger than he'd ever dreamed it was. His coach had lied to him. Life wasn't a basketball game. The spring was gone from his steps as he walked away. God, that made me smile.

I remember almost everything about her. It was as if I was born to be her biographer, and knowing that, I began to take notes from the very beginning. Mostly I wrote those notes somewhere inside my head and my head became a chalk-board. I couldn't bring myself to erase anything I wrote there about her. And now I think I need to empty everything out—so I can have my body back. The thing is this, I know she'll always be inside me. Well, maybe it's not her that's inside me, but there's something. I can feel that something. I feel wings, sometimes. And it's like those wings are all caged up. And I'm the cage, and the wings are trying to find a way to get out. I don't know. It's confusing.

"Everyone's been seeing you with that girl."

"What girl, Dad?" I always pretended I didn't know what the hell was going on. That trick always worked for me.

"Tú sabes cual muchacha," my father said, "no te hagas tonto."

"You should see all the girls that are after me," I said.

"Really?" my little sister said, completely astonished. She was half my age and was addicted to other people's conversations. "Lots of girls are after you, Sammy?"

"Seguro," I said.

"I don't know about that," my father said, "but I know how many girls you're after. Ya te conozco. You're only after one. And her name's Juliana Ríos."

"Really?" Elena asked. "Her sister, Mariana, goes to my school."

I didn't say anything. My father's analysis of the situation sounded like an accusation—like I was committing a crime. "She's nice, Dad."

"Bueno, la muchacha tiene una cara muy bonita, pero eso no quiere decir que she's nice." My father looked down at his plate of food. He was an easy read. Any time he wanted to tell

16

me something, he'd look at his food as if the sopa or the beans on his plate were feeding him words. "You and Juliana aren't doing things, are you?"

"Like what things, Dad?"

"You know what I mean."

"I don't know what you mean," my little sister said.

"No, tell me," I said.

"Yeah," Elena said, "tell us."

"Never mind," my father said. But he couldn't quite give up on the subject, even though Elena was at the table. "What's she like?" he asked.

"She's good and she's pretty." I looked at Elena. "Isn't she pretty, Elena?"

Elena nodded. She was crazy, crazy for me and always ready to be my accomplice. "Beautiful," Elena said.

"And she's smart," I said.

"Does she study?" my dad asked.

"No. She doesn't have to. She just knows things, I guess. I don't know. She doesn't ever take her books home. But I saw her report card. All A's except two B's and one C."

"Not as good as yours," my father said.

"Yeah, but I have to study, Dad."

"Can she teach me how not to study?" Elena asked.

"No," my father told Elena. "It's better to study." He was very literal about earning things. He looked at me. "You don't give her the answers, do you?"

"No, Dad, I don't give her the answers." I wanted to tell him that she sure as hell didn't rely on me for the answers to anything. She found all the answers on her own. He didn't know her, my dad, didn't trust her. He thought she wasn't good enough for me. Nobody thought she was good enough. I wondered what that was like. If people looked at me like they looked at her, I'd be permanently pissed off. "Look, Dad," I said. "We're all the same. We're all from Hollywood."

"No. We're not all the same. Some of us are good, and some of us aren't. You're not like Pifas Espinosa or Joaquín Mesa or René Montoya. Or like Reyes Espinoza. You're not like any of them."

"You won't let me be like them."

"No tiene nada que ver conmigo. You have that wrong, mijo. If you were like those boys, then nothing I would do or say could tame you. You're not like them. You're just not."

I wanted to tell him that sometimes I wanted to be as wild as them. I hated myself sometimes for being so tame, like some docile cat who'd been declawed—good for nothing but sitting on the windowsill. What good was I? In Hollywood, I was useless. "I'm not better than them, Dad."

"Okay," he said.

And then I said, "She's a sweet girl, Dad."

"Sweet?"

"She is, Dad."

He looked at me and shook his head. "I know her family."

"No," I said, "you don't know her, Dad."

"Didn't she tell Mrs. López to—" he stopped and smiled at Elena. "She disrespected Mrs. López in front of the whole neighborhood."

"Mrs. López likes men, Dad."

"What's wrong with liking men?" Elena asked.

"Nothing," I said. I looked at my father. "Mrs. López disrespected Mrs. Ríos by inviting Mr. Ríos into her house. At night." I stopped, nodded at my father, and winked at Elena.

"People aren't supposed to visit each other at night, are they?" Elena asked.

"No," I said, "they're not. They're supposed to stay at home. Right, Dad?"

"Right," my father said, though I knew he thought it was wrong of Juliana to call Mrs. López a "puta desgraciada sinvergüenza" in front of everybody who was buying vegetables at Safeway. My father looked down at his plate again. "Well, I don't want you and Juliana smoking in my car anymore. No se porque fuman. Ya se creen muy grandes. You're just kids."

I nodded. He got up from the table, and he and Elena started cleaning up. Every night, they cleaned the kitchen together, and afterward, they'd eat ice cream and leave the bowls in the sink. I'd see their bowls sitting there on my way out the door in the morning. It was as if I took a piece of them with me. They were good together. Elena always had a hundred questions, and my father tried to answer all of them.

Sometimes, when I'm doing stuff, I picture the two of them, Elena and my dad. And I think about how both me and my dad always fought like hell to protect Elena—as if we could prevent all the crap around us from touching her. You know, the funny thing is that my dad, well, I used to think of him as being as common and decent and ordinary as a piece of gum. But after everything that has happened, well, I think I didn't know shit, not about my Dad anyway. What the hell did I know? What the hell did I know about the things he had to keep in his heart—the things he had to hide from us, the things he had to go through in order to save me and Elena? And why couldn't I have been a thanker like him?

I left them there, in the kitchen that evening. The two of them. As if they were always going to be there. I went to my room and called Juliana. Her father answered the phone and when I asked for her, all he said was: "Don't call here. That puta's not home. Just don't call here anymore. ¡Pinches cabrones, todos! ¡Todos!" I wanted to run out of the house, run down the block, break down his goddamned door and shove my fist down his throat. I pictured me beating on him. It made me feel better. I wonder if things would have turned out different if I had done something like that. Maybe, if I'd done that, the whole history of Hollywood would have turned out for the better.

two

"So what's the symbol for potassium?"

Birdwail, the chemistry teacher, looked right at Juliana. She gave him the right answer. "And the symbol for hydrogen and the symbol for aluminum and the symbol for magnesium and what are their valences?" He kept shooting questions at her. I swear they were bullets and he wanted to kill her. But she wasn't in the mood for dying. She answered them all. One after another, she answered all of Birdwail's useless questions.

"Very good," he said.

"You're surprised, aren't you?" She just stared at him.

"What?" he said.

"That I know."

"I don't know what you're trying to pull, Miss Ríos—"

"I can see it."

Birdwail ignored her question. He told us to turn to page 163 of our textbook.

Juliana got up, turned in her lab notebook and walked toward the door. "Last time, you gave me a B on my lab notebook because you said it was late. It wasn't late. And neither is this one. Now I have witnesses." She walked out the door.

"Come back here!" he yelled. "Come back here!" But she didn't. His face was on fire. "Read Chapter 11," he told us, then sat down at his desk and tried to pretend he was in control. But he kept muttering to himself. He caught me looking at him. I wanted him to see what I was holding in my eyes.

After school, I went looking for Juliana and found her at her locker. "Why did you do that?" I asked. "They're gonna—"

"I went to the principal's office," she said. Her voice was as calm and still as a hot summer afternoon. "I told him some girls liked Chemistry and Biology. Even Mexican girls. I told him Birdwail's job was to teach. To encourage. I told him Birdwail wasn't doing his job. And he said, 'Well, you can drop the class if you want. I'll make sure you won't need it to graduate.' I told him I didn't want to drop the class. I told him that I didn't want any trouble. I told him I earned A's in Birdwail's class and that I expected to get A's. 'A's,' he said. 'A's,' I said. And I just looked at him."

"And what did Fitz have to say after that?"

"He kept nodding, then finally said, 'You won't have any more trouble. I promise.'"

"Well, Birdwail still hates you," I said.

"He hates you, too."

"So?" I said.

"He gave you a B, too," she said. She gave me one of those looks. One of those looks that you didn't quite understand— except that you felt like you were the biggest idiot in southern New Mexico.

"So? It was just a lab notebook. I'll make it up."

"Why should you have to make it up, Sammy? He cheated you—he cheated both of us."

"Okay." I nodded. "So, you talked to the principal, huh?" I knew I was wearing that grin, the one that pissed Carlos Torres off. That grin. "So you won," I said.

"I'm from Hollywood. No one from Hollywood ever wins. We just don't always lose."

She pulled out a pack of cigarettes from her purse. She was a smoker now. A good one. She offered me one. We walked home. It was a long way to Hollywood, but we both hated the bus. "They think we're animals," she said.

"No, they don't."

"They think they're better."

"We don't always behave like—"

"So we don't always behave like them, Sammy. So what? You think those pendejos on the football team behave like people?" She looked at me as she lit her cigarette. Then lit mine. "You want to be like them, don't you?"

"Like the football players? Hell no."

"But you want to be like them, don't you?"

I couldn't look at her. "I don't want to live in Hollywood the rest of my life, that's all."

"I don't either, Sammy. But you don't have to be like them."

"You don't have to worry," I said.

"I worry," she said. She was warning me. Later, I understood what she was warning me about. And I wondered how she knew. She was sixteen. How did she know?

The next day, Birdwail didn't say anything as she walked into class. She was late, and he didn't say a word. Nada.

He handed back our lab notebooks. After what happened, I thought that he would break Juliana and me up as lab partners. But he didn't. He got us started on our experiments. When he came by, he stood over us and watched as Juliana carefully poured some chemicals into a beaker. He watched her every movement. I thought there was going to be more trouble. Maybe he wanted to rattle her cage. She completely ignored him. Finally, he said: "Your hands are steady. Very steady. You may have the hands of a surgeon, Miss Ríos."

"Yes," she said, "I've always been good with knives."

Every day, after school, I'd walk across the street to get my little sister from Mrs. Apodaca's house. I wasn't sure, but I think my father gave her a few bucks for watching Elena. Not that she was much trouble. She was sweet, Elena. One day, sweet Elena was on Mrs. Apodaca's front porch waiting for me. It was late, almost dark. She took my hand and we walked home. I turned on all the lights. I always did that, turned on all the lights. When my dad came home, he'd turn them off. It was like having an argument. I walked into the kitchen and Elena followed me. "Something happened," she whispered.

"What?" I said.

"A boy hit me."

"What?" I picked her up and put her on the kitchen counter. I examined her face. Her cheek was a little swollen. Not much. I kissed it. Elena laughed. "Let's put some ice on it," I said.

"No," she said. "Mrs. Apodaca did that already."

I nodded. "Who? Who hit you?"

"Pico."

"Pico who?"

"Pico Salazar."

"I know his brother," I said. "I'll go over there after supper."

"It's okay," Elena said. "Juliana fixed it."

"How did she fix it?"

"Well, I was playing tether ball with Gabby and Pico comes up to us and says we have to stop, because it's his turn. And I said we were here first. And Gabby says, yeah, and she told him he was nothing but a cucaracha, and I said, yeah, you're a cucaracha, and cucarachas had to wait their turn because we were here first, and if he didn't wait his turn someone was going to come along and step on him because that's what happened to cucarachas. And then Pico says that he's not a pinche cucaracha and if we don't move, he's going to have to hit one of us because girls have to do what boys tell them. And I say I don't have to do what any boy tells me to except my brother, Sammy, and he wasn't Sammy. And so he got mad and he punched me in the cheek. I didn't cry, Sammy. Well, I cried a little bit, but not a lot, and then Juliana comes up to us, and she grabs Pico and she says, 'If I ever see you hit a girl again, I'm going to kick your little Hollywood butt all the way to Mesilla.' And then he starts to cry, and then she tells him she's sorry and to stop crying, and that she didn't mean to hurt his feelings, but he shouldn't go around hitting girls— especially nice girls like me and Gabby, and she tells him again that she's sorry, and she gives him some gum and she gives me and Gabby gum, too—cinnamon—and she made Pico tell me he was sorry, and he said he was sorry and Gabby wanted to know if he still thought girls should do what boys said, and he said no and so Gabby said she was sorry for calling him a cucaracha. And that's what happened, Sammy." When Elena told you a story, it was as if she was running a race—the faster she talked, the better the story. And she never left anything out. I looked at her, and she kissed me. She was always kissing me, that kid. "Juliana likes you," she said.

"How do you know?"

"She said, 'You're Sammy's sister, ¿verdad?' I said yes.

'You're beautiful,' she said, 'just like your brother.' I'm beautiful, Sammy. Juliana said so. But how can boys be beautiful, too?"

"You'll have to ask Dad." I always let Dad handle the questions I had no answers for. I was the brother. Not the father.

That night, I called Juliana. I asked her if she had had a good day. Mostly she said no. But sometimes, sometimes she said yes. And that day, she said, "Yeah, Sammy, I had a good day." And I could almost see her finger on her bottom lip. We talked. Mostly I got her going. And I listened. That's what I wanted to do. Listen to her voice. I kept picturing her telling Elena that I was beautiful. No one had ever said that about me. Finally I said, "Hey, thanks for helping Elena out."

"So she told you, huh?"

"Yeah," I said.

She changed the subject. She started telling me about a dream she'd had. As I listened to her, I thought about what Elena had said. "Gabby says that maybe Juliana's an angel. Angels always appear right when you need them."

1968 was going to be a hot summer. I could tell. The desert had been heating up since March. I was always hot. A week before school let out, Juliana and I went to the Aggie Drive-In. I don't remember the movie. It wasn't anything I was interested in, that's all I know. It's funny about movies—after a few years you forget everything about them. I don't think movies

27

ever showed me anything interesting. Maybe I wanted to learn something. And the movies, well, I guess they didn't make me dream. They did other people, I knew that. Made them dream. But not me. People. People made me dream. And movies weren't like people.

As we were sitting there in the front seat, Juliana took out a cigarette. I told her my dad said we couldn't smoke in his car. Not anymore. A new rule. That's the thing—there was always a new rule. We got out and sat on the hood. We smoked. Just then, Pifas Espinosa and Jaime Rede waved at us from a car just ahead of us. "That you, Sammy?"

"He's drunk," I whispered to Juliana. "Yeah, Pifas, it's me."

Pifas stumbled toward us. "Órale, you wanna beer, ese?" He was in a friendly mood. Pifas was okay.

"Yeah," Juliana said, "a beer sounds good."

I walked back to his car with him. "She's all right, ese," Pifas said. Jaime didn't say anything. I could tell something was wrong. Jaime was one of those kinds of guys—something was always wrong. "She'll dump you," Jaime said after a while. "Same as she dumped me."

I nodded. "Maybe. Maybe not."

"You're not so special," Jaime said.

I wanted to punch him out, but more than that I just wanted to get back to Juliana. "No. I'm not so special," I said. I took the two beers Pifas handed me and walked back to the car. The beers were cold and I was happy. Juliana and I drank them down slowly. And we smoked. "You like to drink, Sammy?"

"It's okay," I said. The truth was that I'd only had two beers in my whole life—and I'd stolen those beers from the bars I cleaned. I didn't hang out much. Not with anybody.

"Have you ever smoked pot, Sammy?"

"Nope," I said. "You?"

"People are starting to do that a lot," she said. "Especially gringos. They're hippies. That's what they call them."

"I know," I said.

"Do you want to be one?"

"No," I said.

"You don't have to be a hippie to smoke pot."

"I know," I said.

"I thought that smoking weed would help me forget," she said, "about stuff. But it didn't. There's not anything you can drink or smoke that can make you forget. Not one damned thing. And that's sad, Sammy." She finished her beer and looked at me. I think she was waiting for me to kiss her. So I did. And then she asked me if I'd ever been with a girl. "Have you, Sammy?"

I shook my head.

"How come?"

"Just haven't."

"Serious?"

"Serious."

"Do you want to?" She kissed me again. I kissed her back. I was shaking. "Do you want to make love to me, Sammy?"

I think that's when I first felt the wings. That's when they woke up and started flapping around inside me.

I don't know how we did it exactly, there, in the backseat of my father's car, but it was good. It was good. I was scared. Not too scared. Not scared enough to stop. That's the thing— I didn't want to stop. Not then. Not ever.

It wasn't her first time. I knew that. Not that I cared. I told her I loved her when she wrapped her bare legs around me. I didn't know anything could feel that perfect. And when it was over, I told her again that I loved her.

"You shouldn't say that," she said.

"But I do, Juliana. I love you."

"Even if you do, Sammy, you shouldn't say things like that."

"Why not?"

"Some girl might believe you some day—and then what?"

I didn't say anything after that. We did it again. Only slower. And after, I wanted to lie there, in the backseat. With her. Forever. Finally, we put our clothes back on. She helped me with my shirt. For a long time after that, I felt her fingers on my bare back. We laughed. I kissed her. Then we sat outside on the hood of my father's car. The movie on the outdoor screen didn't matter. What mattered is that we smelled like each other. We smoked. We looked up at the stars, and she told me that she was going to leave Hollywood. "Next year, after I graduate. I'm packing."

"Where will you go?"

"Maybe to the real Hollywood."

"Nothing's more real than our Hollywood," I said.

"That's the problem," she said. "I don't want real."

Take me with you. That's what I wanted to say. But I thought maybe I shouldn't say anything. I looked up at the stars. Right then, sitting next to her, I felt as big as the sky.

three

Mrs. Apodaca was always ready with a speech or a sermon. Always. Bet your ass. Or just one of her disapproving looks. She referred to us as *demonios*. Demons, devils, ungodly, unclean. That's what she thought about us.

She was just another person ready to put us down.

One Saturday afternoon, she stepped out of her house and marched over to the empty lot behind her house where we were playing baseball. Hands on her sides. Shit. Mad. Mad as hell. "Which one of you used that word? ¿A ver? ¿Cuál de ustedes?" She waited for one of us to answer. Hands on her sides. Mad as hell. She'd wait—forever if she had to.

"What word?" Jaime Rede asked.

"No se hagan tontos. You know what I'm talking about. Tú sabes."

Jaime Rede shook his head. One by one, we all shook our heads. She reduced us to acting like five-year-olds. Shrunk us down with that look of hers. With that voice. God.

But we could wait, too. Yeah. Just like her. We weren't gonna squeal on who'd shouted out the "F" word. And no one was about to confess, either. There wasn't one of us on that field who wouldn't have rather faced his father's belt than one of Mrs. Apodaca's penances. She stared us all in the face. We stared back. This was a war we actually had a chance of winning. Not many opportunities. No, not many. Finally she said. "Play. I want to watch." She grabbed Pifas Espinosa by the shoulder. "There's a chair on my porch. Tráemela." Pifas ran for the chair. When he ran back with it, she sat. As if she were the Empress Carlota. "Play," she said. We all looked at each other. She'd found a way to beat us. Damn. Not one bad word came out of our mouths for the rest of the game. Not much fun, no fun, nope, no fun at all. Damn. I think that Mrs. Apodaca had the time of her life that afternoon. I swear I could almost see her smile. Except she never smiled.

It is impossible to underestimate the important role Mrs. Apodaca played in the lives of the citizens of Hollywood. We elected her to be hated above all the others. Hers was a sacred and necessary office. By hating her, we created a perfect balance in that small barrio of ours. It was not a question of whether she deserved her fate. And it wasn't a question of fairness or justice. It was all a question of survival. That's what I told myself. It helped us to hate her. It helped us to go on living.

One morning she handed out novenas in honor of the Blessed Mother to Susie Hernández and Francisca (aka Frances) Sánchez as they passed in front of her house to catch the bus to go to school. "Go to the priest," she said firmly. She pointed at their skirts.

"God made my legs," Susie said, then slapped her thigh as if with that slap she could make Mrs. Apodaca appreciate not only the danger but the beauty of a woman's legs.

"But who made the dress?" Mrs. Apodaca shot back.

Actually, it wasn't so bad living across the street from Mrs. Apodaca. Any time I got bored, I'd wander out to the front porch. Sit. Wait. I was always rewarded for my patience. Something always happened. It was her habit to stop people as they passed in front of her house. She was a gatekeeper, and now, as I think about it, I swear she would have made one helluva border patrol officer. "Who made the dress?" Even from across the street, I could hear her clearly, could see the deep furrows of her scowl, her face becoming a map of the world. "Who made that dress?"

Susie didn't shrink. "I did." She looked Mrs. Apodaca in the eye and stuck out her chin. It was the universal gesture of defiance in Hollywood, a vestige of the ancestors we still carried in our blood and on our faces. She looked like an Aztec princess in a hieroglyphic. "I made the dress," Susie repeated, "to go with the legs God made."

"Your mother let you?"

"My mother's proud I can sew."

"Proud? Un hombre puede ver todo!"

"God gave men eyes to see."

"To see the good—not to fall into temptation."

"God's glory is a woman's legs."

"God will punish you for that."

"Well, if he doesn't, you will."

"Eres una muchachita muy malcriada."

"I don't like Spanish," Susie said.

"Learn to like it. You live in Hollywood."

"My father's a gringo." Susie crossed her arms.

"Your father is a no-good drunk mojado. He's passed out in some cantina in Mesilla. Ahí se mantiene. En las cantinas. Always drunk. Is that what you want? Is that why you wear dresses like that?" Mrs. Apodaca crossed herself.

"Stop that!" Susie yelled. "Just stop it!"

"Necesitas una bendición."

"I don't need blessings," Susie said, "I need money."

"Money's a curse."

"How would you know? How would anyone in this god-damned neighborhood know?"

"No seas tan malhablada. Es falta de respeto."

"You're just like the gringos. You think you can tell us how to talk." She spit on the ground.

I watched as Susie and Frances turned their back on Mrs. Apodaca and slowly walked away. I couldn't help but feel bad for her. Bad. Bad. Even though Susie was right. There she was, Mrs. Apodaca, standing in her front yard, a large, stubborn figure like a lone tree trying to dig deep enough to find water. Enough water for a tree like that was hard to come by. I wanted to tell her that her morals were useless in the face of a revolutionary like Susie Hernández. It wouldn't have done any good if I had told her.

I watched as Mrs. Apodaca turned and walked toward her house, a rosary swaying in her hand. She slammed her door. It sounded like a gun shot.

She would live to fight another day.

She didn't have a first name. She was just Mrs. Apodaca. Even to her husband. He was always nodding and repeating "Sí, señora," like a beaten down parrot. I don't think anyone ever saw him. He was like a ghost.

And she liked clean, Mrs. Apodaca. She had this lawn, not big, not a big lawn, but it was green. I mean green. Green, green. I swear she watched over her husband like a gargoyle as he worked on the yard every week. Not a weed in sight. Not a roach. She cleaned her sidewalk every damned day of the year. "Así lo hacen en Alemania," she said. "The Germans are very clean." She looked at me with that disapproving gaze. She could have made money giving lessons on how to make people feel like shit with just a glance. "In Hollywood," she said, "there's nothing but filth. Todo está desordenado. There's nothing but chaos." She studied me for a moment. "You know that word?"

"Yes," I said, "I know that word." Words. That's what we had in common. We both liked them. Every time I used the dictionary, I imagined Mrs. Apodaca doing the same thing. I wondered if she had a library lined with shelves of books in her house. Maybe she just had hundreds of thousands of yellowing novenas piled up in a room full of dusty saints. And somewhere in those novenas was the word *chaos*.

"Okay, what does it mean? Give me a definition."

"Chaos," I said, "it's a synonym for Hollywood." I was proud.

She shook her head. "Yo pensaba que eras más respetuoso. But you're not respectful at all." In my rush to exhibit my knowledge, I'd forgotten that she didn't like anyone to criticize our neighborhood. Only she had earned that right. She was funny that way.

"I'm sorry," I said. Around Mrs. Apodaca, it was best to apologize. Immediately. For everything. The more often you apologized, the better.

She looked me over. "How long have you been wearing those jeans?"

"I don't know."

"Apestan. I can smell them from here."

"I'm sorry," I said.

"Don't be sorry," she said. "Just go home and wash them."

37

That was Mrs. Apodaca.

My dad said I was too hard on Mrs. Apodaca. He said she was decent and hardworking. Maybe my dad was right. The problem was that she wanted everyone to know it. That was it, that was the problem. She liked to exhibit her virtues same as she liked to exhibit the roses in her front yard. Or her green grass. I think we were all supposed to cross ourselves and genuflect in the aroma of all that virtue.

She wasn't mean. Not really mean. Not mean like Juliana's father. Not like that. But she wasn't kind either. Just wasn't her way. When she cared, she'd say things like, "Tell your dad that Elena shouldn't wear that dress anymore. It's almost worn out, and anyway it doesn't fit her anymore. ¿Que no ven? La gente va decir que no les importa. Is that what you want for people to think—that you don't care?"

I think my father liked that she was the clothes police—and the confession police—and the yard police. She did his dirty work for him. He never had to tell me to clean the yard. He didn't have to. I mean, Mrs. Apodaca gave me a rake as a birthday gift when I turned twelve. My father made me knock on her front door and thank her. She nodded and asked, "You know how to use it?"

I nodded. "It's a nice rake," I said. I remember smiling. I remember practicing my smile. "The nicest rake I've ever owned," I said. I think I went overboard with my gratitude. I must have sounded insincere. *But I was insincere.* What normal boy wants a rake for his twelfth birthday?

As it turned out, the first time I took the rake in my hands was also the last. One Saturday morning, a bunch of pachucos were running after Pifas Espinosa as I raked the front yard. As he ran past my house, Pifas grabbed the rake, turned around and broke it over some guy's back. I'll never forget the sound of that crack or the look on that poor pinche's face. Mrs. Apodaca never counted on her gift being used as a weapon. It saved Pifas' ass. One day she asked me what happened to my rake.

"It got stolen," I said.

She shook her head. "You should learn to take care of your things." She never bought me another gift. Somehow, I was glad about that.

Once, I saw her in church and she was crying. I could tell. I watched her from the back row of the empty church. I listened to her sobs for a long time. I think I fell asleep to the sounds of her moaning. I used to fall asleep every chance I got. My job at Speed Sweep Janitor Service was getting to me. She shook me awake. "It's a sin to sleep in church," she told me.

"It's a sin to cry in church, too," I said.

Mrs. Apodaca looked at me.

"No, it isn't. And I wasn't crying."

"It's a sin to lie," I said.

"I suppose you'll go and tell everyone in Hollywood that

I was crying in church."

"I might," I said.

"Go ahead," she said. Then, I saw her do something I'd never seen: I saw her smile. God. "No one will believe you," she said. "No one will believe Mrs. Apodaca knows how to cry." She walked out of the church. A few minutes later, she was standing over me again like an angel about to swoop me up in her arms and toss me into the pits of hell.

"What are you doing in here, anyway? A ver ¿qué té pasa?"

"I'm praying," I said.

"Why are you praying?"

"Do I need a reason?"

She nodded. "Did you do something you weren't supposed to do? ¿Qué hiciste?"

I shook my head. "Nada. No hice nada. I was just talking to my mom," I said.

And then she changed. And for a little while she was someone else. She even looked different. I mean, she looked at me and she placed her hand under my chin. It was warm, her hand. Not soft. She worked too hard for soft. "You look like her," she whispered. "Era muy bonita tú mamá. Y muy linda." It occurred to me then that she had loved my mother. And that she missed her. And that she took care of Elena every day after school not for the small amount of money my father gave her, but out of devotion to my mother's memory. I almost liked her, then.

"I miss her," I said.

Then she changed back to being Mrs. Apodaca. The one I knew. "We all belong to God," she said. "Just remember that. Así es." She patted my face and walked away.

We all belong to God. I didn't want to belong to him. I wanted to belong to Juliana *and* to my mother. But it was hard to belong to someone who didn't have a body, who didn't talk. I wanted to run after her and argue with her. And after I finished arguing with her, I wanted to ask her why she'd been crying. Not that she would have told me. I would find out soon enough.

Maybe a week or two later, Mrs. Apodaca called me in when I went to pick up Elena at her house after school. She sent Elena out of the room. "Tengo que hablar con tu hermano." Elena nodded and walked back to Gabriela's room. I held my breath. I knew I was about to get a lecture. It was like bracing for a hundred-mile-an-hour spring wind. "School is going to let out in a month," she said. "What are you planning to do?"

"I'm thinking of quitting my job," I said.

"Are you just going to sit around and let yourself rot like an apple on a tree someone forgot to pick?"

I didn't like apples. "No," I said, "I put in an application at the university. You know, working on the grounds."

She nodded. "Good. It'll keep you away from Juliana Ríos."

I didn't say anything.

"I saw you with her," she said. "You let her kiss you."

I nodded.

"She doesn't come from a good family."

"I don't either," I said.

"Your mother was a saint. Está cantando con los ángeles."

I nodded. Yes, yes, a saint singing with angels, but—

"I don't like her."

I shrugged.

"¿Qué no puedes hablar?"

"Yes," I said, "I can talk." I looked at her eyes, black as a night without stars. "I like her. And it was me who kissed her."

"I know what I saw," she said.

"I like her," I said again.

"I can see that. Everyone can see that. She's not what your mother would want for you."

"I don't think we should be bringing up my mother," I said. I felt my bottom lip trembling.

"Juliana's not the kind of girl—"

"I don't want to talk about Juliana," I said.

"She'll bring you bad luck."

"Maybe it's me who'll bring her bad luck."

"You're a good boy."

"No, I'm not." I wanted to tell her I liked smoking cigarettes and hated going to confession. I wanted to tell her I thought endlessly about sex and that I liked to cuss. I wanted to let out a whole litany of cusswords. I wanted to tell her that

I hated her. What kind of good boy was that? "I like her more than I like God," I said.

"What?"

"You heard me." I walked out of her house. I wasn't a political candidate. She didn't get to sit me down and voice her opinion about the issues she cared about. She didn't get to vote on who I should like. She told my dad I was disrespectful. I told my dad I was absolutely disrespectful. "I told her I liked Juliana more than I liked God."

"You told her that, Sammy?"

"Yes." I looked into my father's serious eyes. I had trouble figuring him out, sometimes. "It's true," I said.

He nodded. "No," he said, "it's not true. It just seems that way." He took my face in his hands and he kissed me on the forehead. He was always doing things like that. "Go on over there," he said. "Vete. You have to apologize."

"I'm not sorry," I said.

"Dile que te perdone."

I didn't give a damn if she forgave me or not. "Just tell me what to say," I said.

"But you won't mean it."

"No. I won't mean it." Adults wanted everything. They thought the world belonged to them. I wondered sometimes why they had children. It wasn't good enough that you said what they wanted you to say. You had to feel it, too. "If I could thank her for a rake," I said, "I can tell her I'm sorry for disrespecting

43

her." I walked out of the kitchen.

I heard Elena talking to my father as I left the room. "He's maaaahhhd," she said.

The next day, after school, I knocked on Mrs. Apodaca's door and told her I was sorry. "Favor de perdonarme, Señora."

She looked at me for a long time. Then nodded. Her forgiveness was as half-hearted as my apology. And hadn't she been my mother's friend? But she had no use for Juliana. I hated her for that.

four

A few weeks later, I saw Mrs. Apodaca in church again. It was just me and her in that small church on the corner of Idaho and Espina. Juliana hadn't gone to school that day. I stopped into the church, not really knowing why. I was alone. Maybe it seemed okay to be alone when you were kneeling in the pew of an empty church. I wandered in, knelt, made the sign of the cross. I tried to pray. Really, I only thought about Juliana. I wasn't fooling anyone. Not God. Not myself. I think I was in the church wanting to ask God to make her love me. Or something like that. It took me a while before I noticed Mrs. Apodaca. She was sobbing quietly near the front of the church. Maybe I should have gone up to her, asked her what was wrong. I should have made some kind of offer. But it would have been an awkward and graceless gesture. I let her cry in peace. I felt bad. I had to admit it.

One Saturday, Reyes Espinoza and I were playing catch in

the empty lot behind Mrs. Apodaca's house. Not that I liked Reyes Espinoza. He was a complete jack off. The kind of guy who would grow up to be a complete and total pendejo. He didn't have it in him to be any other way. I felt sorry for him. But I hated him, too. That's why I always avoided him. But that Saturday, he'd come over to play catch. Guess he was bored. Guess I was too. And right away he made my life miserable. He was good at that. So we're playing catch, and after about five minutes, he says, "Hey, Sammy, heads up," and he throws my baseball right into Mrs. Apodaca's yard.

He laughed. "Better get it," he said.

"You get it," I said. I wasn't about to go into Mrs. Apodaca's immaculate backyard without permission.

"I'm not gonna get it," he said. "It's not my ball."

I wanted to pop him one. I did. "I'll get it later," I said.

"Just jump over her fence and get it. C'mon, Sammy."

"Hell no."

"Chicken. No huevos, baby."

"Sí, cabrón," I said. "If your balls are so big, you get it."

"Nah," he said. "I jump over that fence and that pinche ruca will have me tossed en el mero bote. Not gonna do no jail just for a piss-ant baseball."

"She won't throw you in jail," I said.

"Like hell she won't. That ruquita's mean. And she hates my ass."

We argued for a while. I hated arguing with pendejos like

46

Reyes Espinoza. "You threw it in there. Now you get it," I said. "Just knock on the door and ask her."

"Hell no. You do it."

"Later," I said. I walked away. But I knew if I wanted that ball, I'd have to find my own way of getting it back. Reyes Espinoza didn't care about it. He didn't care about anything. Not about me. Not about my baseball. I'd have to apologize, and Mrs. Apodaca would give me a lecture about respecting other people's property and she'd give me my baseball back and that would be the end of it. I told Reyes Espinoza he was a cabrón and had no huevos and that he was a pinche to boot. He threw me a finger. I pointed my chin at him. That Aztec hieroglyphic thing again. I went home. I listened to the radio. K-G-R-T was playing some okay music. I gave myself a lecture *relax, relax.* I'd been telling myself to relax ever since I was a kid. *Relax, it's Saturday.* My Dad had taken Elena and Mrs. Apodaca's daughter, Gabriela, to an afternoon movie. They liked movies. Everyone liked movies. Except me. Movies bored me. I listened to the radio for a while, tried to relax, but then I got to thinking about my baseball. I was still mad about Mrs. Apodaca not liking Juliana. None of her damned business anyway. It's funny how we have arguments with people in our heads. We're better arguers when the people we're arguing with aren't around. And in those arguments, we always win. So that's why we liked doing stuff like that in our heads. So I lay there in my bed and argued with Mrs. Apodaca for a while.

Then I thought about my baseball. I saw it sitting there like a golden egg in the middle of her backyard. I decided to go get it. I don't know what I was thinking. Maybe I just needed to trespass against her. Trespass. I always liked that word—ever since I'd made my first communion.

Jumping over her fence wasn't so hard. It was maybe six feet and made of cinder block. If you took a running jump, you could pull yourself over. That's exactly what I did. I looked around and saw my baseball. It was right under one of her rose bushes. The yard wasn't as perfect as I'd thought. Everything was neat and orderly but the rose bushes looked like they needed trimming and the grass definitely needed mowing. I thought that was strange. I'd never known the Apodacas to let the grass grow. Not like that.

I took the ball. Looked around. It's a funny feeling to be in a place where you know you don't belong. I was all in knots. And I thought I was going to throw up. Relax, relax. I wasn't stealing anything. I looked around again. I looked at the ball in my trembling hand—then tossed it into the empty lot. It was safe now. There. The world was right again. Except that I was still standing in the middle of Mrs. Apodaca's backyard. I made my way back to the fence. That's when I heard the back door opening. I didn't even bother to look. I could hear my heart. I hated that. It was never a good thing when you heard your own heart. I jumped. I could feel the scrape of the cinder blocks against my knees. I fell to the ground. I don't know how. Shit, shit. I wasn't thinking. But I could see the huge pomegranate bush in the corner of the yard. A place to hide. That was all I could think of. Shit. I found myself hiding behind the bush. God. God himself couldn't have seen me. Not that I was worried about Him. It was Mrs. Apodaca I was worried about.

I closed my eyes and prayed. And then I heard a wailing, just like the sounds that came out of people when they went to a funeral. And then I wasn't afraid anymore. It was like my heart changed--went from being scared to being sad. I peeked out from behind the bush and saw Mr. Apodaca raising his fists toward heaven. Tears were falling down his face. And then he started shouting: "¡No me quiero morir! ¡No me quiero morir!" His face was all contorted. Rage did that, twisted your face and made you look like an animal. He looked completely different. Not passive. Not like a cement sidewalk you stepped on. But like a man. He was challenging God to a fistfight. I swear, if God would've come down, Mr. Apodaca would have knocked him to the ground. That's when I saw him fall on his knees and howl.

Everything in the world seemed to stop. There was nothing else. Just Mr. Apodaca on his knees wailing like a coyote. I could have watched him forever. It made me sad. But, somehow, I couldn't stop watching. Then I realized that I was seeing him. For the first time, I was seeing *him, Mr. Apodaca,*

49

a man. A real man. Not just somebody's husband. I'd never noticed how small he was. Smaller than me. And skinny.

He was sick. It was easy to see.

I lived across the street from him. How could I have not known? I wanted to hold him. I'd never wanted to hold a grown man—except my father when my mother died. And I had held him. My dad. I had.

His sobs got quieter and quieter. And yet, they seemed to get louder and louder. There was nothing else in the world except the sound of his sobbing. He curled up like a baby in the womb. He cried. And cried. And I thought maybe he'd die right there. Right then, right there. Crying. I didn't know what to do. I wanted to save him but I didn't know how. I didn't. I didn't know how to do anything. I was about to come out from behind the bush. I don't know what I was planning to do. Hug him, maybe. Take him inside. Take him inside—that wasn't such a bad idea. That's when I saw Mrs. Apodaca come out into the yard. She didn't march out. That's what she usually did. She walked, slowly. I'd never seen her walk like that. She knelt down next to him. Slow. Careful. She looked at him. I'll never forget that look on her face. Like she was seeing the face of God. She bit her trembling lip, then took a breath. Then another. And then she held him. She rocked and rocked him in her arms. Rocked and rocked him until he stopped crying and she kept saying, "Amor, no llores. No llores." Then, as if she was as strong as one of the sentries who guarded the gates of heaven, she picked him up—and carried him into the house.

I stayed behind that bush for a while. Just didn't want to leave. I played the scene over and over in my mind. I'd never seen a man yelling at God. I'd never seen a woman picking up a man and carrying him. Everything in the world was bigger than I'd ever thought.

Something happened in a backyard. Something small. And everything changed.

I don't remember how long I hid there. Behind that bush. I half expected to turn to stone. I kept feeling my own skin. Just to make sure I was still flesh. Or maybe I thought I'd changed. I don't know. I just know that I finally managed to leave the Apodacas' garden. I jumped the fence. Went back home. But I was restless.

I called Juliana. She wasn't there.

My own house felt strange to me. I don't know. I wanted my Dad and Elena to come home. But I guess they decided to go do other stuff after the movie. Maybe that was a good thing. Because the Apodacas' daughter was with them. And the Apodacas needed time to recover. They would be calm again when their daughter walked through the door. It occurred to me right then that my father knew everything about what was happening with the Apodacas. Fathers knew a lot of things. I wondered why fathers kept so many secrets from their sons. Maybe that's the way it was supposed to be.

About an hour later I went out and sat on the front porch. I wondered why the Apodacas had never moved to another neighborhood. They never really belonged. I studied their house. The nicest, neatest house on the block. Maybe even the nicest house in the whole neighborhood. Anyone would have thought a gringo lived there—well, except for the fact that Mrs. Apodaca's house was as pink as a flamingo.

I suddenly realized that the front lawn needed mowing. I even thought I spotted a weed. It just wasn't right. I don't remember walking across the street. I just know I found myself standing at the Apodacas' front door. I was there—so I knocked. Mrs. Apodaca came to the door. Her eyes were dry. She looked at me. The same face. There was a question on her lips. But she didn't ask it.

"Hi," I said.

Her question was gone. She looked at me blankly. She looked tired.

"I can do the lawn," I said.

"We can do our own lawn," she said.

"Oh." I shrugged. "I just needed some extra money," I said.

"No te necesito," she said.

I nodded. "Okay," I said.

I started to walk away.

"How much do you charge?" She asked. "I'll pay you a dollar. Front and back."

I nodded. "A dollar?"

"No soy una mujer rica. I can't afford more than that."

"No, that's okay," I said. "A dollar's good. I can start now. If you want."

She nodded.

She taught me about rose bushes that afternoon. The right way to trim them. There were rules. There were rules for everything. She knew them all. She pointed at a branch on one of her bushes. "That one," she said. "See how those leaves are turning brown? There's always a part that's dying. You have to know which part of a plant is dying—and which part is being born. That's the key to trimming. You have to look. You have to see. ¿Me entiendes? Mira."

I nodded. I listened.

And then she starts in with her religious stuff. I knew it was coming. She started talking about Eden, and how we carried the memory of paradise around with us, and that was why so many of us needed to have gardens. "We all have leaves from that original garden in our hearts." That's what she said, and according to her, they were there so we wouldn't forget. "When you work for something good, hijo," she said, "you're working your way back to Eden." So that was her problem. She really believed most people wanted to be pure. She believed we all wanted to go back to Eden. And even though I knew anything was better than Hollywood, I wasn't convinced most of us cared anything about Eden. Not that I told her what I was thinking.

Mrs. Apodaca just looked at me. "You don't believe me, do you?"

I sort of shrugged. "I want to," I said. I wasn't lying.

After that Saturday afternoon, I kept up the Apodacas' yard until Mr. Apodaca died.

He was nothing but bone in the end. We begin as water and end up as bone. Brittle bone that breaks. That turns to dust. Nothing anybody can do about it. Not a damn thing.

Mrs. Apodaca was damned stoic about the whole thing. And every time she got bossy about how I should take care of the yard, well, I kind of just listened. I took it. She was entitled to her bad days. Once, Juliana came over to her house and watched me trim the roses. Mrs. Apodaca offered her a Coke and a novena, and told her, "the Virgin Mary didn't dress like that." I looked at Juliana and smiled. I knew what she was thinking: The Virgin Mary never had to live in Hollywood.

Mrs. Apodaca didn't change much during the last few months of her husband's life. Stayed the same. Dressed the same. Her and her hats. Sometimes, she stuck her chin out at me. I liked that.

I think Mrs. Apodaca was a woman who understood life as a series of burdens. Someone had to carry them. That's where she came in. That was her job, the one God had given her. That was her sacred duty. That's where she found salvation.

I never thought of her as being pure. But she was. I think she was. She didn't wear disguises for people like the rest of us. She didn't. She didn't soften herself. She didn't make herself more acceptable to the people around her. She didn't know how.

I dressed up nice for Mr. Apodaca's funeral. I remember how she broke down when she saw me at the church. I felt a little funny holding her. I wished to God I hadn't been such an awkward kid. I always felt like there was too much of me to stuff into my own flesh. I wanted to tell her something. We, who both liked words so much, we had so little to say. Juliana was right. Words didn't mean as much as I thought. Still, I wanted to tell her things. A hundred things. That I knew she loved her husband. That she did her best and God knew. That the heart stopped hurting. At least enough to go on living. I knew about that. I did know. But maybe losing a husband or a wife was different than losing a mother. So maybe I didn't know. Maybe I didn't know anything. I wanted to tell her I really did believe that God planted leaves in our hearts so we could remember Eden, and maybe Mr. Apodaca could turn in his leaves now, and get into heaven. I wanted to say all those things to her, but I got myself all tangled up in the conversation I was having with myself—so I wound up not saying anything. Maybe I did say something. Maybe I said, "It's okay," as she sobbed into my shoulder. What a thing to say.

I thought about how I'd seen her carry her husband back

into the house. It was like watching someone make love. I hadn't earned the right to see that. Not by a long shot. I'd stolen something from her. From both of them. I wanted to tell her, I saw you. He was breaking and you made sure he stayed whole. I saw you. I'm sorry. I'm sorry. And then, abruptly, she pulled away from me. And stopped crying. She looked up at me and shook her head. "You need a haircut," she said.

I nodded. "I'll get one tomorrow."

"What's wrong with this afternoon?"

"Okay," I said. I was onto her. The days of fooling me were over. Sometimes, you find things out about people. And after that, you can't hate them anymore.

five

I quit my job at Speed Sweep Janitor Service. I was tired of getting up at four in the morning. I got a full-time job for the summer with the landscape crews at the university. Pifas Espinosa got a job there, too. He'd just graduated from Las Cruces High. He looked like he'd be permanently hung over for the rest of his life from all that celebrating. The first day on the job, Pifas said working there was the same thing as going to college. Pifas. He just didn't get it.

When I got my first paycheck, I ran into Juliana at the Pic Quick. She was buying a pack of cigarettes. I was buying a Pepsi. We walked back home together. We didn't say anything for a long time. Finally, I said, "You want to go out tomorrow night?" I didn't look at her.

"Yeah," she said, "that would be nice."

I thought maybe she'd say no because the last few times I'd asked her out, she'd told me she was busy. She seemed sad to me. I thought maybe it was me who made her sad. Maybe I hurt her.

I stopped walking. I thought a while. Maybe I'd just beg her to stay with me, tell her I was sorry if I'd hurt her. Beg. And then she stopped walking, too. And she looked at me. I thought she was going to kiss me. But she didn't. I didn't see any anger in her eyes, no remnants of her father. I didn't see any pieces of Hollywood or Las Cruces High or any of the other parts of the world that had hurt her. Her eyes were like a book and there were words written there: *I might be a knife. I might cut you. Sammy, tell me that you'll bleed. For me.* And then her eyes became a desert, calm and large and I didn't care if they swallowed me up. And I understood. Standing right there. That she loved me. That she loved me the only way she knew how. And then I kissed her. And she put her hand on my heart, and I knew she could feel those wings that were throwing themselves against my rib cage.

We walked back to Hollywood as slow as our legs could take us.

Every time we went out, she always came to my house. Because of the way her dad was. The next evening, I walked out of the house and sat on the front porch. Waited. Saturday night *I need you, ba-a-by…* I looked at my shirt. Maybe it wasn't right. I never knew what to wear. Not that I had a lot of shirts. I just wanted to look fine. Hated to wait—gave me too much time to think about stupid things, things that didn't matter. Like shirts. Seven thirty came and went. She didn't show. Fifteen minutes later, I was still there. Waiting. Eight o'clock. No Juliana. That's when I heard the ambulance. It passed right in front of our house and kept on moving down the street. I don't know why, but I ran after it. I felt my heart beating in my chest like a bird flapping its wings, trying to find his way out of a cage. I ran and ran after the ambulance. When it stopped in front of Juliana's house, I stood still and stared at the crowd. I heard myself screaming, but I wasn't me anymore. "What's wrong? ¿Qué pasó? ¿Dónde está Juliana?" I started to follow the guys in the ambulance into the house, but a policeman stopped me. "Sorry, son, can't let you go in there."

"But Juliana—"

"Sorry, son, you'll have to move back toward the street."

"No. No!" I was yelling. "Juliana! She's in there! She's my girl—"

I felt the policeman's firm hand on my arm. He led me to the street. He looked at me like he was real sad. Like he was real sorry. "It'll be okay, son," he said. He left me there, staring at the house. Surrounded by most of the citizens of Hollywood.

Everyone around me was talking, and some lady, Mrs. Moreno, was saying how Mrs. Ríos had left the house screaming and yelling, swearing to God that she was never coming back. "¡Parecía loca! Y el Señor Ríos, he told her to go ahead and leave, que se fuera mucho a la chingada—but when she came back don't expect to find your children. ¡Me la vas a pagar, cabrona! I'm gonna get your ass! And he went back inside the house. That's when I heard the gunshots."

I stopped listening.

Another ambulance came.

I saw Pifas and I asked him for a cigarette. "She's okay," he said, "don't worry, ese. You know how it is, big family, ese. They fight, ¿sabes, Sammy?" He kept talking. I saw him moving his lips. But he was far away.

More cop cars came. And a black car. A white guy in a tie got out of the car and went into the house. All those gringos. In Juliana's house.

They took Mr. Ríos away in handcuffs. I tried to see his eyes, but I couldn't get close enough. *What have you done to Juliana? What have you done?*

It got dark. And then the moon came up. It wasn't full, but it gave enough light. I could see everything. They started wheeling out the dead. Juliana and her four brothers and her two sisters. All of them. Hollywood had never been so quiet. When there isn't any hope, it doesn't do any good to say anything.

I sat on the sidewalk. Pifas sat there with me. He kept giving me cigarettes. I kept smoking them. We didn't try to talk.

Mrs. Apodaca made a wooden cross and planted it in front

of the house. She hung a rosary on the cross and said a prayer. Half of Hollywood brought candles and lit them. And whispered things. Prayers. The yard looked like a cemetery. On the Day of the Dead.

After a few hours, it was only me and Pifas. By then we'd finished his cigarettes and he wandered away.

And then it was only me.

I don't know how long I sat there. I looked at the stars and the moon and I thought maybe nothing had happened. Juliana was sitting right next to me on the hood of my father's car. We were at the Aggie Drive-In. I was kissing her. I was lighting a cigarette for her. I must have fallen asleep at the foot of Mrs. Apodaca's cross. Sometime in the night, I felt someone shaking me awake. "You can't stay here, mi'jo." When I saw it was my dad, I started to cry. He kept kissing me and whispering things to make me feel better. I couldn't hear, nothing, not the words, not the sound of his voice. But I could feel his arms around me. And I wanted him to carry me home in those arms. I wanted him to tell me that when I woke, Juliana would be alive. In the morning, she would be waking up from a long sleep. She would be lying next to me in bed. In my house. But when I woke up, I knew it was all true. That she was gone. And I didn't have anything inside me anymore. The wings were gone. And, maybe, I thought, that it was a good thing, that those wings were gone, because now they were free. I don't know. I didn't care. Not about anything. Not anymore.

I was driving around in my father's car. It was raining and thundering and the sky was acting exactly like Juliana's eyes. I had tried not to think of her, but somehow, she always came back. And that morning, in the newspaper, I'd seen a picture of Juliana's father. They were sending him to prison, and there he was on the front page. The Hollywood Murderer. That's what people called him. All afternoon, I felt sick. And driving home, it all came back to me. And that damned song came on the radio, Frankie Valli singing *You're just too good . . .* and all of a sudden I saw myself handing Juliana a pack of cigarettes. I pictured her in the backless dress she never wore—the one I was going to buy her. I pictured her giving Birdwail all the right answers. I pictured us on the hood of my father's car. She was looking at me. I was cold and shivering, and I knew I had to pull over to the side of the road. I didn't know what was happening. I just knew I had to get out of the car. I stepped out into the rain, and as I stood there, I swore I heard Juliana's voice *Someone's gonna hurt you some day, Sammy.* Maybe it was the thunder. Maybe it was the rain. I knew I was yelling and shouting only it wasn't me. It was someone I used to be. I didn't know if I was crying. Maybe I was. Maybe I wasn't. Maybe it was the rain.

Somehow, I managed to get back in the truck and drive myself home. I remember walking in the door and feeling like I was on fire. My dad made me take a hot shower. He put me to bed. "What were you doing out in the rain, Sammy? You're burning up." I was in bed for three days. I had dreams. I was wandering around the streets of Hollywood—alone—knocking on doors. No one was home. Everyone had moved away. And I prayed to God. I prayed, God, God, take away my heart.

Pifas and Gigi and the Politics of Hollywood

"Every day, just take a breath and keep trying, Gigi."

"What for, Sammy?"

"Cause if we don't, we'll all be dead. We're too young for that."

"Ha, ha, Sammy. Ha, ha."

six

I don't know what summer meant for most people, but for me, summer meant work. At least I didn't have to go to school. Summer. Work. Pifas had just graduated—"At the bottom ten percent of my class," to use his own words against him. "Screw it. Who cares? No one cares. Maybe our moms, maybe they care, but only for about five minutes, and then they move on to worry about lots of other stuff, you know, like money and food and clothes and where to find someone to fix your car for free and shit like that."

We both called ourselves Mexicans even though we didn't have a peso's worth of knowledge about Mexico. We were both raised in Hollywood—the only country either of us knew. We both smoked Marlboros. And we were both guys. That just about exhausted the list of things we had in common.

I worked with Pifas all that summer. Working the grounds of the university. "Fucking minimum wage job for minimum wage Mexicans." That's how Pifas put it. Not that Pifas was prepared to do anything else. And not that he worked, either. Work was not something he was interested in. Took up space, that's what he was good at—that, and complaining and eating his lunch. Oh yeah, and he was damn good at making like he was busy when the foreman showed up. "How you guys doin'?" the foreman asked every time he came by. He'd smile that idiot grin of his. Not smiling at me. Not at me. He was smiling at Pifas. People who weren't interested in work had a way of finding each other.

"Fuckin' A," Pifas would say. "Fuckin' A," the foreman would say. What was that? I never understood that fuckin' A business. Not then, not now. Then the two of them would smoke a cigarette and talk about what needed to be done. They were good at that. Talking. I'd keep working. I felt better about collecting a paycheck when I worked for it. A curse I inherited from my father. And anyway, I liked to smoke my cigarettes by myself. I'd tell Pifas I had to find a bathroom, and I'd go and smoke a cigarette and get some peace.

Aside from spouting his theories and asking me personal questions, Pifas spent a lot of time watching girls. "They're all into sex now, ¿sabes, Sammy? All of 'em. Think of it, man, it's all too beautiful, Sammy. 1968 and they all drink and smoke pot and don't wear bras and listen to rock. Man, man, man. Women are equal now, ¿sabes, Sammy? That's the word. Equality, baby. And you know what that means? That means they're all into sex, just like me and you. I never knew equality could be so beautiful. Man, man, man." Man, man, man. That and fuckin' A and far out and far fucking out—that's what he said all summer. Pifas was dangerous with the English language. He was dangerous with any language. At least he didn't say groovy. Groovy was too much of a gringo thing for Pifas. Good thing, too, or I'd have popped him one. I swear I would've.

I got sick of him asking me if I was still thinking of Juliana. I'd be turning up the ground with my shovel, digging a bed for some new plants, and he'd say, "Hey, Sammy, you thinkin' of Juliana?"

"No," I'd say. But if I was thinking of her, it would really get to me that he was asking. Because really it was none of his damned business. And if I wasn't thinking of her, it would get to me even more because he would remind me of her. And it still hurt, that whole sad thing about Juliana and her family, and her good-for-nothing father who'd confessed to the whole damned thing. "I feel bad about this. Me muero de tristeza," that's what that bastard said—as if feeling bad and telling the world that you were dying of sadness because you'd killed your children was somehow going to make everything all better. Screw him. He felt bad. What was that? Juliana was dead. His daughter, the one he'd hated, his beautiful Juliana. She was dead. And all because he got mad at his wife. Such bullshit. It still hurt. The whole damn thing still hurt. And I missed the wings that had been beating inside of me when I was with Juliana. I missed them—even though those wings had scared me. And I got into my head that those wings had belonged to a bird, and that the bird was beginning to grow inside of me, and that all of that meant something. Something important—like the leaves Mrs. Apodaca talked about—as important as that. But now it was all gone. And part of me hoped the wings would come back. And part of me just didn't give a damn about anything.

But the thing of it was that every time I thought of Juliana I could picture my insides and I could picture two broken wings lying inside my gut. They were just lying there.

Once, when I was thinking of Juliana, I took a match and burned the tip of one of my fingers. Burned it like it was a piece of paper. Or an exam that got handed back to me by a teacher who hated me. Burned it. Like that. And I got this huge blister all over my finger. I just looked at it. Just stared at what I'd done to myself. But I didn't worry too much about it. I mean, it was easier to think of my burned finger than it was to think about Juliana. She was so beautiful. That kind of beauty left scars. Anywhere it touched you. And I got touched all over.

So one day, right before the Fourth of July, I'd just mowed one of the campus lawns. And Pifas was supposed to be raking. But he wasn't. He wasn't raking. He was just standing there watching me. Like I was worth watching. I picked up a rake and got to work. No use in thinking Pifas was going to help me out. Then he looks at me. "So," he says, "you thinkin' of Juliana?"

"Look," I said, "if you ask me that one more damned time, I'm gonna stick a firecracker up your ass and you'll never take another shit in peace the rest of your natural life, you got that, Pifas?"

"Órale, don't be such a cabrón. I was just askin', ese."

"Just don't be asking about her anymore," I said.

He really got on my nerves, Pifas. Such an asshole. And the thing is, he always had to be talking. What was wrong with listening to the wind blow? What was wrong with that? What was wrong with smoking a cigarette and listening to the sound of your own lungs as you took in all that poison into your body? It was such a good thing, really, to listen to yourself smoke. Yeah, I know it was bad for me. Everyone said so. Bad for me. Yeah, yeah.

And every Friday, Pifas asks me if I want to go hang with him and his friends. "Hang," he says, "let's just hang. Drink a few cold ones, shoot the breeze." He was good at that, shooting the breeze.

I always tried to say no, but my excuses sounded lame, even to me. So one Friday Pifas says to me, "They think you're a real culo, ese. Know what I mean, Sammy? You know what they say? They say, 'He thinks he's too fuckin' good.' They call you the Librarian, you know that? Cuz you read too many fuckin' books. Books, Sammy, what the hell's that?"

"I know why they call me the Librarian, Pifas."

"Es una pinche vergüenza. Aren't you embarrassed, ese?"

"I don't give a damn ¿sabes? You think I care what a bunch of pendejos think?"

For some reason, he got this hurt look on his face. I hated that. "Okay," I said, "okay. I'll go." Anyway, I didn't have anything better to do. Okay. That word seemed to make Pifas happy. For some reason, he liked me.

I shouldn't have said okay. Sometimes okay can bring you a lot of trouble.

So that Friday, Pifas picked me up. I was sitting on the porch waiting for him. Shit, I said to myself when I saw his car pull up. There was Joaquín Mesa, Jaime Rede, and Reyes Espinoza—all of them sitting in the backseat of his car, a whole convention of assholes. And right away, Reyes Espinoza starts in on me. "Órale, how come you get to ride shotgun?"

"Look," I said, "you were all sitting in the backseat of the car—shit. Shit! You want shotgun?" I said. "Pifas, stop the car."

"Órale. Relax, ese."

"Stop this good-for-nothing-pinche car, Pifas."

Pifas stopped the car. I got out. I opened the back door. I looked at Reyes. "You want shotgun. You want to act like my little sister, Elena. Here! Take shotgun, you pinche."

Reyes didn't say a word. He just got out of the car and got in the front seat. I got in the back and slammed the door. "Do we need any more changes here?" I looked at Jaime Rede who was sitting in the middle. "Are you happy? Is everyone happy? I'm happy. Are you happy, Jaime? Are you, Reyes?"

Pifas started up the car. "You're in one pissed off mood," Joaquín Mesa said. He tossed me a cigarette. "Here."

I reached in my pocket, took out a book of matches and lit it.

"Órale, Sammy, I gave you a cigarette. Say thank you, cabrón."

"Yeah, yeah. Thanks. Eternal fucking gratitude."

That made Jaime Rede laugh. It was weird to hear him laugh. He didn't laugh at anything. Then, pretty soon, everyone in the car was laughing. Even me.

Pifas drove over to his brother's house who lived in some trailer park near Mesilla. His trailer park was all trashed out, even by Hollywood standards. Pifas goes in and then comes right back out with a cold case of beer. Joaquín smiled like someone had just told him he'd won the pinche lottery. So we go riding around and everyone's drinking and Jaime Rede's complaining about Gigi Carmona who dumped him. "She wouldn't even put out," he said. "I should have dumped her first." That's what really got him—that she dumped him before he got the chance. It was hard to feel bad for him. All the girls thought he was good-looking. And he was. But the word was out on him. He was permanently in a bad mood.

"Chicks are a pain in the ass," Reyes said.

"How would you know?" Joaquín laughed. "Who the shit would go out with you?"

"Shut up," Pifas said.

"Sí, mamón, no one'll go out with you either, Pifas."

"Órale, pinche," Pifas said, "that's why you're out with us, cuz you got girls lining up to spread their legs for you."

Joaquín laughed. Chugged his beer. "Didn't feel like gettin' laid tonight, ¿sabes?"

"Me neither," Jaime said.

"Me neither," Reyes said.

And we all lost it. Laughed our asses off. Maybe we would have an all right time. I'd finished my first beer and was thinking about having another when we're cruising down El Paseo and this guy from Chiva Town, Tony Guerra, yells something at Pifas. Pifas, of course, thinks the worst. The guy could have been yelling "Ese, how you guys doin'?" He could've been inviting us to a keg party at the river. No, but right away Pifas takes offense. "Órale, I'm gonna kick your ass," he says and he's hanging out the window and trying to drive all at the same time.

"Órale, chingazos," Joaquín says. Always ready to throw a few punches, Joaquín. And I'm thinking, shit. Shit. Then all of a sudden we're all driving toward some abandoned farmhouse right behind Las Cruces High. There's about four cars and when we get there, everyone leaves their lights on. I guess if there was gonna be some blood, they wanted to get a good look at it. What good was blood if you couldn't see it spilling out on the ground? And then there's chingazos everywhere. Pifas and this guy Tony are beating the crap out of each other, and then Joaquín Mesa starts in on one of Tony's friends, and then Jaime Rede who was probably still mad over the fact that Gigi Carmona dumped him decides he just has to hit someone. So he jumps in, too. And Reyes Espinoza, who just hated to be left out, he jumps in and just starts swinging a lo loco. He didn't care who he was swinging it, just so long as he got a piece of the action. So there's about seven or eight guys fighting in front of this abandoned farmhouse, and I'm just sitting there shaking my head and cussing myself out for being there. Who's the pendejo here? I ask myself.

And then I see Pifas on the ground, and Tony's still punching him. Shit. I have to pull Tony off of him and tell him, "¡Órale! Look! He's down. Ya párale. You win, damnit. What do you say you leave the pobre pendejo alone, ese."

And Tony, who doesn't look too good himself, doesn't say anything. He looks at me. "What if I don't want to stop?" He looks down at Pifas who's lying there. He lights a cigarette. He looks at me.

I look at him.

He figures he's tired. He figures I'm not so tired.

So he takes a drag from his cigarette and nods. Then he calls his guys off. "Ya cabrones," he says. And everybody stops fighting just like that. And then everyone is standing around like a bunch of pendejos.

I help Pifas up. His lip is cut. "You all right, Pifas?"

"Yeah, yeah," he says. He lights a cigarette, too. Then he decides to get real friendly and says, "Órale, you guys want some beer?"

And Tony says, "Sure, ese, why not?" So Pifas hands out a Budweiser to everyone, and they're all hanging out together. Best friends. And there I am, hanging out with them. Who's the pendejo here?

And then Jaime Rede, who always hated me, says, "Órale, Sammy, you're a chicken shit, you know that? Everyone else was fighting, and you're just sitting there like a vieja, watching us. You should ask Darlene Díaz to lend you her cheerleading skirt. Pinche joto."

I wanted to pound him. I lit a cigarette. I blew out the smoke through my nose, real cool. Sometimes, I thought I was so fucking cool. "You know what, Jaime," I said, "next time you talk to me that way, I'm gonna use your pinche Mexican face for an ashtray." I took his beer out of his hand and poured it out on the ground. Real slow. Real cool. It was easy to be cool around Jaime. I knew he wouldn't screw with me.

"Man, man, man," Pifas said.

Man, man, man. I turned around and walked. Just kept walking.

I was pissed. These guys, what was wrong with them anyway? What was it with all the fighting? So what if they were pissed off? I was pissed off, too. I was pissed off about a lot of things. About my mom. About Juliana. About living in Hollywood. About working all the time, and having to save every dime, every nickel, every penny, just so I could go to college. About having teachers and friends who looked at me like I was wasting my time by working so goddamned hard at being a good student. About being called *the Librarian* behind my back by every asshole who thought being a man meant ignoring the fact that he was born with a fucking mind. Damnit to hell! I was pissed off, too. But I didn't go around kicking people's asses just because I was pissed off. Shit, sometimes, having these conversations with myself only made me madder. I lit a cigarette. Once I calmed down, I just enjoyed the walk. It was a nice night. Hot. And it smelled like rain.

It was good to be alone. I always liked that, being alone. Maybe it was because Hollywood felt so crowded. It's funny, how much time I could spend in my head. I had a whole life up there. The people I knew, they put things in that life. Like my Dad and everyone else I ran into and the whole population of Hollywood. I was always telling my little sister, Elena, that every time we did something good, every time—then we got a little closer to the garden. She wanted to know which garden. I told her the garden that was in the Bible—the garden where everything had been perfect. Of course, I got that idea from Mrs. Apodaca—not that I told Elena about where my idea came from. And really, it didn't matter that it was Mrs.

Apodaca's idea because all the stuff that was in the garden was different for everyone. The stuff that was in my garden was different from the stuff that was in Mrs. Apodaca's garden. So, really the garden was mine. And I was always making up the garden in my head. And it didn't have run-down houses and it didn't have crappy jobs and it didn't have teachers who looked at you like you were in the wrong place, and it didn't have guys who liked to take out their fists and, well, I stayed up nights thinking of what the garden did and didn't have. And I lived there. That's where I lived. God, I wondered if I wanted guys like Pifas in my garden. But if I wouldn't have them, who would? Who the hell would?

After a while, just walking, I got relaxed. And I got to whistling. I was good at that. When I got to Solano, a car passed me real slow. Then the car turned around and I thought, "Shit, what now?" I just kept walking, and then I took a side street, which really wasn't very smart. Why did people think I was so smart? Because I read books? Books don't make you smart. I was always doing dumb things. So my heart starts to pound— and then I hear this voice, "Hey, Sammy, what's up?"

I knew that voice. I looked up—just who I thought it was. "That you, Gigi?" She was with a car full of girls.

"What's up, Sammy? How come you're walking down the street all by yourself?"

"There a law against that?"

"No seas así, Sammy. Can't you be friendly?"

"Mr. Friendly, that's me." I smiled. "I was just with your friend, Jaime Rede."

"He's a piece of shit."

"Be nice, Gigi."

"Fuck you, Sammy."

"No seas así."

She laughed. She had a nice laugh, Gigi did. But she wore tons of makeup, and her hair was always teased and stiff from all that hairspray. She always looked like she was auditioning for the part of a Go-Go Girl on one of those dumbass T.V. shows. "So," she says, "I didn't know you and Jaime were friends."

"He's from Hollywood. I'm from Hollywood."

"We're all from Hollywood."

"Does that make us friends?"

"No, Sammy, I think it just means we're all stuck with each other. For now, anyway." She played with the crucifix that was hanging from her gold chain. "I'll tell you one thing, though, I'm not sticking with Jaime Rede. He's a cabrón and a pinche."

"Nice mouth."

"Oh, right. Guys can talk how they want. Girls. They just gotta look good."

"Everyone has to look good, Gigi. This is America."

She laughed. I liked that she laughed.

"I didn't know you could be funny."

I nodded. Smiled. I guess I smiled. "Look," I said. "I gotta go."

"We'll give you a ride if you give us some cigarettes."

"If you can't afford to buy 'em, don't smoke 'em."

"Don't be mean," she said.

I tossed her the pack. "Keep 'em." I kept walking.

"Don't you want a ride?"

"Nope."

"I hate you," she said. She sounded mad. She threw the cigarettes back at me. Hit me with them. Not that it hurt.

"Good," I said. I wondered why she'd said that. I'd given her my pack of cigarettes. So what if I'd turned down a ride?

I was tired when I got home. I mean tired. I sat on the porch and smoked a cigarette. My dad came out. "You okay, mi'jo?"

"Yeah, Dad."

"I didn't hear a car."

"I walked."

He didn't ask. I didn't tell. It started raining. We sat there—my dad and me—on the porch watching the rain. He asked me for a cigarette. So we sat there and smoked. And right then, it didn't feel bad to be Sammy Santos. Being with my dad, it always felt right. Maybe I didn't have a mom anymore. But I had a dad.

When I went to bed, it was still raining. I liked the thunder, the sound of it. I liked the breeze that was coming through the open window. I kept going over everything in my mind like the soil I turned over at work. I always did that when I went to bed, turned everything over. So I start talking to myself. *So this is what I get for saying okay to Pifas? I get to watch a bunch of guys beat the crap out of each other. I get to play referee. I get called names by Jaime Rede and then the son-ofabitch threatens me. So I resort to threatening him back. Then I get mad and walk home. I get stopped by Gigi Carmona who informs me that she hates me. Fun. A summer night in Las Cruces, New Mexico. Fun.*

seven

The next Friday, Pifas asks me if I want to go out again. "Friday, my man," he says. "Órale, it's time to party, ese." I told him I didn't like hanging out with Jaime Rede. He said Jaime Rede wasn't going. I told him I didn't like hanging out with Reyes Espinoza. He said Reyes Espinoza wasn't going.

"C'mon, ese, we'll have a good time. There's a party. Some chick named Hatty Garrison, her parents are out of town."

I knew Hatty. I couldn't believe she'd actually invited Pifas to her party. "Are you invited or you just crashing?"

"No, maaan, she told me to bring my friends. C'mon, ese. Lots of chicks, ese. A lo mejor we'll get lucky."

"Yeah, sure. We have a better chance of getting busted than getting laid."

"Don't be that way, ese."

I wondered why Pifas was so optimistic about things.

"C'mon, Sammy. Last week we had fun."

We had fun? "Okay," I said. I said it again. I said okay. So Pifas picks me up and he's with René Montoya. René wasn't an asshole. I liked him. Only thing is, he liked trouble. He couldn't help himself. I knew he had a record. I'd even seen him in handcuffs before, right there in front of my house. Busted. I never asked what for. None of my business. Trouble. My dad said he was going to die young if he didn't watch it. "He'll wind up in the can, just watch, en la mera pinta." And Mrs. Apodaca, I swear if he came anywhere within a block of her, she'd get out her holy water. But if you were around him, you wouldn't know any of those things, wouldn't even guess it. He was clean cut, almost wholesome. Could have done a commercial for Colgate toothpaste—well, except that you could tell he was Mexican, which wasn't a good thing if you wanted to be in a commercial.

We went driving around, and we go to this place, a drive-in liquor place called The Welcome Inn that sold beer to René because he looked a lot older. We drive around and have a couple of beers. We talk. Pifas asks René why the cops stick to him like flies on shit. "Why do you think, pendejo? They like picking on Mexicans. We're like weeds. And they're the men with hoes."

"You think so?" Pifas says.

"You think they go around busting keg parties the gringos throw? Hell no. Hell no, they don't. You think they arrest gringos when they get in a fight? Do you, Pifas?"

He starts getting mad. I can hear it in his voice.

"Doesn't matter what cops think," I said.

"I like you, Sammy. You're smart. But you're full of shit."

"Thanks," I said. "You're full of shit, too." I tossed him a cigarette.

"It matters, Sammy." That's what René said. "It matters what the cops think. Just like it matters what our fucking teachers think." He licked the cigarette he was holding. "Toss me a light," he said. "Sammy, the only thing that doesn't matter is us."

We get to the party around nine o'clock. Nice. Hollywood didn't have houses like the one Hatty Garrison lived in. Cars everywhere on her street. I knew there'd be trouble. Already the neighbors looked like they were ready to swoop down. So Pifas and René Montoya and me, we go to the door. Hatty's there with this big smile. "Pifas!" she says. She was nice, Hatty. Always liked her. "Sammy!" she says. And she hugs me. I could smell the beer on her. Well on her way to being drunk. Not a good sign, I thought. I hated that I was such a worrier. Was Pifas worried? Was René worried? Was Hatty worried? No one was worried. We had a house full of Alfred E. Neumans.

We made our way through the crowd. The music was loud as shit. I never liked that. I mean, I liked rock. I liked the song that was on. I liked the Rolling Stones. But I didn't like loud. I pushed my way through the crowd and made my way to the backyard. Lots of gringos. Lots of Chicanos, too. Integration. Yeah, yeah. I tried to see if anyone else from Hollywood was there. Didn't see anyone, mostly people I knew from school. People I'd be ashamed to take to my house. I hated that I was ashamed. Where did that come from?

Someone handed me a plastic cup. I walked over to the keg and some guy says, "Sammy! Fucking A! Sammy!" He takes my empty cup and fills it up from the keg. There's always a keg watcher. Afraid everybody will drink all the beer and leave nothing for him.

"Hey, Michael, how is it?" That's what I always say. How is it? It was a Sammy Santos thing.

Michael nodded his head to the music and handed me the cup full of beer. "It's good, Sammy. Everything's good."

"Good," I said. "I'm good, too." That's when I see Gigi talking to some girl. She was wearing a mini-skirt, and her white go-go boots and really pink lipstick. Pink as Mrs. Apodaca's house. She had a body, Gigi did. Liked having it. Liked it a lot. I walk over to her. "Gigi. How is it?"

"It's you," she said.

"Yeah. Me, Gigi. Just me."

"What do you want?"

"Nothing," I said. I walked away. I didn't get her. I just didn't.

It was an okay party. People were dancing. People were talking. People were drinking. People were making out. That sort of thing. You know the scene. Funny thing, I wasn't into it. Maybe it was Juliana. Maybe my head was still in another place. With her. At the Aggie Drive-In. I was always a watcher. But now, I was even more of a watcher. I wasn't a part of anything. Not anything real. Maybe something would happen. If not to me, to someone else. Didn't matter if it was something good or something bad. Just anything to make me feel like I was alive. Maybe, deep down, I knew why Pifas and Joaquín and René and Reyes liked to fight. They wanted to feel something. Maybe I was just like them. Maybe that wasn't such a bad thing. So there I was, at a party at Hatty Garrison's house, a beer in my hand and about to light a cigarette, when Gigi comes up to me and says, "You know, Sammy, you're a real asshole."

"Did I do something to you, Gigi? Did I?"

"You have your head stuck so far up your ass you can see what you ate for dinner."

"Nice mouth."

"Don't nice mouth me, Sammy."

"You wanna tell me why we're fighting a war?" I offered her a cigarette. She took it—like she was doing me a favor.

"Why do you tell everyone my name's Ramona?"

"Well, because that's your name."

"I hate that name."

"Pick it up with your mom and dad."

She really shot me a look. You know. The look. The one

that makes you feel like a worm about to be stepped on.

"Okay. Look, I don't go around telling everyone your real name's not Gigi. I don't know—"

"You told Jaime Rede."

"Big deal."

"Now he knows."

"He was in the first grade with us, Gigi."

"What does that mean?"

"That's how I know what your name is—from first grade. That's what the teacher used to call you."

"You remember that?"

"How the hell else would I know what your name is, Gigi?"

"Well, you shouldn't have told him. Everyone he knows has started calling me Ramona. And it's all your fault. I feel like a pendeja."

She didn't smoke a cigarette like a real smoker. She didn't like it. I think a cigarette just went with the outfit—that's why she wanted to hold one.

"That's why you're mad at me?"

"I have other reasons."

"You wanna tell me about 'em?"

"No."

Great. I hated that. "No?"

"No." She inhaled the cigarette I'd given her like she was real cool, like she'd been practicing in front of a mirror. "See ya, Sammy." She disappeared into the house, got swallowed up by the song that was blaring out *I'm getting closer to my home* . . . I look over and see Jaime Rede talking to this guy that was in my Spanish class, Eric Fry. And the two of them are talking real quiet. I wondered if they were making some kind of dope deal. Someone told me Jaime was into that. And Eric Fry, well, I didn't know anything about him—except that he spoke perfect Spanish, something pretty odd for a gringo, spoke it better than most Mexicans. But he was a little too proud of himself. He liked to correct people in our Spanish class. I hated that. I didn't like him much. I don't care if he did speak Spanish. No. I didn't like him. Not that he wasn't nice to me. He was. It wasn't that. Anyway, whatever they were talking about, they were really into it. I wondered if I shouldn't walk over there and say "How is it?" but then I thought, what would I say after that?

Just then, I thought I'd light a cigarette. That's when I heard someone yell, "Fight! Fight!" Somehow the whole party had pushed itself out to the front yard. There was a big circle around two guys who were going at it. I had a feeling. I did. So I elbow my way to the front. And there's René and some guy who played football named Scott. And they were really fighting. They hated each other. Nobody could fight like that if they didn't hate. Shit. Shit. And then someone yells, "Cops! Cops!" And Scott and René don't care. They keep fighting. But I care. And if the cops came, I knew they'd just haul René in again. I hated that. I jumped in. Crazy. I was crazy. "Goddamnit, René, let's get the hell outta here!" He looked at me—then we just ran.

I couldn't believe it, there I was running down some street, didn't even really know where I was running. And then I start getting mad. This is what I get for saying okay. This is what I get for dancing with the fucking devil—I wind up in hell. What did I expect? Shit, when I get a hold of Pifas—I kept looking back to see if there was a cop car following us. And then I saw these headlights, and I thought, busted. Cabrón, Pifas, when I get a hold of that little shit—busted, busted. My heart was pounding right up to my throat. Right there. In my throat. And then, when I turned I could see it wasn't a cop car, just an old beat up '57 Chevy, but that didn't stop me from running. I just ran, René still running behind me. And as the car caught up to us, I heard a voice, "Hop in." Gigi! It was Gigi! Thank God. Thank God for Gigi. We didn't ask questions, we just hopped in the car.

"You guys aren't too smart, you know that? How many times have you been hauled in, René? And you, Sammy?" The thing about Gigi was that she was pretty straight. I mean, she played tough, but she wasn't. Not really. There were some girls in Hollywood that were really tough. But Gigi wasn't one of them. She was a nice girl trying to pretend she wasn't.

"Can I catch my breath?" I said.

No one said anything for a while. René and I, we just

wanted to catch our breath. God, breathing can be loud. In a car. When no one's talking. I wiped the sweat off my face with the shoulder of my shirt. "Thanks, Gigi," I said. "You saved our asses."

"Yeah, well, look, give me a smoke." So I gave her a smoke. I watched her light it, then noticed who was driving the car. A girl who lived down the block. Angelina. Quiet. Never stood out much. Everyone called her Angel. Good girl type. What was she doing at a keg party?

"Hi Angel," I said.

"Hi Sammy." She had a nice voice. Soft. Maybe too soft for a girl from Hollywood.

"So where we going?" René says. "It's early."

"I'm not taking you anywhere. I'm gonna dump your Raza ass at home—unless you promise not to start anymore fights. What is it with you, anyway? You're such a bofo. Estás loco ¿o qué?"

"I didn't start that fight. That pinche gringo has it in for me. Y yo no me dejo. Hell no. I don't bow to cabrones like that. No way. Next time I see that cabrón I'm gonna kick his ass all the way to Minneapolis or wherever the shit his people come from."

"You know why Gloria broke up with you? Because you think with your fists, that's why. That's even worse than thinking with your dick."

"Hey, hey, Gigi," I said.

"Cállate, Samuel. Just shut up."

"I don't want to talk about Gloria."

"Guess you don't. She loved your stupid pinche brown ass. Did you care?"

"I cared."

"Oye el agua. Está lloviendo. Look, just shut up."

"This is fun," I said. "We're having fun, aren't we, Angel?"

Angel smiles but she's a good driver. She nods and just keeps driving. By then, we were on El Paseo just cruising. And then René says, "Hey, there's Pifas! Honk, Angel." Angel, good girl that she was, does exactly what René says.

René hangs out the window, "Hey, Pifas!"

Pifas looks up, and does that Aztec chin thing. We both pull over to a side street.

"There was cops everywhere! Chingao, and everyone's running, and I'm thinking, shit, *all that wasted beer.* And people are hiding all over the house, and Hatty's crying, felt bad for her, and I'm just tryin' like hell to boogie, ¿sabes?" Sometimes when Pifas got going, you couldn't shut the guy up. "Bunch of people got busted. And, cabrones, you left without me. Órale ¿qué pues?" But already, he'd forgiven us. "Let's go to the river. I got some Boone's Farm." And he just takes off.

"Follow 'em," René says. And Angel does what she's told.

"Pifas is all screwed up, ¿sabes?" Gigi does this thing with her cigarette like she's writing a sentence in the air.

"He's all right, Pifas." René was loyal. I liked that. "Buena gente. He's there when you need him."

Gigi was into lecturing. If she didn't watch herself she was gonna grow up and be Mrs. Apodaca. "He finds trouble. He smells it. Just like you, René. If you could only smell money like you smelled trouble."

"Yeah, yeah. If only, if only," René said. He kind of went away for a second. I could tell. I wondered where he went. He did that sometimes, went somewhere in his head. Just like me.

At the river, we parked the cars. God, you could see everything in the moonlight. The river looked clean and pure—even though it wasn't. In the light of that summer moon, everything seemed calm. Even us. Even Pifas and René. God, I liked it there. I think the garden in my head was lit up like this. Better than any party.

Gigi and Angel and René and Pifas and me, we sat there and drank Boone's Farm Apple Wine. And we smoked. Mostly Angel didn't say anything, she just listened. But one thing I noticed about her. She was there. She was really there. Not like me. I was somewhere else. In my heart. Pifas and René were drinking a lot. Gigi and I only drank a little. Then, out of nowhere, Angel says, "Let's play a game. Let's play, What-are-we-going-to-do-when-we-leave-Hollywood?"

No one said anything. Everyone was thinking she was stupid. But before anyone said that, I said, "College. I'm going to college."

"Me, too," Angel said.

René looked at us like we were crazy. "Not me. No gringo-ass college for me. More teachers and more gringos. No way. I'm gonna go be a boxer in L.A. That's where I'm headed."

"A boxer?" Gigi said. "Estás loco. Te van a matar."

"Nobody's gonna get killed," René laughed. He took a big swig from the bottle of wine and passed it to me.

"I joined up."

We all looked at Pifas.

"What?" Gigi said.

"I said I joined up." Pifas had this really serious expression on his face.

"You're drunk, Pifas."

"Fuckin' A, René," he said. "¿Y qué? But I'm goin' in the pinche Army."

René had this sick look on his face, like he just couldn't believe it. "Órale, Pifas, don't be a pendejo. What are you gonna do in the army? There's a war goin' on, ese. Don't you pay attention? Hollywood isn't enough for you? Shit, ese, you're joining the system instead of fucking fighting it. You should join the Brown Berets, not the fucking Army."

"Órale, I'm not a pendejo. What the shit am I supposed to do? It's either enlist or get drafted. Brown Berets, my ass. When they draft me, what are the fuckin' Brown Berets gonna do? What are they gonna do for Pifas Espinosa? Fight the system, shit! Shit! That's what I say. Who's the pendejo, René? What do you want me to do, run through the shithole streets of Hollywood yelling, 'Come out of your goddamned good-for-nothing houses and fight the fuckin' system! Come out! Come out!'" Pifas got up from the hood of his car and started running around throwing his arms in the air like a bird flapping his wings—a bird that couldn't fly no matter how hard he flapped. And he kept yelling, "Come out!" like a crazy man. "Citizens of Hollywood, rise up! Rise up against the fucking system!" We all watched him, didn't say anything, just watched, looked at each other like maybe we were supposed to do something. But what do you do when someone loses it? Right there, in front of you. Right there. He threw himself on the ground and just lay there, "Rise up! Fucking rise up!" Then he laughed. I thought he would laugh forever. And right then, the laughing sounded like crying. And maybe he was crying. Then, he stopped. Just stopped. Got up and sat back on the hood of his car. "I enlisted," he said, his voice completely normal again.

"Are you okay?" Gigi whispered.

He nodded. "Yeah. I enlisted. And, anyway, what if they send me to Germany instead of Nam?"

"Yeah, right."

"It could happen, ese." Pifas looked away from René, then looked at me. "It could happen, couldn't it, Sammy?"

"Yeah," I said. He knew. I knew. Everyone knew. But I said yeah.

"Nothing's gonna happen to me," he said. Then he twisted

open a new bottle of wine.

"Yeah," I said. "Remember that time those guys were after you, all those pachucos, and you grabbed my rake as you ran by, then turned around and bashed one of those guys with it? Broke my rake on that poor bastard. Right in half, broke my rake. All those vatos after you, and nothing happened. Not to you, Pifas."

Pifas laughed. "Fuckin' A."

No one said anything for a long time. We just sat there. Just another summer night. Five of us from Hollywood, at the river, having a good time. We had smokes and wine. We didn't have anything to be sad about. But for a minute, we all went to our separtate corners, all of us like the boxers René wanted to be, all of us tired, all of us wanting to rest for a minute before we got in the ring again. I don't know what everybody else was thinking. Maybe they were thinking what I was thinking—that Pifas would go to a place called Viet Nam. That maybe he wouldn't come back. That maybe we weren't kids anymore and that last summer's baseball games in the empty lot behind the Apodacas' house were something that we'd lost. Lost without even knowing it. That was the problem with growing up—you lost things you didn't know you had.

Finally, after a while, Gigi reached over and kissed Pifas on the cheek. Like a sister. "Oh, Pifas, estás más loco que un perro suelto."

They were both sitting on the hood of Pifas' car. And I

could tell Pifas, well, he got a little embarrassed. He was a year older, almost nineteen, but right then, he looked like he was ten. Ten and going off to the Army.

I don't know why—maybe I just didn't want to think about Pifas going off to the military. I don't know, I just wanted to think about something else. So I looked at Gigi and asked, "Hey, Gigi, what do you want to do when you leave Hollywood?"

She grabbed the bottle of wine away from Pifas. "What if I don't want to tell you?"

"Ah c'mon," Pifas said. "Tell us."

She took a swig from the bottle of wine. "No laughing."

"No laughing," I said.

"Tell them, Gigi." Angel said it like she already knew.

"Okay," she said. There was that word that got you into trouble. She nodded. "I'm gonna be a singer."

"A singer?" René said.

Angel shot him a look. "You said no laughing."

"A singer?" Pifas said. "Yeah?"

"Yeah," she said. She smiled. Gigi had a killer smile.

"Sing something," Pifas said.

"Nah." But she wanted to sing. We could tell.

"C'mon," I said. "Sing something for us, Gigi."

Even Angel, quiet Angel, told her to sing.

"I don't know," she said. She was backing down.

"C'mon, Gigi," Pifas said, "sing." He sounded sad. Sounded

as if he'd break down and cry if she didn't.

She smiled at him. "Okay," she said. "If anyone laughs they'll be sorry. I swear there'll be trouble." She took a breath. She stopped. Took another breath. Then she started. Soft and unsure. At first. But then clearer and clearer. She sang. God, I didn't know. I didn't know anybody could sing like that. And the song she was singing, it was an old Mexican love song entitled *La gloria eres tú*. I'd expected her to start singing some rock and roll song or something that matched her go-go boots or maybe a Joan Baez tune—but that's not what she was singing. She was singing in Spanish. She was singing from a different place. In a language that didn't matter a damn. But it mattered to Gigi. And it mattered to us—to Pifas and René and to Angel. *La gloria eres tú*. God, she could sing. And in the moonlight, she didn't seem like a girl at all. She was a woman with a voice. Any man would die just to hear that voice. I swear—just to hear it. I thought the world had stopped to listen to Gigi—Gigi Carmona from Hollywood. I could see tears rolling down Pifas' face. As pure as Gigi's voice. I could feel those wings inside me again—like they were coming back to life, like all they needed was just one beautiful song for them to get up and start beating again. Everything was so perfect, I mean really perfect. Maybe this was what the garden was like. Maybe this was the way the world should end. Not with me and my own thoughts, not with high school boys using their fists on each other, not with Pifas going off to

97

war—but with the tears of boys falling to the beat of a woman's song, the sounds of guns and bombs and fists against flesh disappearing. This is the way the world should end: with boys turning into men as they listen to a woman sing.

I wish Juliana had been there.

eight

"You think I'm a dumbass, don't you, Sammy?"

We were sitting on my front porch one night, a week before Pifas was leaving. Leaving—I've always hated that word. It was beginning to thunder. Rain. August was like that. "Toss me a cigarette," I said. "I'm out." He tossed me one. I lit it. "No," I said. "I don't think that."

"Yeah, you do. You don't respect me. Dime la verdad. I can take it."

"No seas pendejo. I respect you, Pifas."

"Since when?"

"Since that night. When Juliana—you know. Since that night."

"And before that?"

"Before that? I thought you were a dumbass."

He laughed. We both laughed.

He nodded. I watched him—then joined in the nodding.

"I've always been a screwup," he said. "Not you, Sammy. Ever since grade school, you were one serious kid. Always working—puro trabajar, trabajar, trabajar. Mano, tienes que re-laaaaaaax. Even when you play, it's work for you. Me, I do too much relaxing."

"You're not a screwup," I said.

"I didn't enlist."

"What? What are you saying, Pifas?"

"I got drafted. I didn't want anyone to know, know what I mean? ¿Sabes? Me dio vergüenza. So I made out like I enlisted. Everyone knows only losers get drafted."

"Don't do that, Pifas. It's a system. It's just a system."

"There are winners in that system, Sammy. Look, I know the score. Look, we both know, don't we, Sammy? There's two kinds of people in this fucking world—those who make it and those who don't. We're on different sides of that coin, ¿sabes? And when that coin was tossed, your side landed facing the sky and my side landed facing the fucking ground. And we both know, don't we, Sammy? And there's not a damn thing we can do about it. Let's not waste time cryin' about what's never gonna change."

"You're not a loser," I said. It was storming now. The rain was coming down, the sky crackling like it was a piece of dry wood on fire. "You're not a loser, Pifas."

"You used to think so."

"Damnit to hell, I was wrong." I looked at him. So many

times, I hadn't seen him. "Pifas, listen. Listen to me. I was wrong about you."

They were rioting in Chicago. Rioting. Not that riots were something foreign. I grew up watching that sort of thing. Normal stuff. Blood was normal. People exploding like boxes of ammunition—that was normal. The grotesque, twisted faces of men and women shouting, being hit. The reflex of an arm going up to protect a face. Faces were sacred. The Aztecs knew that. *Not there, don't hit me there.* I grew up like a lot of people—being a witness to all that from the safe distance of my own home. Television did that. Made you far from things. Made you a watcher. Made you believe you were safe. We watched the footage, my father and I, on the news. He was addicted to the news, needed to watch like I had come to need cigarettes. Never missed, not if he could help it. He pointed at the screen. "Look, hijo. Mira. Cabrones. This is not democracy." My father didn't cuss much. But he cussed when he watched the news. There was always something on to make him mad. He could get pretty fierce about things. His children. His politics. He looked at me, "Do you think this is democracy?"

"No, Dad," I said, "it's a riot. It's a bunch of cops beating up on demonstrators."

"And you think this is a good thing?"

"No, Dad." I'd had these conversations with him before. I

knew how they went. He wanted me to think. He wanted to make sure I wasn't brain dead. *You can't just think about yourself. You can't just think about school. There's a world, mi'jo. You have to think about what's going on in it. You have to figure out your place.* That was his standard lecture. Or some variation.

He shook his finger at the television screen again. "Mayor Daley's a pinche," he said. "You watch. Because of this, that sinvergüenza Nixon's going to win the election." My dad hated Nixon. I hated him, too. I hated him for my dad.

"What about the protesters?" I said. "They beat the hell out of them, Dad. What about them?"

My dad shook his head. He had no answer. "Están chingados. Pobres," he said, "they thought they were going to change the world."

"The world's not worth changing," I said.

My father looked at me and shook his head. "A veces no te conozco." He'd switched to Spanish. That meant he was mad. Not good. Sometimes, I disappointed him. "Estás muy joven para pensar así."

He was right—I was too young to be so cynical. I was tired. I was sad. Pifas was going off to the Army. Pifas was right about me, about what I felt. I hadn't liked him before, but now, everything was different. I liked him. He'd grown on me. Had a good heart even though he could be a real pain in the ass. Didn't mean any harm. And here he was, off to get himself killed. I wasn't in the mood for thinking good thoughts.

Blood on the streets of Chicago didn't do anything for my bad mood. "I'm sorry," I said.

"The world's a good place, Sammy." He shook his head. "Even though this damned country's falling apart, I'm telling you the world's a good place." He laughed. "Me estoy volviendo loco."

"No, Dad, you're not crazy." I hated when he got down on himself. I wanted to kiss him. He kissed me all the time, my dad. So how come I couldn't get my ass off the couch and kiss him? I got up, walked into the kitchen and brought him a beer. "You want a cigarette, Dad?"

"Yeah," he said. "Give me one."

I handed him one. He lit it. "Summer's almost over."

"Yeah," I said.

"Next year you're going to college?"

He asked that about once a week. He wanted to be sure.

"Yeah, Dad."

"And Pifas is off to the Army?"

"Yeah, Dad. There's a party for him tomorrow night."

"His mom told me. This is going to kill her, Sammy. She loves that boy."

"Yeah, Dad," I said. "She's a nice lady."

"Ese muchacho, yo no sé. He never made one good decision in his life." He just kept shaking his head. "No sense, he just doesn't have any sense." My dad took a long, slow drag off his cigarette. "Don't ever join the Army."

"I won't."

He looked at me. "Never. ¿Me entiendes?"

"I understand, Dad." Joining the Army had never crossed my mind. He knew that. I'm not the Army type—I'd told him that a hundred times. But I understood what he was trying to tell me. He was afraid. Of losing me—just like Mrs. Espinosa was losing Pifas.

"My brother was killed in Korea," he said.

We had a picture of my uncle in the living room—next to the picture of John Kennedy. "I know, Dad."

"He was all I had."

"I know, Dad."

"They threw me out of the Army, did you know that?"

"Yeah, Dad, you told me."

"They said I was retarded. That's why they threw me out. That's what it says on my discharge papers. My commanding officer thought Mexicans were about as smart as dogs. That's why, that's the real reason. Desgraciados. Just threw me out. Like I didn't belong. Retarded."

I'd heard the story too many times. That hurt in his voice. I wanted it to stop. But I knew it would always be there. I hated them for that. For giving him a hurt he'd carry for a lifetime. I was starting to know a lot of things about hurt. I thought about the dead wings lying somewhere inside me. They were kind of rotting by now, I guess. And my father, well, he must've had those dead wings inside him, too. Only I figured, because he was a lot older, he had a whole dead bird buried somewhere and it was making him old. Maybe that bird died the same time as my mother. Yeah, that was it, that's how I was beginning to see the whole thing. I don't know. I think a lot about stuff. Anyway, I just looked at my dad and said, "Screw them, Dad, it doesn't matter."

"Don't ever let them treat you like that."

"I won't." I watched him smoke his cigarette. "Dad," I said. "You're the best, ¿me entiendes?" He smiled. I loved to see him smile.

nine

Pifas' party was at his brother's trailer house. They'd cleaned it all up for the occasion. All kinds of people were there—Gigi Carmona and Susie Hernández and Frances Sánchez and Angel and Jaime Rede and Joaquín and René and Reyes, and all of Pifas' brothers—all five of them. Hatty Garrison was there with her friends, Pauline and Sandra. They were both Mexican, but they didn't look Mexican. That happens. Lots of other people I didn't know so well were there, people I knew from Hollywood, some of Huicho's brothers whom I hated. I had my reasons. And some other people I knew from high school.

The music was really going. Someone had put on Carlos Santana. Everybody in Hollywood loved Santana. Loved, loved him. He was Pifas' favorite musician. *Man, man, man,* that's what Pifas said every time one of his songs came on the radio at work. *Fuckin' A, fuckin' A.* Maybe we'd be listening to

Santana all night. That was okay with me.

Everybody was having a good time. Lots of laughing. I liked that about parties. Mostly people were hanging around outside. Someone had hung a string of Christmas-tree lights across the front yard that crisscrossed from Pifas' brother's trailer to the trailer next door.

Someone was smoking dope. I could smell it. The smell was good. I liked it. I looked at the corner of the yard, and there was a group of older guys huddled around. Long hair and beards like they were trying to copy an album cover of Credence Clearwater Revival. I watched them for a while. I wondered what it would be like to smoke some. Bet it was good. But I wasn't about to do any weed. Nope. Not tonight.

I didn't notice her standing next to me.

"You like to watch people, don't you?"

I smiled at her. Too much makeup. The short dress was good, though. "How is it, Gigi?"

"I'm good, Sammy. You didn't answer my question."

"Yeah, I like to watch people. People are good."

"Maybe it's easier to watch people than to talk to them."

"I like to talk to people, Gigi."

"Maybe you just don't like to talk to me."

"Where do you get this idea that I have something against you? You know, I think you're the best. Really, Gigi. You're fine."

"Don't bullshit me, Sammy."

"Don't start, Gigi." I looked at her. "I'm not gonna fight a war with you. I'm just not. You wanna dance?"

"You asking me to dance?"

I grabbed her hand. That scared me. Why did I grab her hand? And maybe I heard a flutter of wings—but then the sound went away. We walked to where everyone was dancing. And then we danced. She was a good dancer. Not that I had any doubts. I mean, I guess I thought that anybody who could sing could dance, too. Me, I didn't do either of those things. Not a singer, not a dancer. But you don't always have to be good at something to do it. And I was in the mood to dance. I don't know. It was a nice night and I just wanted to dance.

I don't know how long we danced. Long time. It was good. We looked at each other. I'd smile. She'd smile. Her smile was different than mine. I didn't like that. It scared me. "Let's get a beer," she said over the loud music.

I went over to the keg and poured a beer for me, and one for Gigi. We sat a little away from the music. And Gigi was singing along with Santana and nodding her head. She was happy. Like the music was inside her. Then Pifas comes over and sits with us. "This is it. Fuckin' A, Sammy."

"You're okay, Pifas," I said. I lifted my plastic cup. He lifted his. So did Gigi. "Here's to the Army. Watch your ass, baby."

Gigi started to cry.

"No, no, no," Pifas said. "Don't do that. Man, man, man, don't do that, Gigi." He hugged her.

Then she laughed. "I'm better," she said. Then she hit him on the shoulder. "Just don't get your ass shot, okay?"

"Look, when I come back, I'm gonna go to college on the G.I. Bill."

"Oh yeah?" I said.

"Yeah. I'm gonna be a college man—just like you, Sammy."

I could feel myself starting to leave. I did that, sometimes, I just left. It was hard to be there. To look at him. To play this game like everything was fine, like he was just going away to camp or on vacation or like he was just moving away to California. I wasn't good at pretending. But I knew that's the only way people survived. Stay, I told myself. Just stay. Pretend. Like the rest of the world. We talked a while. Angel and René and Reyes and Jaime and Susie and Frances, they came over—and we all stood around and made fun of each other. It was good. We were laughing. We were really laughing. We were just kids.

Somewhere along the line that night, I decided to get really drunk. I'd never been drunk before. And I wanted to know what it was like. No, that's not it. It was another way of pretending.

I remember posing for a picture with Pifas and the rest of us Hollywood types. We were all in it. All of us. I still have that picture. I don't know how I wound up with it—but I still have it. Pifas is right in the center. And I'm standing right next to him. And we're all smiling.

I remember throwing up behind the trailer house. I remember hearing Jaime's voice, "The fucking Librarian's throwing up." I remember Gigi being so nice to me. Maybe she didn't want to fight with me anymore.

And I remember promising to meet Pifas at the bus station.

Gigi drove me home in my dad's car. Someone must've followed us, because she kissed me as we stood in front of my house. Like a sister. But there was more behind the kiss. I knew there was, even though I was drunk. And that's when I really understood that Gigi had a beautiful bird living inside her— really beautiful—and I could almost see it and hear it, and I knew that someday that bird was gonna make Gigi free. Well, maybe I was just thinking all this crap because I was drunk. But how come I couldn't shut down all these crazy thoughts? I thought booze was supposed to make you forget about things.

I sat there, still as a rock, and watched Gigi as she ran off and got in some car. Pifas. Pifas was in the car.

The next morning, I felt like a cat had crawled in my mouth and shed all its fur in there. The room spun around if I closed my eyes. My head felt like someone had been using it for a sidewalk. I drank lots of water, took three aspirin. I looked at the clock. There was a note on the kitchen table, my dad informing me that he'd taken Elena bowling. She loved to bowl on Saturday mornings, that little sister of mine. How the hell was I gonna get to the bus station? I called René. His mother said that he was still asleep.

"Can you wake him up?"

I heard nothing on the other end.

"Please, Mrs. Montoya. Please." I must've sounded desperate. When I heard René's voice on the other end, all I said was, "Get your ass over here. I need a ride to see Pifas at the bus station."

"Órale," he said, then hung up.

When we got to the bus station, Pifas was there with his whole family. I didn't say much. Pifas didn't say much either. Mrs. Espinosa started crying. Pifas told her not to cry. "No llores, Mamá. Be back before you know it." Mr. Espinosa held her, and he had this sick look on his face. He looked like someone was punching him. He stood there and took it.

I'd never said good-bye to anybody. I didn't know what you were supposed to do. There must have been rules. But what the hell was there to say, anyway? Why not just speak in all the clichés we'd been taught? Why not? What was wrong with saying, *Take care of yourself, don't get your ass shot, we'll miss you, write.* What was wrong with saying any of those things?

"Listen, Pifas," I said, "if you write, I'll write back. I promise."

He nodded. He looked like maybe he was gonna break down and cry. Cry right there. God, he looked closer to fifteen than eighteen. Right there, I wanted to say, "Look, Pifas, René and I, we'll take you to Canada. Fuck the Army. We'll take you to Canada." That's what I should have said. But I didn't. And what the hell was Pifas supposed to do in Canada anyway? Loiter?

Pifas nodded at me. "I'll write, ese. Fuckin' A, I'll write." We shook hands. I should have at least hugged him. But I didn't. We shook hands. Even René hugged him. What was wrong with me? Why did I always freeze up at all the important moments? Damnit, I hated myself. And I felt those wings beating inside me again—only it wasn't love that woke those wings up from their sleep. It wasn't. It was something bad, something mean. It was anger. I didn't know anger could do that. When Juliana made those wings appear, I thought it was because of love. But it wasn't true. Hate could make the wings grow strong. And the thought scared me. It really scared me. Damnit! Why were all these bad things happening? Juliana getting killed, and Pifas going off to war, and my insides being torn up.

I sat there. Still as a stone. I watched Pifas climbing on the bus. He was leaving. And all I'd done was shake his hand. I couldn't let him—"Pifas!" It was me. I was yelling his name. It was me. I wasn't even thinking. "Look! Look, take this." I took off the chain I was wearing—the crucifix my mom had given me. I never took it off. Never. "Here," I said, "wear it. Don't ever take it off. It'll bring you luck." He looked at it, then looked at me. Don't cry. Just don't do that. He clutched the crucifix in his fist. He kept nodding. He got on the bus. He opened the window and waved. His hands were big. I'd never noticed that. He was a small guy. But his hands were big.

See ya, Pifas. See ya around.

His family lingered awhile. They looked lost—then finally they just wandered home. Mrs. Espinosa told us to visit her. A nice lady. She promised to make tortillas for us. As if she didn't have enough to do. "Todos son mis hijos," she said. She was one sweet lady. She was. We told her we'd visit. We wouldn't. There was nothing to do but lie to her.

René and I, we hung around for a while longer. We looked at each other. "I think Gigi was with Pifas last night, ¿sabes?"

I nodded.

"I don't think he's ever been laid."

Some guys would have thought less of Gigi for doing that—but not me. She wanted to give him something. She wanted to make him feel like he was worth something.

"I'm dead," René said.

I felt for the place around my neck where my crucifix used to hang. I thought of my mom. I thought of Juliana. "I'm dead, too," I said.

ten

With Pifas gone, my job wasn't much fun. I missed his commentaries. The last two weeks of worked dragged on and on. I thought they'd never end. But like everything else, they *would* end. On the last day of work, the foreman came by. He nodded at me. He didn't like me much. I didn't blame him. I hadn't been all that nice to him. "Want a cigarette?" I said.

He nodded. "Fuckin' A," he said.

"Fuckin' A," I said.

The summer of 1968 was over. It was time for the leaves to change. School started. It would be my last year. I wouldn't miss it when it was all over. I swore I wouldn't. It felt strange to walk the halls. I felt like I was a foreigner. An alien. I didn't belong there anymore. But I had to finish out the last season.

I walked by Juliana's old locker. I heard two girls talking. "Yeah, you didn't hear? Remember, at the beginning of the summer, her dad goes all crazy and shoots them all, Juliana and all her brothers and sisters."

"Oh, yeah, I heard about that—that was Juliana? My God? It's really awful. And she was so pretty." I just kept walking.

Spanish IV-S was my homeroom class. S. For Spanish Speakers. That meant me and Jaime Rede and René Montoya. And that gringo, Eric Fry, who was too good to be in one of the Spanish IV-E classes. E. For English speakers. Mrs. Scott was our homeroom teacher. Ofelia Montes Scott. She was "one of *us* who'd married one of *them*." That's how René put it. René had it in for gringos. He said I had it all wrong. "They have it in for us. It's them, Sammy. Them. ¿Qué pues, Sammy? You're really a pendejo about these things." Yeah, yeah. I don't know where he got the idea that I was on the other side of the issue—it's just that he talked about the same damn thing over and over. *Just give it a rest, René.* That's what I'd tell him. Not that he did. René never gave anything a rest. Maybe Gigi was wrong, maybe he would make a good boxer. He sure as hell liked to fight.

First thing that happened on the first day of school is that they gave us all the new rules. The new rules, they were a lot like the old ones. We'd heard it all. But they liked to tell us. Just in case we'd all forgotten. They figured summers were for forgetting. Maybe they figured right. So they read the rules. Boys, no hair below your collar. Girls, skirts two inches above the knee—any higher and you go home. Boys, tuck your shirts in.

Wear belts. You know what those are, those things your father has to take off once in a while and threaten you with. No patches on your pants. No T-shirts. Girls, no pants. Pants are for boys. And no shorts. No shorts for girls. No shorts for boys. And boys, no hair allowed on your face. Clean cut. Oh, and one more thing, boys: no taps on your shoes. That was meant for all the pachucos who loved to wear taps on their shoes. "Saves your shoes," René said. He had taps. "Órale, the nuns wear 'em, why the shit can't we?" Oh, and one last thing, no public displays of affection. No holding hands. No kissing. Mrs. Scott seemed to enjoy reading the rules. Then she switched to Spanish. We got them in two languages. "Jaime Rede, are you rolling your eyes?" She hated Jaime Rede. She had that in her favor.

"Sí Señora, I'm rolling my eyes." I had to hand it to Jaime. He didn't hold back.

"We're not going to have a good year, are we, Jaime?"

"We're going to have a great year," he said. He actually sounded happy. I wondered what was wrong with him. Happy and Jaime Rede didn't go together. I swear. What was the matter with him?

The dialogue between teacher and student was cut short when the principal, Marvin C. Fitz, got on the intercom to make an announcement. "Welcome back, all of you. Welcome to all new students, and welcome especially to the Senior Class, the Class of 1969…" I hated his voice. He sounded like he was made of plastic. He sort of looked like that, too.

I tuned out. I wasn't what you'd call a good citizen. I wasn't involved. There was a poster going around: "Drop out and drop acid." I liked that. Not that I was about to drop out. To drop out, you had to be in. I'd never been in. I'd always been just, well, looking in. And to drop acid, you had to have money—mine was all going toward college.

I did my homework. I studied. I went home. School was, as Pifas would say, "a fucking drag." If I was a good student, that only meant I wanted to go to college. It didn't mean anything else. Not to me. I only had two questions on my mind when it came to my relationship with my teachers or the school administration: What do you want? And when do you want it? I'd yes-sirred and no-ma'amed my way through my public education. If I had a rebellious mind, I didn't let my body in on it. My body was a good soldier.

It was only during lunch that Gigi caught me up on what I'd missed in Marvin C. Fitz's long-winded intercom announcement. "Sammy, I want you to be my campaign manager." I was outside, in the back of the cafeteria. The smoking section. All those rules, and they let us smoke—but only on that one piece of earth.

I looked at her blankly. Then I looked at Susie Hernández. Then I looked at Frances Sánchez. Then I looked at Angel. "What is she talking about?"

"I'm running for Senior Class President."

"We already have one. Her name's Sandy Ikard."

"And she moved, pendejo. She up and moved."

"Isn't that what a vice president's for?"

"He up and moved, too," Susie said. "His dad got transferred from White Sands."

I shrugged. "Wish my dad would have been transferred. Guess they don't transfer janitors." I took a drag from my cigarette. "So where do you come by all this new information?"

"Baboso. Menso. Weren't you listening to the announcement this morning?"

"Baboso? Nice mouth." I shrugged. "Guess I wasn't."

"So I'm running."

Shit, I thought. Why did people set themselves up for heartbreak? How many times did you have to lie down on a busy street before you got run over? "Good for you, Gigi," I said.

"So I want you to be my campaign manager."

"I don't know how to do that."

"There's nothing to it," Frances said. She gave me this look. Angel gave me a look, too. She was a looker, that Angel. But right then she looked at me the same way Susie and Frances were looking at me. I knew what the looks meant. *She's asking you. Don't be a piece of shit.*

Why do you want to run, Gigi? But I knew the answer. She had the right, didn't she? Why not her? She didn't have a prayer. I should have told her not to run. I should have told

118

her that Pifas had a better shot at being stationed in Germany than she had at being elected. Gigi Carmona from Hollywood wasn't going to be the President of the Class of 1969. She wasn't. No way. Nice dream, nothing wrong with dreaming. You won't win. That would have been the honest thing to say. But I wasn't always honest. And she was standing right there in front of me. She looked so happy. Like the world had given her a chance at something. And she wasn't going to let the moment pass. She was beautiful—even with all that makeup that she didn't need to be wearing. I thought of the girl who'd sang that song. That song that broke my heart that night at the river. I thought of the girl that went with Pifas the night before he left. I loved that girl. Not like I had loved Juliana. But I loved her. "Okay," I said. Even though she was going to get massacred. Even though her heart was going to break like it was nothing more than one of those cheap plastic rulers. I said okay. I'd said that word again, okay. That word always got me into trouble.

"We have two weeks," she said, "before the assembly."

"Let's do it," I said. "We need twenty people." I said it as if I knew what the hell I was talking about. "Twenty hard-core people. Twenty people who'll work night and day for two weeks." I looked at Angel and Susie and Frances. "There's three. And we're gonna need some money."

"Money?" Gigi looked at me.

"Elections aren't free, Gigi. This is America. We're gonna

need a roll of butcher paper and some tempera paints and some construction paper to make you some buttons and, well, maybe some balloons." Shit, I thought. I was going to have to put my money where my mouth was. I had a five-dollar bill in my wallet. I had it there for emergencies. I'd carried it around for two years. And I'd never spent it. I figured now was the time. I took the five out of my wallet. "Here." I gave it to Angel. I trusted her. Susie and Frances, I wasn't so sure. "You're the treasurer." I looked at Susie and Frances. "How much money do you have?"

"I have seventy-five cents," Frances said.

I pointed at Angel. "Give it to her."

Frances reached in her purse. "And what about you?" I said. I gave Susie the same look she'd given me. She reached in her purse and took out a dollar.

"Good. Good. We've started. Let's spread out. Let's hit the people we know. It's lunchtime. It's a good time to hit people up. Gigi, make a list. You need twenty hard-core people. And not Hollywood types either. Get Eric Fry—he'll help you. I hate his ass, but he'll help you. And get Hatty Garrison. She'll help you, too. It's gotta be a coalition thing," I said. "Know what I mean?" They knew. They knew exactly what I was talking about. *Don't just get a bunch of Mexicans.* That's what I meant. They knew. "And let's try to raise twenty-five dollars. We already have $6.75—"

"$8.75," Angel said. "I threw in two more."

I smiled at her. God. She was pretty. "We're a third of the way there. Let's see what we have at the end of the day."

"I'll throw in two more dollars," Gigi said. She started reaching into her purse.

"Nope," I said. "Candidates can't give."

"Why not? Why can't I give to my own campaign?"

"You are giving, Gigi. Don't you know the rules? You're putting your Hollywood ass on the line, ¿sabes?" All of a sudden I was directing all the traffic. "Put your money back in your purse. You pay your way. We pay our way." I clapped my hands, then rubbed them together like a miser. *Where did I get this stuff?* "Okay, let's collect our money. Let's get our people. We can meet right here after school. Right here. Two weeks. Two weeks." I clapped my hands. Like a fucking football coach.

I won't lie to you. Even thinking back to that day makes me smile. I was really into it. I wasn't on the sidelines. Just watching. I was a part of something. It was good. Really. I was part of a cause. I was part of something that wasn't about me—that wasn't about Sammy Santos. Gigi for President. Wouldn't that be something? I saw the four of them walking toward the cafeteria. Susie, Frances, Angel, and Gigi. Good for them, I thought. And good for me. I was on the right side. We didn't have a prayer. I stood there. I decided to skip lunch. I thought about lighting another cigarette. I looked down at the ground. I saw a pair of shoes. I looked up. Gigi was standing there. She looked at me. Then she came right up to me and kissed me on the cheek.

"What was that for?"

"You know," she said. "You know exactly what that was for."

"They can kick you out for doing that, Gigi," I said. "Public display of affection." We looked at each other.

"Yeah, yeah," she said.

"Yeah, yeah," I said.

So the rest of the day I'm trying to hit people up for money. I wasn't too bad at it. I managed to collect $4.50—all in quarters. Between fifth and sixth periods, I asked this guy Eddie Montague for some money. He was a doctor's son. I knew him a little. He went to confession every Saturday at Immaculate Heart of Mary Church. Either he was a good person or a bad person who had plenty to confess. "Give generously," I said.

"Why don't you run, Sammy?"

"Why would I run?"

"Because people like you."

"People don't even know me."

"Everyone knows you."

"People don't know me," I said again. They didn't. No one knew me.

"Look, Sammy, people take you seriously."

"Not interested. My money's on Gigi."

"No one takes her seriously."

"I do."

"She won't win."

"Why not?"

"You know why not."

"No, I don't. Why don't you enlighten me?"

"Okay. Gigi doesn't know the word *enlighten.* For starters."

"Don't sell her short."

"Wake up, Sammy."

"You wake up, you sonofabitch."

"Don't get mad."

"Screw you."

"Look, don't get mad. I'm just tellin' you how it is." He stuck a five-dollar bill in my hand. "Here."

"But you won't vote for her, will you?"

"No, Sammy."

I shoved it back in his hand. "Keep your fucking money."

I went straight to the bathroom. I slammed my fist against one of the doors. "Damnit to hell!" The campaign was a few hours old, and already I was losing it. It pissed me off the way he said Gigi doesn't know the word *enlighten.* He'd already decided she was stupid, that she didn't measure up. He'd sized her up. She was just a brainless Mexican broad from Hollywood. I hated him for thinking that about Gigi. But I'd thought it, too. I guess I couldn't hate him without hating myself.

eleven

There were twelve of us—not counting the candidate. Not twenty. But twelve. We stood right behind the cafeteria, right where we'd stood at lunchtime. Eric Fry stood with us. And Hatty Garrison—and her new boyfriend, Kent Volkmer. Some guy from Chiva Town named Jorge North. Jorge North—what kind of name was that? Jaime Rede. He and Eric seemed to be pretty tight. Maybe there was something to the talk of him and Eric smoking pot together. Mota. Weed. And Charlie Gladstein was with us, he who was Jewish and who liked Mexicans more than he liked Protestants. I knew that because he told me. "Fucking Protestants," he told me one time at some party. He was drunk. "I hate them. They own the fucking world." I liked him. I liked his anger even though he was kind of rich. Still, he was like the words I used to write in the margins of the novels I read. Not a real part of the story. I think he had a thing for Gigi. And the Torres brothers were there, Larry and Mike, who didn't live in Hollywood but who wanted to. They were the only Mexicans I knew who wanted to live in a poorer neighborhood than the one they lived in.

We all looked at each other. It was my show. I'd said okay. And now I had to come through. Okay, I thought. This is what okay means. I didn't like it that we were all gathered at the back of the school. In the smoking section. Bad idea. Not a good way to start. "Let's go sit on the front lawn," I said. So that's what we did. We all sat around, talking. And Gigi told us why she wanted to be class president. "Because I'm not mainstream." That's what she said. I knew exactly what she was saying. "And because I work hard. And because this screwed-up rat's nest of a school needs a little shakin' up." She did a little dance. We all clapped. *Go Gigi.* "And besides, which one of us voted for Sandy Ikard? And which one of us voted for fuck-face, what was his name, the vice president who moved?" We all laughed. "Okay," she said. She looked at me. "Sammy's the organizer. He's gonna show us how to do this thing." I nodded. What the hell did I know? But what did we have to lose? It wasn't like Pifas who'd been drafted. No one was going to get shot. It wasn't like the protesters on the streets of Chicago. No one was going to get hurt.

There wouldn't be any blood.

I gave out assignments like I knew what I was doing. A committee to come up with a slogan. A committee to plaster the school with signs. A committee to make ¡Viva Gigi!

buttons out of construction paper. And everyone agreed to get everyone they knew to vote for Gigi. "How much money do we have?" I asked Angel.

"Twenty-six dollars! We've collected twenty-six dollars in one day!" She couldn't hide the excitement in her voice. I'd never seen Angel so animated. She wasn't this passive female thing—she was alive. Really. God, she was so beautiful. She reminded me of Juliana. A little. Only a little. Juliana was a lot tougher. I liked tough. "Twenty-six dollars!" she said again.

"Good," I said. I reached in my pocket. "Here's $4.50 more. That brings us up to over thirty. Great. Great!" I clapped my hands. I thought of Eddie Montague, what he'd said. "Let's win this thing," I said.

And we got to work.

I called Gigi that night. I told her, "Gigi, you gotta work on your campaign speech. You gotta make it really good. What are the rules? Did you get the rules?"

"Yes, I have the rules." I could tell I'd pissed her off, like she didn't know what she was supposed to do. "I signed up at the office, shithead. And they gave me this piece of paper. And my parents have to sign it. And it says my speech can't be longer than five minutes or they'll make me sit down. And my speech has to be pre-approved by the principal."

"What?"

"Es lo que dice, Sammy. It says, 'All speeches must be turned into the principal's office for approval two days prior to the student assembly.'"

"It says that? In English? I can't believe that shit!"

"So what am I supposed to do about it?"

"I don't know, Gigi, but that really sucks."

"So, tell me, Sammy. What am I supposed to do about that?"

"Write two speeches," I said.

"Two speeches. I can barely write one."

"Write two, Gigi. One for the principal. And one, well, say what Gigi would say."

"What am I gonna do with two speeches, Sammy?"

"I have a plan," I said. "Trust me."

For two weeks, we lived, slept, and ate Gigi's campaign. We passed out flyers. We plastered the school with posters on butcher paper. Charlie Gladstein and Eric Fry and Jaime Rede—who seemed to be a changed man—made all the posters. They hung them up everywhere. Even in the boys' bathrooms. We had three opponents. I thought we had them all on the run. I was beginning to think we might win. Maybe. Maybe was one of those words like okay. Those two words alone could kill you. Stay away from those words.

Every night, I went over to Gigi's and made her practice her speech. She wrote it herself. It was great. Really. She'd wanted me to write it. She'd begged me. "No," I said. "Look, this is you, Gigi. It's gotta be all you." Okay, so I did a little editing. I swear, not a lot. It was all her. And I made her practice every night. "This is stupid," she said.

"No," I said. Not stupid. No one won an election by accident. Every night she practiced. It was like preparing for a concert. That's what I told her. "Pretend you're singing. Remember that night when you sang for us at the river? Do that. Okay? If you can do that, then you win."

Two days before the election, Gigi turned in one of her speeches to the principal. That same day, we marched—Gigi's twelve—that's what we called ourselves—we marched down the hall between second and third period shouting, "¡Viva Gigi! What? ¡Viva Gigi! What? ¡Viva Gigi!" It wasn't a great idea to do that. Not really great. But Angel said we should do it. So we did it. Beautiful Angel. And guess what? We were so hip. We were hip. The twelve. Viva Gigi.

The night before the election, Gigi called me. "What should I wear?"

"Not my category," I said.

"C'mon, Sammy, no seas así."

"Chingao," I said, "I'm a guy. Wrong sex. Call Angel."

"Damnit, Sammy, what should I wear?"

I wanted to tell her not to tease her hair. I wanted to tell her not to wear so much makeup. I wanted to tell her not to fuck things up. "Wear blue," I said. "And follow the script. Just like we practiced."

"Okay," she said. "I'm really scared."

"Smoke a cigarette," I said.

"Cabrón. You're no help. You're just a pinche."

"After all I've done?"

"You were drafted." I thought of Pifas. I'd written him a letter. His mother gave me his address. I'd sent him a campaign button made of blue construction paper that said ¡Viva Gigi! "Yeah," I said, "I was drafted. But I might have enlisted, anyway." I thought of Pifas again.

We talked for a while. Me and Gigi. That's all she needed. To talk. I liked her voice. And she was funny. And smart. And I still hated Eddie Montague for saying those things. I would never forgive him. I wouldn't. I was becoming hard. That wasn't a good thing. I couldn't stop what I was turning into.

That night, I couldn't sleep. I thought of Pifas. I thought of Gigi. I thought of them together. In the back of some car, making love. Like me and Juliana. But I knew it wasn't like me and Juliana at all. Juliana and I, well, we trembled. She never told me she loved me, but I knew she did. But Gigi didn't love Pifas. There were other reasons to have sex. I knew that. Love wasn't the only reason. And why was I thinking about Pifas and Gigi together in the backseat of a car? *Focus*, I said, *focus on the election*. I ran through a list in my mind. Was everything done? Had we done everything that was humanly possible? Had we talked to enough people? Had we—and then I stopped. I was doing it again. Relax. Relax. Why did I give myself lectures that didn't work? I tossed. I turned. Sleep wasn't going to come. I got up, put on an old pair of cutoffs

129

and went out on the porch. I lit a cigarette. That's what I always did. I sat there for a while, trying not to think of tomorrow.

I heard the front door open. I knew it was Dad. "¿Qué no puedes dormir?"

"Se me espantó el sueño."

"It's easy to scare sleep off," he said. It was a joke. So I laughed. Not convincingly. But I laughed.

He sat next to me on the front steps of the porch.

"What's the worst thing that could happen?"

"The worst thing? Lose."

"Losing isn't so bad."

"Sure would be nice to win, Dad." I flicked my cigarette out on the front yard. "We already know what it's like to lose."

I woke up nervous. You know the feeling. Your stomach is churning. You want to go back to bed. Only if you did, you wouldn't be able to fall back asleep. Your stomach feels like you swallowed a pigeon, and it was slamming against your insides, trying to get out. Panic city. I tried to pretend it was a normal day. I fixed breakfast for Elena. Scrambled eggs. "Come back to me, Sammy," she said.

"I haven't gone anywhere, mamacita," I said. She liked when I called her mamacita.

"Yes, you have, Sammy. You're away."

"Where am I?"

"You're doing something for Gigi. It makes you go away."
That meant I hadn't read to her for two weeks.

I nodded. "I'm coming back. I promise."

"When?"

"Tonight. Tonight I'm coming back."

"You'll read to me?"

"Seguro, mamacita." She smiled. She had my dad's smile.
My mom's eyes. A killer combination. I felt better. I walked to
school.

The assembly was for seniors only. Since it was a special election, there were special rules. The runner-up would automat-
ically be the vice president. Our classes marched in. There
were about six hundred of us in our class—give or take. I
won't lie. I was nervous as hell. My palms were sweating. The
twelve—we all sat together. We listened to the speeches, dull
stuff. *I promise to represent the students I promise that our
dances will be really far out and the bands will be far out and I
promise that I'll do everything to make our senior year the
grooviest year of your life are you fat are you short I want your
vote I'm just like you so vote for me that way you're voting
for you.*

Every one had their partisans. They made a big deal, like
their candidate had really said something. Then it was Gigi's
turn. Stick to the plan, Gigi. Just stick to the plan. The dress
was nice. Serious. Too much makeup. Again. But that was

Gigi. *Relax. Relax.* She didn't look nervous. Maybe all the practicing had paid off. She smiled at everyone. She raised the pages of her speech in the air. "This is my speech," she said. "Mr. Fitz approved it. He approved all our speeches. That's the system." She paused—just like we'd practiced. She waved the pages of her speech in the air—then took it in her hands, and ripped it right in half. She tossed the ripped pages aside. Everyone watched as the pages floated to the floor. She might as well have ripped the pages out of the Bible. You could hear people breathe—that's how quiet it was. Everyone had stopped. Everyone was listening. "My name is Gigi Carmona and I want to be your president. You know why? Because nobody owns me. Nobody owns Gigi Carmona." She'd changed the speech. Shit! She'd changed everything. I could hear my heart. Okay, Gigi, okay.

"You know," she said—just like she was having a conversation, "you know, I don't care about school dances. Maybe I'd care more if someone actually asked me out." Everyone laughed. She had them. God. She had them. "I know. I know. I wear too much makeup." She smiled. "I like it, baby ¿y qué?" Attitude. She was giving them attitude. They roared. They roared for Gigi. She waited for them to stop laughing and clapping—and then she started again. "I don't care about football games. Maybe I'd care more if the guys who played that game walked around the school with a little more respect in their walk. The school doesn't belong to football players—

132

it belongs to us. To everybody. I care about what happens in this school. I think we need to change the way we do things around here. I do. You know what I'm gonna do once you elect me president of the senior class? I'm going to lead the charge to change the dress code. I don't know about you, but I don't want to be a nun. And I don't want to dress like one. You think if I'd said that in the speech I turned into the principal, that he'd have let me say it? No way!" God, she was going for all the marbles. This was her chance to say something—and damnit she was gonna make the most of it. Gigi Carmona had never stood in front of a microphone. And she was making it count. She pointed at the principal who was sitting next to all the candidates. "He would not have let me say what I wanted to say." She stopped. She looked at all of us. "This is America. I believe in free speech, baby. Do you? If you don't, I want to know why not?" She paused again. "My name is Gigi Carmona and I say it's time we opened our mouths and raised some hell." As those words came out of her, the senior class exploded. The whole world was yelling her name. The whole world was stomping their feet. Our teachers had lost control. We didn't belong to them. We belonged to ourselves.

Gigi was happy. God, she was. And we were happy, too. Because we'd seen somebody—and the somebody she was had given us something. It was as if we were the last piece of America that was waking up. And Gigi was the one who was nudging us out of our slumber. It was good. God. Yeah, Gigi!

I wondered what Eddie Montague was thinking now. I wanted to find him. I wanted to see the look on his face. I wanted to ask him if Gigi had said anything enlightening. But it wasn't fair of me to think those things. It was mean. It was small. I knew that. And he hadn't been the only one to sell her short. I had, too. Me. Sammy Santos. I'd sold her short. I didn't think she had it in her. I'd mistaken her for the makeup she wore. And even as I watched her standing in front of us glowing like she was on fire with the same kind of grace that a candle has when it burns in a church—even as she stood there—I was ashamed. For not believing. Gigi had told the truth. I hadn't enlisted. I'd been drafted. I started yelling, "Gigi! Gigi! Gigi!" Maybe by yelling her name, I could wash away my guilt. And then, like magic, everybody was shouting, "Gigi! Gigi! Gigi!" and she stood there in front of all of us, and I knew that the bird she had inside her was free. She had found a way to set it free. She tossed us all a kiss and I thought she was the most beautiful thing I'd ever seen.

Politics is never easy. This was our first lesson. There would be more lessons. All of them would hurt. We may have won the battle—but we lost the war. Nobody doubted that Gigi had gotten the votes. Even one of her opponents confessed to voting for her. It didn't matter. Our votes didn't count. Democracy wasn't always a simple thing. She'd broken the rules. This was a coloring book, and Gigi had colored outside the lines. They disqualified her. "You're lucky we're not suspending you." They always say that. How undeserving and lucky you were. How generous and virtuous and forgiving they were. You're lucky. That's what they told her. They appointed a new president and a new vice president. But everybody knew the truth—Gigi Carmona from Hollywood had beaten them. She'd stood up there and spit at them. They'd forgotten to remind us of that particular rule on the first day of school: no spitting. No spitting in public.

Gigi came over that evening. Sat on my front porch and cried. "They stole it from me, Sammy."

It was my fault. I was the one who'd given her the advice to switch the speeches. My big idea. But it was Gigi who was paying the price. "I'm sorry," I whispered. "If it wasn't for me, you'd have won. I was supposed to help you, Gigi. I screwed you over."

"No," she said.

"Yes," I said, "it's true. I shoved you out on a busy street— and a car was coming. I screwed you over."

"No," she said. "That's not right. You know what Fitz said? *You brought this on yourself.* That's what he said. Don't believe them, Sammy. If you believe them, then we lose."

We did lose. That's what I wanted to say. I put my arm around her.

"I was great. Don't you think so, Sammy?" She broke down. Right there. Right there on my porch.

"God, Gigi, you were the most beautiful thing on the earth."

I don't know if she heard me or not.

Her tears had become a river. We both took a dive and swam there. Nothing else to do but swim.

Right after we'd finished Gigi's campaign, my father began a campaign of his own. He and Frances Sánchez' father were working the precinct for Hubert Humphrey. They walked the neighborhood, and not just ours. They handed out pamphlets put out by the Democratic National Committee. Meetings, meetings, meetings. Meetings with the local unions. Meetings with the Knights of Columbus. Meetings with the precinct chairs. Democrats loved meetings. My father was always gone. He'd come home late every night. I'd be sitting at the kitchen table doing my homework. I'd warm up dinner for him. He'd talk politics. I'd listen. I loved his voice.

When Halloween came along, I had to take Elena trick-or-treating. We had fun, me and Elena. I let her stay up and count her stash. She counted it over and over. But we missed our father. "He's gone," Elena said, "just like you when you were helping Gigi."

"Yes," I said. "He'll be back. Be patient. He'll be back."

On election day, we joined my father in front of my sister's school, Hollywood Heights. Not the real name of the school—but that's what we called it. That's where the people of Hollywood voted. Our polling place. My father held his Humphrey sign like he was related to him. He greeted everyone as they walked in to vote. He knew everyone by name. All the men shook my father's hand. He was acting just like Father Fallon—that's what he did when people were coming out of Mass, shook everyone's hands.

Dad and Mr. Sánchez were proud. Their people had come out to vote. They'd done their job. When the polls closed, my father bought us hamburgers at LotaBurger. We went home, hamburgers in hand, to watch the results on television.

Humphrey won by a landslide—in my dad's precinct. Humphrey had taken Hollywood by storm. The nation went a different way. Like Gigi Carmona, Hubert Humphrey would never be president. We were always out of step. Out of line, some people would say. Way out of line.

That night, my father and I went to our version of the wailing wall—the front porch. He had a beer. I smoked a cigarette. "No me gusta perder," my dad said.

I nodded. "I hate losing, too, Dad."

Then all of a sudden, he broke out laughing. At first I thought he might be crying. But he wasn't. "Maybe we shouldn't hate losing so much, you know that, Sammy? I mean—it's the only thing we're good at." He laughed and laughed. God, his laugh made me smile. But that's when I understood that there wasn't much of a difference between Gigi's tears and my father's laughter.

another name for exile

"Sammy, how come everybody
wants to be in love?"

"Because everybody's crazy,
that's why."

"Were Mom and Dad crazy
when they were in love?"

"Probably, Elena.
That's the way it is."

twelve

I was fearless when I was a boy. Not afraid of anything. Didn't have bad dreams. Wasn't afraid of the devil. Pifas Espinosa, he had dreams. Bad ones. He used to tell me all about them at recess, how the devil would come, how he wore disguises. How the devil always dressed like someone he knew, his father, his mother, one of his brothers, a teacher, the guy behind the counter at Rexall drugs. And then he'd move in for the kill. "He takes me with him." He was afraid. I felt bad for Pifas. Even though I hadn't liked him back then. Me, I never had dreams like that. I had a guardian angel. And, as insurance, my Mom hung a picture of the Sacred Heart of Jesus in my room. His heart burned like his eyes. For me. His heart.

I didn't have to be afraid.

And I wasn't afraid of school. Lots of kids in Hollywood were afraid of school. There were rumors about what went on in there. "They make you hate your mom and dad. They turn you into a gringo." I heard a kid say that at the Pic Quick. I knew it wasn't true. If you weren't born a gringo, you couldn't become one. I knew that. I wasn't afraid of school, even though my English wasn't so great. Not at first. My parents spoke it, but they liked Spanish more. I liked Spanish more, too. School, well, school was an all-English thing. But that didn't scare me. English. Spanish. They were languages. What was scary about that? Uno, dos, tres, cuatro. One, two, three, four. Was that scary?

Even scary teachers didn't scare me. I think that's why so many of my teachers didn't like me. They looked at me, saw the lack of fear in my eyes. That's what they saw. I think they mistook that fearless look of mine for a lack of respect.

No, I wasn't afraid of bad dreams or devils or English or school or teachers. And I wasn't afraid of the neighborhood I lived in. When I was in sixth grade, I overheard a man at the Safeway say he wouldn't walk through the streets of Hollywood at night. "Not in that neighborhood." Even Mrs. Apodaca was afraid of our barrio. Said it wasn't decent. Anything could happen. Like what? I'd been walking through the streets of Hollywood my whole life. Walked and walked. Found things. Saw stuff. Talked to people. Asked them questions. What was there to be afraid of?

My mom was always chasing me down. Always trying to escape. Streets, alleys, the aisles of Surplus City. Every chance

142

I got, I made good my escape. Mama always found me. She was crazy about me. My dad, too. Always hugging me and kissing me and holding me. For the longest time, I was an only child. I was an entire world for my mom and dad. I was heaven. I was Eden.

And they were gods.

I was eight when Elena was born. Old enough to be jealous, I guess. But I never was. Jealousy wasn't ever my thing. I loved the idea of having a sister. When my mom was pregnant, I told her that's what I wanted. A sister. That's what I wanted. That's what I got. I thought my mom was giving me a present. I thought Elena was for me. When my mom went into the hospital, René asked me if I was afraid. "Why?" I said.

"What if she doesn't come back?"

I wasn't afraid. Maybe I should have been. But I wasn't. Fear was something in my future. Something I was bound to learn sooner or later. We learned to read, to write, to think, to sin, to love—and to be afraid. That's what we learned in living. For me, fear was something I learned in the confessional booth of Immaculate Heart of Mary Church. If I was heaven to my parents, I was hell to Father Fallon. Sammy Santos wasn't Eden. No, not to Fallon. Everybody's garden was different.

I don't know why. I took an instant dislike to that priest in catechism classes when I was seven. He was big and white. Not fat really. But not skinny. Thick. Like the trunk of a tree. He came to our class and spoke about sin. His topic was as serious as his voice. Gravel, like gravel in a cement mixer. He smoked a lot. I could smell it. Maybe that's why he always talked like he needed to clear his throat. Like he was about to spit.

Sin and repentance. That was his topic. He told us how holy God was and how not-holy we were. I took notes. That's what I always did. Took notes. *God wants to redeem me* that's what I wrote. That's what he said. That's what I wrote. And then I wrote. *Heaven is something you have to want.* That's what he said. That's what I wrote. I wondered how badly I wanted heaven. I wondered if I had to love Father Fallon in order to get there. Probably I did. I was in trouble. Serious. I don't know why, but I told Larry Torres that I didn't like Father Fallon. "No one likes him," Larry said. "He's just an F.B.I. anyway." I didn't ask him what that meant. I didn't want Larry to think he knew more than me. Later I asked Pifas what that meant. "Foreign Born Irish," he said. "Oh," I said. I guess I'd known that. I mean, everybody knew Father Fallon was from Ireland. It was supposed to be a good thing. It was better to be from Ireland than to be from Mexico. I knew that.

I studied hard to make my first communion. I had reached the age of reason. That's what they told me. It sounded important. I learned my Baltimore Catechism. I didn't know where Baltimore was. Didn't know why they'd named a catechism after a city. No one ever explained that to me. I guess if it was important, they would have told me. I sometimes got distracted by side issues. I still do that. But the main thing—the main thing was that I learned about God. Learned about the seven sacraments. Learned to pray the rosary. Learned the Apostle's Creed and the Act of Contrition. Sister Joseph taught me the prayers in English. My mom taught me the prayers in Spanish. Two women. Two teachers. Two languages. Two of everything. I was lucky. That's what I thought.

For the longest time I was confused about the theology of sin. But this is what I was told: there were mortal sins and there were venial sins. That sounded simple enough. Mortal sins were big sins. Serious. Things like missing Mass, using God's name in vain, stealing, coveting your neighbor's wife— whatever that meant—and killing. I knew what killing meant. I never understood exactly why missing Mass was as serious as killing someone. I guess I figured it was a good way of getting people to go to Mass every Sunday, of keeping order. Order was important. Couldn't have a church that was in chaos. No. Mrs. Apodaca wouldn't have stood for it. Mass. Every Sunday. Serious business. Mortal.

Then there were venial sins. They were smaller—things like getting mad and yelling and not obeying your parents and cussing. I figured most of my sins fell under this category. Maybe I was kidding myself. Maybe there were mortal sins I didn't even know about. And maybe I'd committed them. All of them. Without even knowing it.

145

Larry Torres informed me that sex was a mortal sin. I didn't know anything about that. "If you're married," he said, "then it's okay." I took his word for it. Larry Torres seemed to know a lot of things. "Getting a hard-on, that's a mortal sin, too." I didn't know what that was. But he had two older brothers. They must've told him these things. How else would he know? I nodded. *Hard-ons*, I thought. Serious. Mortal.

My first confession was pretty uneventful. There was about eighty of us who were waiting in line. We sat in the pews, kneeling, preparing ourselves. To make our hearts contrite. That's how Sister Joseph put it. I remember kneeling in my pew listening to Larry Torres and Reyes Espinoza endlessly discussing what they were going to tell the priest. "I'm going to tell him I killed someone," Reyes Espinoza whispered. Even as a kid he was a liar and a jerk. Even back then.

"And did you kill anyone?" Larry whispered back.

"Nope."

"Then you're lying."

"That's the plan," he said. "I'm going to tell Father Fallon that I killed someone. And then I'm going to tell him that I lied." Reyes had it all figured out.

I rolled my eyes.

Reyes caught me in the act. Rolling my eyes. "I'm gonna kick your ass," he whispered. He had no respect. We were in church. And there he was threatening me. He was a real cabrón. He didn't have a contrite heart. I knew that. I was right about that.

I rolled my eyes again. Reyes Espinoza never scared me. If scary teachers didn't scare me, why would Reyes Espinoza? "Go ahead," I said real soft. "I need something to tell the priest. I can tell him that I beat you up. Right here. Right in front of God and all the angels. Maybe that's good enough to count as a mortal sin."

"You're a joto," he said.

I hated when people called me that. That was the worst. "I hate you," I said. Now I really did have something to tell the priest. I wondered if hating someone was mortal or venial. I hated Reyes enough for it to count as mortal. One mortal, I thought, and about eight or nine venials. That was my list.

Larry wanted to know exactly what I was going to tell the priest. I shook my head. I told him it was a sin to tell.

"It isn't," he said.

"It is," I said. "You can only tell a priest."

"Shhh," Sister Joseph said. She gave us that look. That nun look. Even nice nuns could give you that look. They learned it in the monastery. They had to pass a test before they could take final vows. The look was on the test. "Shhhh," she said. She stood there a while.

I wasn't afraid. Not then. I had my sins in order, including my newly acquired one regarding Reyes Espinoza. I had a

147

contrite heart. I was ready. It went okay. Nothing special. My sins weren't that special. I knew that. The confessional wasn't as dark as people said it was. I remember that. And I remember reciting the Act of Contrition perfectly. I was proud. I thought about reciting it in Spanish, too. So Father Fallon would know that I knew how to talk to God in two languages. I didn't, though. When I walked out of there, I felt clean. Real clean. That's the way it was supposed to be. I liked that. It was better than taking a bath. Clean. I liked that.

At first, I went to confession almost every week. Father Fallon wasn't nice. He wasn't mean. But he wasn't nice. Sometimes he mumbled. But I never got the feeling he actually cared very much. I figured it was me. My sins were pretty dull. Venial was dull. That was okay.

When I got to high school, things began to change. That's when I began to be afraid. Maybe not afraid of confession. Maybe just afraid of Father Fallon.

For Lent, I'd given up eating Payday candy bars—and I'd given up drinking Pepsis. Loved that drink, loved it like anything. Giving up something was supposed to hurt. If it didn't hurt, then what was the point? I missed my Paydays. I'd also made a promise to do something nice once a day. Maybe I'd make an effort to do more than grunt at my teachers, not that I grunted on the outside. I did most of my grunting on the inside. But Mrs. Apodaca said God saw the words you said—even the ones you said to yourself.

The first Saturday after Ash Wednesday, I decided to go to confession. Actually, Mrs. Apodaca felt God had personally appointed her for overseeing my salvation. She's the one who actually decided for me. She knocked at the door and reminded me that it was Lent, and Lent was a time for humbling yourself before God. And what better way of humbling yourself than partaking of the sacrament of confession. "Yes, yes," I told her. I already had plans. *Mil gracias, Señora for the reminder. Thank you, thank you, thank you.* "And don't forget," she said, "to tell the priest you missed Mass last Sunday."

"I was sick," I said.

"Yes, but tell him. It's up to him to decide if it's excused."

I nodded. *Mil gracias, Señora. Thank you, thank you.* I felt like handing her a piece of paper and pen. *You wanna write down my sins, Señora?*

When she left, I shook my head and looked at my dad. "How can you be friends with that woman? Híjole."

"Tiene su gracia," he said.

"Meaning?"

"Meaning she's a good woman."

I smiled. He was right. Of course he was. I knew that. Still, she was pushy as hell. I smiled. Let them think you were a good sport. Crap. Confession. It wasn't so much that I objected to the sacrament—it was just that I was lazy. And I was in the middle of reading a novel. And it was a Saturday.

And I'd gotten up at four in the morning—again—to clean those pinche bars for my pinche boss who I fucking hated and I was being nice to. I was getting mad. I just wanted to stay home. Sloth was a sin. Rage must have been a sin, too. Okay, okay, I was going.

Like usual, I walked to confession. My dad wouldn't lend me the car. He looked at me. "¿Tienes polio?"

Do I have polio? Ha, ha, ha. Don't quit your day job, Dad. So I walked. Anyway, back then, everyone walked everywhere.

I was walking through Chiva Town. That's the way you got to Immaculate Heart of Mary Church—by walking through Chiva Town. As I was passing Larry and Mike Torres' house, I heard a whistle. Larry. He whistled for everything. I stuck out my chin at him, the Aztec greeting thing. He gave it back to me. "Where you goin', Sam?" I didn't like being called Sam. I wasn't a Sam.

"Confession," I said. I gave him a look. Don't start. Just don't fucking start.

He smiled. I knew that smile. Sucker. Pendejo. Good luck, keep warm and well fed. Wish I were goin', too. Yeah, I knew that smile.

His mother happened to be overhearing.

"Ándale pues, vete con él," she said as she came to the door. Larry got this really sick look on his face. Mrs. Torres smiled at me—then looked back at Larry. "He's from Hollywood, and he's going. You go, too. Vete." She did that thing with her arms *Go! Go!* I tried not to be insulted by her comment. "How are you, Sammy?" she said. "How's your dad?"

"Fine," I said.

"I bet he doesn't have to drag you to church like I do mine," she said.

I wanted to tell her I lived across the street from Mrs. Apodaca. One of God's sentinels. Always on alert, always on duty, always sniffing out sin like a dog sniffing out an old bone. I grinned. "No ma'am," I said. I felt like pinche Eddie Haskel on *Leave it to Beaver*.

"Wait up," Larry said. "Let me get Mike." If he had to go, he was gonna drag his younger brother down with him. I would've done the same thing.

I waited. Nobody invited me in. I was from Hollywood. Then, Larry and Mike came out.

"Puto," he said. " *Just cuz of you I have to go to confession.*"

"You're the one that whistled when I was walking by." I grinned. He hated my grin. He always had. Just like I'd always hated his attitude. If we walked to confession together, both of us would have plenty to confess. I remembered the discussion we'd had before our first confession. Things hadn't changed very much. Larry was still an exhibitionist. He liked to wear his sins on his sleeve.

"So, what are you gonna tell the priest? Órale, dime, ¿qué le vas a decir?" No, things hadn't changed one damn bit.

I shook my head. "I haven't thought about it."

"Are you gonna tell him you masturbate?"

"Not everybody masturbates, Larry. Not everybody's fixated on their own dick."

"Fixated? Ay, ay, ya te crees muy psychologist. You don't know shit. And if you don't masturbate, how do you know what it is?"

"You know what, Lencho—" He hated to be called Lencho. So what? I hated to be called Sam. "Not everybody goes around announcing that they masturbate. It's not cool."

"You don't know shit about cool."

Mike was staying out of it. He was just along for the ride.

"Well, it's a mortal sin to masturbate," he said finally. "Because we're committing abortion."

"What?" He was more of a pendejo than I'd ever thought. "What are you talking about?"

"We carry the babies. And when we make love, we deposit the babies in the woman's womb. And the woman, well, she provides the place where the baby can grow." He made that masturbating motion with his hand. "Casqueta," he said. "Puñeta. Every time we do that, we commit an abortion. That's mortal," he said.

I swear Larry Torres had a medieval mind. "You're full of shit," I said.

"¿Y qué? What do you have to worry about? You don't do it, ¿verdad, cabrón?"

"¿Qué te importa? Sins are between God, the priest, and the sinner."

"You talk like a gringo book, sometimes, you know that?"

"You talk like a really brainless bofo," I said.

Mike laughed. Larry shot his brother a look. The I'm-gonna-kick-your-ass-when-I-get-home look. That look.

I didn't say anything. Finally I said, "Well, even if you do masturbate," I told him, "I'm sure it's a small sin. In your case, anyway, ¿sabes? Small pecker. Small sin. Know what I'm sayin'?" I got him right where it hurts.

That's when he reached over and took a swipe at me. He got me right on the side of my cheek. It didn't hurt much—he'd just kind of grazed me. I didn't like to fight. I didn't. I swear, I didn't. But I just had to hit him back. Those were the rules in Hollywood. And right then, right there, we went at it. We punched the hell out of each other. All of a sudden we were on the ground punching at each other. Rolling around on somebody's front lawn. Then I hear this man's voice. "If y'all don't stop that right now, A'hm gonna call the po-lice." I don't know what made me look up. Maybe it was the drawl. Larry looked up, too. Big man. Really big man. We both nodded. "Now, y'all shake hands," he said.

Larry and I looked at each other.

"Go on. Go on. Won't hurtcha."

We shrugged. Shook hands. Kept on walking down the street. "Pinche Texan," Larry said.

"He seemed okay," I said.

"He's a mean bastard," Larry said. "Sonofabitch hits his wife. He married some woman from Jalisco. She doesn't even speak English. He hits her. We can hear. Every night." He looked at Mike. "We hear them, don't we, Mike?"

Mike nodded. "It's bad," he said.

I looked at Larry. "You're gonna have a black eye."

He looked at me. "So are you."

"You stupid s.o.b.," I said.

"Screw you," he said.

We just kept walking toward the church. When we were a couple of blocks away, Larry starts in again. "So what are you gonna tell the priest?"

"Órale, Lencho. I'm not gonna tell you."

"That's a gringo thing," he said.

"What are you talking about?"

"Being private about things—that's something real gringo."

I shook my head. "Well, maybe I'm a gringo."

"Well maybe you're just a fucking Tío Taco."

"Shut up," I said. "Just shut up." I saw the church up ahead. "When you tell the priest you masturbate, tell him your dick is so small that really you're only committing a venial."

I thought he was gonna take another swipe at me. He would've too, except that Sister Joseph was waving at us. "Hi, boys! Coming to confession, are you?"

We smiled. Yes, Sister. Yes, Sister. Larry was glancing at me, sideways. "I fucking hate your ass," he whispered.

"Tell the priest," I said. "Tell him that you're sorry you hate me."

"I'm not sorry."

Nope. Things hadn't changed. He still didn't have a contrite heart.

thirteen

"Bless me, Father, for I have sinned." I paused, thought back. "It's been six weeks since my last confession." Six weeks. Six weeks wasn't bad. I didn't know where to begin, so I thought I'd begin with my walk to church. "I got in a fight on my way to Church."

"What?" Father Fallon asked. "What?" He was in a bad mood.

"I got in a fight on my way to confession."

I tried to explain, but nothing came out of my mouth. I was sorry. Sorry I'd said anything.

"What?" he said.

"It wasn't a bad fight," I said.

"That's what you all do, don't you? You're all animals."

I didn't say anything. Nothing. I just knelt there. Maybe this was a kind of fight, too. Only I couldn't hit back in this one.

"Yes, sir," I said. "I mean, no, sir. No, Father. My friend hit me. I hit him back."

"Your friend? Friend? Animals. Men turn the other cheek. They have minds. They have hearts. Animals, animals are just instinct."

"I'm not an animal, Father." My heart was pounding. I thought my blood was on fire. That's how it felt. My whole body was tight. Tight, like I didn't fit inside myself. "I got in a fight. I'm sorry. I'm not proud of what I did. It was wrong. But I'm not an animal."

"Are you questioning a priest?"

I didn't say anything.

"Are you?"

I could feel myself leaving. I took a breath, closed my eyes, then reached for the door—and opened it. I got up to leave. Nothing seemed real. Nothing. Not me, not the door to the confessional I was opening. Not the church I was in.

"Where are you going? You can't—" I was already walking away. I found myself standing outside the church. I wasn't ever going to go back. I wasn't. I walked to the Pic Quick on Solano. I bought a pack of cigarettes. I stepped outside. I smoked a cigarette. That would help. That's what I thought. Then I walked back into the store and bought a Payday. I ate it. Then I walked back into the store and bought a Pepsi. I went outside and drank. It was good. I lit another cigarette. I noticed Larry and Mike walking toward the store. I waved.

They waved back. We pointed our chins at each other.

"Fallon called me an animal," Larry said. He looked sad. I hated that—the way he looked.

Me too. That's what I wanted to say. But nothing came out of my mouth.

He sat down next to me.

"You want a cigarette?" I said.

"Yeah."

I laughed. "It's not a sin. To smoke."

Larry put the cigarette in his mouth.

"You want one, too?" I asked Mike. Mike never said anything. He looked at Larry. "Yeah," he said. So I gave him one.

We sat, the three of us. Smoked.

"I hate him," Larry said. "I hate him." He looked at me. He wanted me to say something.

I knew what I had to say. "You're not an animal," I said. Then I laughed. "You're an asshole. But you're not an animal." I took a drink from my bottle of Pepsi. "Let's play a game of basketball." He was a better player, always beat me. "Let's play some basketball," I said.

That night, I had a dream. Father Fallon was standing over me. I couldn't move. I couldn't run. It was dark. I couldn't see anything. Just him. I could hear his harsh Irish voice. First soft. Then louder. Then louder. "You've gone and lost it. You've gone and lost heaven." That's what he was saying. Over and over and over. "You've gone and lost heaven." And then there was nothing but fire.

I woke up shaking.

The next day I went to Mass. But only because my father made me. I told him I wasn't feeling well. "No me siento bien. Go without me." He put his hand on my forehead. "You're fine." He looked at my eye. It wasn't bad. "I want you to wash my car after Mass. Will you do that?"

I nodded. My punishment for fighting with Larry.

"You're fine."

"I'm not," I said.

"You've always liked going to Mass."

I hadn't. When my mom was alive, I'd liked it. When she died, it was something I just did. Something I did with my father and Elena. "Okay," I said. But he knew I didn't mean it. All okay meant was that I wasn't going to fight. Not with him. Not on Sunday. "Is Elena dressed?" I went to her room. She was wearing a yellow dress. Pretty. "If I tell Jesus to tell Mom something, do you think he will?"

"Yes," I said.

"Do you really think he will?"

"Yes," I said again. "Yes, yes." What god could refuse Elena?

On the way to Mass, my dad didn't let me smoke. "You want to pray with cigarette on your breath? Es falta de respeto. That's what you should've given up for Lent." Maybe he was right. But smoking was a new thing anyway, too new to give up. As I sat in the backseat, it occurred to me that we'd gotten a new priest at Immaculate Heart of Mary. Maybe the new priest, Father Francis, maybe he would have the 10:30 Mass. I had hope. It made me feel better. Not much. But better. We were a little late. My heart sank. He was there, Fallon, up there on the altar. Mass began *In the name of the Father, and of the Son* and I left somewhere. I don't remember where I went. Just somewhere else. I could feel myself shaking when it was time to go to communion. If I didn't go, my father would want to know why. I was a bad liar. It's not that I never lied to him. I did. But he always knew when I lied. Just because he didn't say anything didn't mean he didn't know. So I went to communion.

As I reached the altar, I could feel myself trembling. I looked at Father Fallon's eyes. "The Body of Christ."

"Amen," I said. I closed my eyes and took the host on my tongue. Like a true penitent. He hadn't known it was me, the guy who'd walked out of confession. He hadn't known. I was just another young man, another communicant, another face. Another animal.

All that Lent, I avoided going to confession. I lied to my father, told him I was going. But I didn't. But I didn't eat any more Paydays or drink any more Pepsis. I'd stop in at church on my way home. I prayed. Mostly I just sat there. My heart didn't feel any more alive than the wood pews I was sitting on. I thought maybe I was losing my faith or whatever was left of it.

Maybe it had left when Juliana was killed. I don't know. I don't. I'd heard people talk about that, about people who'd lost their faith. I thought about my dream. When you lost your faith, you lost heaven. I didn't want to lose heaven. My mom was there. And Juliana, too.

I thought about all the lost souls I knew. That's how Mrs. Apodaca put it. And she wasn't wrong. "They just wander about. Almas perdidas. Es una tristeza." I hated to agree with her, but she was right. So many people walking around the world, lost. And it was sad. And I was becoming one of them. I didn't want that. But I didn't know what to do about myself. If I thought about what Father Fallon had said, I would get angry. I'd have to smoke a cigarette or two before I calmed down. But I'd turned my back on a sacrament. My mom had told me that a man never turned his back on a sacrament. Maybe she was watching. Maybe she knew. Or maybe she had better things to do than watch me.

That day, after I'd tried to pray at the church, I stopped by to see Larry on the way home. He was watching television. The house was loud and crowded with all his older brothers. Everyone fighting. They liked to fight in that family. "Let's go buy a Coke," he said.

"A Pepsi," I said.

"A Coke," he said.

We just had to fight. About everything.

On the way back from the store, I asked him. "Did you

161

ever go to confession again?" I asked. "After that day?"

"Hell no," he said. "And I'm never going back."

"You're not afraid?"

"Of what?"

I nodded. I realized that I'd never been afraid of anything. And now I was afraid of everything. I was afraid something would happen to my Dad or that something would happen to my sister. Hadn't something happened to Juliana? Didn't bad things happen to the people of Hollywood all the time? And I was afraid of Father Fallon. Afraid he had the power to take heaven away from me. Maybe he had the power. Maybe he didn't. I wasn't sure. But I was afraid. I wasn't so fearless anymore.

"Of what?" Larry asked again. "Afraid of fucking what?"

"Nada," I said, "never mind."

"You're too serious, ¿sabes? Pifas says you have to learn how to relax. ¿Entiendes, Méndez?"

"Yeah, yeah. Cómo chingan."

"God doesn't give a rat's ass about confession, anyway." This from the theologian who thought that masturbation was the same thing as having an abortion.

"What if he does?"

"Then we're completely screwed. ¿Sabes?"

"Yeah, yeah," I said. Talking to Larry never made me feel any better.

* * *

It was a sad Lent. I was sad about everything. On Holy Saturday, my dad thought it would be a good idea if we all went to confession together. Me and him and Elena. Shit. Shit. "Okay," I said.

There were two confessional lines that Saturday. One line for Father Francis and one line for Father Fallon. Father Francis definitely had the longest line. Dad got in the shorter line. He didn't seem to care if he was in Father Fallon's line or not. What sins did he have, anyway? Me, I got in Father Francis' line. Maybe it would all work out. Why do we always hope? I saw Father Fallon's line get shorter and shorter. And then there was no one left on his side of the church. He came out of the confessional. He walked up to the row where I was sitting. "Over here," he whispered. All of us in that row looked at each other. He waited. We nodded. It was over for all of us. We who'd had such hope.

My heart was pounding. God. It was really pounding.

I took a breath. I went first. What good would it do to sit there and listen to my heart thumping against my chest. "Bless me, Father, for I have sinned . . . " I stopped. "The last time I came to confession, I walked out." There. I'd said it.

"You?" he said. "You turned your back on a sacrament."

"Yes," I said. "I am heartily sorry. I am, Father." I wasn't sorry. Why was I lying? And my dumb heart just kept pounding as if my body was a locked door and my heart was a fist. Pounding and pounding. And I thought maybe the wings had

163

come back. Those wings, they came and went, came alive, then went dead. I couldn't think. I don't remember anything else. I know I was in there for a long time. I kept saying, "Yes, sir, yes, Father, I'm sorry, I'm sorry." Sometimes, you find yourself in the middle of a storm and you don't know anything, you're just scared and confused and everything around you is chaos and turmoil and you don't know what to do, so you don't do anything, just close your eyes, and when you finally open them, you don't know how it is that you're still standing there. The storm gone—and you're standing there. In all that calmness. I heard myself reciting the Act of Contrition. *Oh my God I am heartily sorry for having offended thee, and I detest all my sins because I dread the loss of heaven and the pains of hell. But most of all because I offended thee my God who art all good and deserving of all my love . . .* Fallon gave me a severe penance, an entire rosary. He lectured me. I didn't listen. Then I heard the words of absolution. And his final words "Go and sin no more." When I walked out of the confessional, I didn't feel clean. Not clean, dirtier than before. Dirtier than I'd ever been. Even after praying the rosary. Even after completing my penance. I wasn't clean.

I watched Elena as she looked for eggs on Easter Sunday. My dad had bought her a new dress. Blue and pink. And new shoes. White. She was clean. My dad had bought me a new shirt, too. I didn't feel any better, any cleaner, any purer because I was wearing something new.

I kept watching Elena. She laughed every time she found an egg. "Look!" she yelled. "Look, Sammy!" I wanted to be her voice. I wanted to be her laughter. She was eight, almost nine, and yet she seemed to be younger than that. I wondered if I had ever been like her. I didn't think so. I had never been that pure.

I didn't go to confession for a long time after that. When I thought about going, I remembered I'd never confessed that Juliana and I had had sex. But what was the point? What was the point in telling the priest you had sex with a girl who was dead?

One afternoon, I was walking to the store to get a Pepsi. The sun was setting, and the light was beautiful, like there was a halo around the earth. I saw Father Fallon walking down the street, walking toward me. Maybe it was just a dream. But he kept walking. He was real. He was there. Walking. I guess he was just enjoying the evening. Who knows? I didn't know anything about what priests did when they weren't on duty. As he came nearer and nearer, I could hear my heart pounding again. I took a breath. And then he was four feet away. "Hello, Father," I said.

He looked at me. He didn't say anything. He just kept walking. I turned around and watched him. "Hey!" I said. Then ran after him. "Father. Father."

He turned around. I caught up to him. "Yes?" He looked at me. He wanted to know why I was bothering him. I wasn't anything to him, a fly on a plate.

"Father." I looked at him. "Why do you hate us?" The question just came out. Like it had been there on my tongue all this time, just waiting for a chance to escape.

"What?" he said. I could see it in his eyes. He did hate us.

"Why do you hate us?"

He was going to say something. But he saw something in my eyes. My heart had stopped pounding. I wasn't afraid. I don't know why. I just wasn't. I think it was him—he was afraid. Of me. Of Sammy Santos. I could see that. He turned. And started to walk away. Then he turned back and looked at me. "I don't," he whispered. "I don't." But there was no conviction in his voice. No hope of being believed. He turned away again. I watched him until he disappeared. I just stood there.

As I walked back home, I got to thinking. And then I knew what I'd been afraid of all those months. I hadn't been afraid of confession. I hadn't been afraid of Father Fallon. I was afraid of what I had inside. That I was bad. But I wasn't. What I had in there, it wasn't all bad. There was some good there. I knew that.

A part of me had believed Father Fallon when he'd called me animal. I'd believed him. Why had I believed him? And then I kept thinking and thinking and then it occurred to me that I should run after him. Because I'd said the wrong thing.

Why do you hate us? That wasn't it. I should've called him what he was. *You're a damned liar.* And then I shook my head and thought. *Hell, Sammy, let the poor man alone.* Let him alone.

I whistled as I walked back home. Lent was over.

fourteen

I wasn't thinking about love. That's the last thing I was thinking of. I'd already learned that lots of things could kill the bruise in my heart I called love. Cancer, that would do it. A bullet, that would do it. I suppose that other, more subtle poisons could kill it, too. But there was nothing subtle about the world I lived in, nothing subtle about cancer. Or a bullet blasting out of a gun. Or the barrio I lived in.

But at school, everybody was obsessed with finding some love. The end of October—1968—and people went around desperate. Passing notes. Investigating who might be interested in going out with them on weekends. As if being alone was a sickness. Like the flu that was going around. There was a lot of talk about who was going out with who, and who put out and who was a good kisser and who wouldn't let you touch her. Guys like to talk. About girls they wanted—but would never have.

People went around looking at people from a distance, observing them. Are you the one? What made most of us so desperate? I hated desperate. And I didn't want to have anything to do with all that note-passing, please-look-at-me stuff that was going around. No thanks, no, not a good time. Not me. Love, not what I was looking for. René told me my bad attitude was all because of Juliana. I just told him to shut up. I told him high school kids didn't know crap about love, and to just shut the hell up. He just kinda looked at me like I was having a bad day. I hate when people look at me that way. And I wasn't gonna let him have the last word with that look of his, so I just yelled, "René, you piece of shit, what do you know? The summer of love just passed us by, shithead— didn't you know that? It just passed us by. It's over." I didn't know why I was yelling. And old René, he just flipped me the bird and kept walking.

That September, I'd gotten a job working at the Dairy Queen on Saturdays. One day a week and sometimes I'd substitute. Dad said no more working during the week. Plenty of time for working when I got older. Okay, I said. The Dairy Queen job was the compromise. I needed to work. But I didn't need love. Sometimes I'd flirt. Not much. Just some. It depended on the girl, but I'd stop if she did something that reminded me of Juliana. And I hated all that, thinking about her and seeing her in other girls even though that was impossible, because those girls were alive and Juliana was dead. But still I tried to flirt as if everything inside me was normal. It depended on my mood. If I had a lot of homework on my mind, I'd be in my head. I didn't mind thinking about my homework. Better than thinking about Juliana.

Gigi would come by the Dairy Queen on Saturday afternoons. With her friends. She wanted me to flirt with her in front of the whole world. I never did. I knew her game. She was starting to give me those looks again, those you're-a-shit looks. Those looks—I wanted to run from them.

Yeah, yeah. She lost her bid for the presidency of the Senior class. Maybe so, but I didn't feel so sorry for her after a while. She'd become a celebrity for that speech of hers. Gigi Carmona had made it big at Las Cruces High. Free Speech Queen. She'd made the principal blush—in front of everybody. Everything was Gigi this and Gigi that. The whole thing was getting on my nerves. Gigi, Gigi. The Mexicans loved her—especially the Mexicans from Hollywood and Chiva Town. The first Mexican-American princess Hollywood ever produced. Gringos loved her, too. Radical chic. Gigi Gigi. She got invited to all the parties, wanted me to go with her. No thanks. Never went. She'd get mad at me. I'd bring her back to earth by whispering her real name. Ramona Carmona. Ramona Carmona. "You're a real pinche," that's what she'd say.

She even went out on a date with this gringo named Adam. No comment. "How was the date?"

170

"How was what date?" I didn't like coy. She'd told half of Hollywood.

I didn't say anything. I looked at Angel who was standing right next to her.

"You mean Adam?"

"Did you have a good time?" I smiled. At Angel.

"He's got blue eyes."

"My pen's got blue ink."

Angel laughed. Gigi gave her a look. You know which look.

"He's got a Camaro."

"His father paid for it."

"What's wrong with that?"

"Nothing. Did he pick you up?"

"Yes."

"Met your mom and dad?"

"Yes. He's a nice boy."

"You step out of Hollywood, the world's full of nice boys. Glad he's one of 'em."

She looked at me. "He's not so different from Hollywood boys. He tried to kiss me."

"You shoulda let him," I said. "Mighta been fun."

"I'm not a puta, you know. You're a pinche."

"No one said you were a puta. A little kiss on a date, what's the big deal? Especially on a date." I handed her the sundae she'd ordered. I put extra pineapples. On the house. She loved pineapples. Genetic memory. A Mexican thing. Like the Aztec greeting. She took it and walked away. Then she turns around and says, "He wasn't that special."

"I know that," I said. All of Las Cruces knew that.

Pissed her off. Really did. I looked at Angel, handed her an ice cream cone.

"I didn't order this," she said.

"On the house," I said.

"OOUUH, big man."

I just looked at her. I'd never heard her pop off before. "You're hanging around Gigi too much."

"Gigi didn't give me a voice, you know? I had one before Gigi."

Fair enough. I nodded.

"Keep the ice cream," she said. She handed it back to me.

"Your friend's waiting for you," I said. I did that Aztec thing with my chin. I couldn't help but watch her as she walked away.

I paid for the ice cream cone I'd made for Angel. Ate it. Good. I liked ice cream. And right then I was thinking that I was more hungry for ice cream than I was hungry for girls.

Appetites came and went. Like a spring wind.

Quitting time that evening, I decided to walk home. I called my dad, told him I was walking. Just felt like it. "Just like your mother," he said. "She loved to walk." As I was walking up Lohman, a car passes me. Stops. Nice car. Mustang. Brand spanking new. Absolutely. A beauty. Cherry red. Baby, baby, baby—that was a real car. And Jaime Rede pops his head out. "Sammy! Wanna ride?" He was all smiles. Acted like he was my best friend. I'd known him since I was four. He'd been pissed off for all of the thirteen years I'd known him. And now, now he was all sunshine and lollipops like that dumb 45 Elena played over and over on her record player. I hated that song. Now, Jaime was trying to be my friend. Or maybe he was on pot. Mota. Maybe that put him in a good mood and made him act like that song Elena liked so damned much.

I gave him the Aztec greeting. That chin thing. "Sure," I said. "I'll take a ride." I liked the car. When I got to the car I looked at his eyes, to see if they were red. Nope. Not dilated. Normal. Didn't look like he was smoking weed. There were guys at school—you knew. You just knew. Then I saw who was driving. I shouldn't have been that surprised. "Ese, Sammy."

"What is it, Eric? What is it?" I repeated myself sometimes. If I wasn't happy. Like saying something twice made it sound like it was more real.

He nodded to the song on the radio, keeping the beat. René always said that—you gotta keep the beat. Keep it in your head. Fine, fine, yeah. Except I hated *The Who*. Liked *Chicago*. Loved *Blood, Sweat, and Tears*. Loved brass. Hated *The Who*—but it was *The Who* that was on the radio. And Eric nodding to the music. Keeping the beat. "Órale, Sammy, ¿qué dices, Sammy?" I hated that. Talking to me in Spanish. Fry.

Eric Fry. I knew English. Knew it better than he did. I know for a fact he'd never read *Great Expectations.* God, that boy was white. I don't mean that he was just a gringo. I mean his skin. God, it was white.

"Nothing," I said, "just comin' home from work." I wanted to ask him if he knew what that was. I knew he hadn't paid for the Mustang he was driving. Just like that Adam guy Gigi had gone out with. Knew where Eric lived, too. In those homes in Mesilla Park Eddie's father had built. Work. Can you spell it? It starts with a W, ends with a K. K as in suck. I nodded, smiled. "Just comin' home from work," I said again. "You?"

"Nada, nada," he said, "no hay nada que hacer." I mean, his accent was perfect. Spoke like a native of Chihuahua. That's what pissed me off. Here he was, this rich gringo, nice looking, sort of, if that was your type, had everything, was nice to everybody, the works, the whole package—and everybody thought he was so fucking far-out and groovy because he spoke Spanish. Nobody thought Mexicans were far-out and groovy because we spoke English. Nope. That's not the way it worked. Nope, I didn't like gringos who got to be more Mexican than Mexicans. "Nope," I said, "there's nothing to do in this town." I wasn't gonna use one word of Spanish in that car. Hell no. Not me. Not Sammy Santos. American all the way.

"So," Jaime says, "you goin' out tonight?"

"Yeah," I said.

"Goin' out with Gigi?"

"Nope," I said. I didn't feel like talking to these guys. Neither one of them. It was like telling them what I was gonna tell the priest at confession.

"How come? She's got it bad for you, ese."

"Don't think so."

"What are you, Sammy? Blind? ¿Ciego? ¿Qué no puedes ver? That girl would go to hell for you."

"Is that right?" That was my father's line. "She's a good girl, Gigi. What would she want with me?"

"You should ask her out."

"Why don't you ask her out?"

"It's not me she likes. She likes you, Sammy."

Eric pulled into the parking lot of a 7-11. I liked the Pic Quick better. I wasn't the one driving. "Órale, ¿quieren algo de tomar?" His Spanish was pissing me off.

"I'll take a Coke," Jaime said.

I shook my head.

"¿Estás seguro?"

"I'm sure," I said. I would know if I wanted something to drink. I watched him walk inside the store—then looked at Jaime. "You're gonna let him buy you a Coke?"

"What's wrong with that?"

"You can't buy your own damn Coke? What's wrong with you, Jaime?"

"Órale, what's wrong with you, Sammy? The guy's buying me a Coke. Big fucking deal. ¿Qué te duele?"

"So you guys smoking pot together—or what? ¿Se ponen grifos? Getting sky high—that's what everyone says."

"Since when do you care what everyone says, Sammy?"

"Never have. Still don't."

"¿Entonces? We hang out together. What's the big deal?"

"Seems weird."

"Why?"

"You know why, Jaime."

"No. Why don't you tell me, cabrón?"

"He doesn't know who you are."

"Oh. You do? *You do?* You know me, Sammy?"

"Since you were four."

"And what do you know about me?"

"You're from Hollywood."

"And that's all you know."

"It's enough."

"No." That's what he said. I almost got out of the car right then. Right there. But there was Eric, two Cokes in his hand. One for him. One for Jaime.

"Mind if I smoke?" I said. I didn't really want one. It was a test.

"Mind if I bum one?"

Shit. I tossed my pack to Jaime. They lit up. Jaime tossed them back. I didn't light one. By then, we were passing The Cork and Bottle. "You can leave me off here," I said.

Eric pulled into the driveway. "You sure?"

"Yeah," I said.

Jaime opened the car door. Pulled the seat up so I get out the backseat. Eric looked at me. "Something eating you?"

"No. Guess I'm just tired."

"You don't like me, do you?"

I decided I wasn't going to lie. Probably wouldn't get any more rides in his car. "No. I guess I don't." I looked at him. "Sorry. Look, thanks for the ride."

I saw the look on Jaime's face. He wasn't smiling anymore.

I didn't feel so good about myself as I walked home. I sure as hell didn't.

The house was empty. My father wasn't home. He was out, doing good somewhere. There was a note on the table. *Your sister's at the Apodacas. Bring her home. I'll be late. If you have to go out, well you have to go out. I'm sure Mrs. Apodaca will take her. I already told her you have my permission, so she won't give you a hard time.* I smiled. Dad was always looking out for me. He knew Mrs. Apodaca was always giving me the third degree. I shook my head. He was a funny guy, my dad, always getting involved with stuff—cleaning up the neighborhood, planting trees, helping the Knights of Columbus raise money for this or that. His way of loving the world. "You've got to love the world, Sammy."

Sundays he took us to breakfast after Mass and Sunday nights he'd cook. Sundays he gave me a day off. Tomorrow was Sunday. Good day. I'd read. *Great Expectations,* that's what I

177

was reading. I'd read it before, liked Dickens. Even if he was English. They weren't all bad. I knew that. I thought of Eric Fry. Yeah, that's what I'd do, I'd read. And then I'd help Elena with her homework. I'd watch football with Dad. It didn't matter that I only halfway paid attention. I'd sit with him, halfway read, halfway watch the game. In the evenings we'd watch *The Wonderful World of Disney* with Elena. Then we'd watch *Ed Sullivan*. Yup, tomorrow was Sunday. But tonight, tonight was Saturday. And I wanted to go out. Because I wanted to feel something else, anything besides what I was feeling. I wanted to go out. Maybe I'd call René. Maybe we'd go out. Cruise. Have a few beers. That's what I thought. I picked up the phone. Dialed. He answered.

"René. What is it?"

"Hey, Sammy, ¿qué dices?"

"Nada, nada. Hey, you got plans tonight?"

"Gotta date, Sammy."

Figures. He was one of those guys who was always looking. Always. Desperate. "Anybody I know?" I asked.

"Yeah, you know her. Angel. Angel Rosas."

He was goin' out with Angel. Shit. Not that I would've ever asked her out. But Angel? I tried to be a good sport. "She's fine," I said.

"Yeah. Wanna ask someone out? We could all four go out." He was being decent.

"Nah," I said.

"Why don't you call Gigi?"

"I don't want to call Gigi."

"C'mon, ask her out."

"She wears too much makeup."

"Ask her out."

"It's almost six o'clock. Yeah, yeah, I'll call her and say, 'Gigi, what is it? You wanna go out? Pick you up in an hour and half.' She'll call me a pendejo and a menso and a pinche and a cabrón and she'll hang the phone up on me. You don't call a girl half hour before you pick her up, ¿sabes?"

"Cálmate, ese." And then he put on this real white hippie voice, "Don't be a bummer, baby, be cool. Stay cool. Everything's far-out and bitchin'." René, he could be funny.

I laughed. "Nah, I'll pass."

He got real quiet. I knew something was up. "I was gonna call you," he said. "Gigi's kinda comin' along on our date."

"What?"

"It's the only way Angel would go out with me. She said she didn't trust me. She said she'd go—only if Gigi was going. So—"

"So that's why you want me to ask her out? Screw you. Forget it."

"Ah, come on."

"To babysit Gigi."

"It's not like that."

"Yeah, you pinche, it's just like that."

"Look, I really like Angel. No seas culo."

"I don't like it when someone makes a pendejo out of me. Look, just pick me up, damnit." I hung up the phone. I wasn't gonna have a good time. Hell no, I wasn't.

I sat on the porch, lit a cigarette, thought about Gigi and what a pain in the ass she was. I thought about René. He was gonna kiss Angel. I hated the thought of that. Then I thought about Eric and Jaime and what a pinche I'd been. They were trying to be friendly. And I was a complete cabrón. And then it came to me that I was thinking less and less about Juliana. That made me sad. The living, they forget. But that's what we do. I didn't want to forget. Didn't matter, though, what I wanted. Each day I forgot a little more.

I wondered if my father had forgotten my mother. But if he had, how come he never went out on dates? I wanted to ask him about that. I mean, he probably carried my mother around with him every day—just like I carried Juliana around. Only it was probably worse for my Dad. But I knew my father would never talk about that kind of thing. Not ever. I guess that maybe my mom and dad had loved each other so much that it just wasn't right to talk about it. When you really loved someone, you wanted other people to know. But you wanted to keep it a secret, too. That's what love was: a secret. Mostly, that's what love was.

fifteen

So we went out. The four of us, me and Gigi and René and Angel. We went riding around. Then we went to get some burgers at Shirley's. Went inside and everything. Not just the drive-in. We talked. About stuff. I didn't like the way René was looking at Angel. But she wasn't looking at him the same way. That was good. "There's a party at Charlie Gladstein's," Gigi said. "We're invited. He wants us to come."

Yup. That Charlie had a thing for Gigi. I knew that. I did. "He wants you to come to his party," I said.

"Don't be like that, Sammy. He's nice. He likes you."

I nodded. "I like him, too. Nice guy. Yeah, yeah, everyone likes everyone." I laughed, remembering what he'd told me. "Except Charlie doesn't like Protestants."

"What?"

"He was at a party once, and that's what he told me. Said that Protestants thought they owned the fucking world. Hates them. That's what he said."

Angel laughed. "Well then, he doesn't like a lot of people."

"Guess not."

And I thought right there, right then, that the good thing about hating a whole group of people was that you didn't have to be specific. You could stay nice and general. And vague. I don't know why I thought that. I did that, sometimes, left the conversation and thought things.

I paid for Gigi's burger. "It's not a date," I said. "I'm just paying for a friend. Friends can pay."

"Next time, I'll pay," she said. "Then we'll be even."

"Fine," I said.

"Fine," she said. But I could tell she was mad. She was touchy, Gigi was.

So then we go to Charlie's party. Lots of Protestants there, far as I could tell. A keg, no parents, no shitkickers, no Future Farmers of America types. When those types came, there was always a fight. No fights. Not tonight. Nice house. Nicer than Hatty Garrison's—who was there. Party girl. "Hey Hatty," I said, "how is it?"

"Sammy!" she said. Always nice. Didn't know if I liked her boyfriend, Kent. Hey, but he'd helped Gigi on her campaign. Couldn't be all bad.

Everyone was in the backyard, which was bigger than three Hollywood lots. People were dancing. Rolling Stones. Didn't like Mick Jagger. Soon as we got there, Charlie heads straight for Gigi, asks her to dance. Half drunk already, that Charlie. So they dance most of the night. So did René and Angel. I sat there, drinking a beer, watching. I thought of Juliana and got sad, but I didn't want to sit there and feel like that.

I saw Jaime and Eric pouring themselves a beer at the keg. I wondered if they'd been here a long time. I decided I should go up to them, you know, make nice. Why not? *Make love, not war.* Such bullshit, really. More people were into war than were into love. Sex didn't count. Sex was sex. Hell, everybody knew that. So I go up to Eric and Jaime. I offer them a smoke. "Peace," I said. Then I laughed. I just couldn't say that kind of crap with a straight face. Charlie. Charlie could get away with stuff like that. But not me. Then I felt like a pendejo for laughing. "I was in a bad mood this afternoon. Sorry."

"I'm not a pendejo," Eric said.

"No one said you were a pendejo."

"You always look at me like I am."

"Sorry."

"Really?"

"Yeah. Sorry."

So we stood around the keg and talked about things. Jaime said he wanted to go to college. I never knew that about him. "U.C.L.A.," he said. "I'm getting the hell outta Dodge." I wondered if his grades were any good. Didn't know. Didn't know anything about him—except that he'd hung out with Pifas and Reyes. And they weren't good for each other. Always getting into fights. As bad as René. Maybe worse. But we'd lost Pifas to the Army. And Reyes, well, the last time I'd seen him, he was all strung out on heroin. Looked like shit. Threatened to kick my ass if I didn't give him my cigarettes. So now, Jaime hung out with Eric. Maybe it was his way of leaving Hollywood without having to leave town. Maybe I didn't blame him. Maybe I did. "I hear you're going to college, too," Jaime said.

"Yeah," I said. Not U.C.L.A. "Probably staying here. New Mexico State. Local boy. Local college." I made like that was okay with me. I didn't mean it. But I smiled.

"You should leave," Jaime said. "Everyone knows you get good grades." I always wondered how people knew these things about me. "You could get into all kinds of schools."

I thought about my dad and Elena. What would they do? If I left? "Maybe," I said. "Maybe I'll leave. Who knows?"

But I knew. "You, Eric?" I was trying. I could be nice. I could.

"Penn State," he said. "That's home. Pennsylvania. We moved here because my dad works at Johnson Space Center." The way he'd said Penn State like he already knew that school belonged to him. I nodded. And kept smoking my cigarette. I went back to watching René and Angel dance. Time went by real slow that night.

Later, I saw Jaime dancing with Pauline. Eric was dancing

with Susie Hernández . Bad dancers both of them. Worse than me. But Pauline and Susie, they could dance. And God. Susie's dresses were getting shorter and shorter. Mrs. Apodaca would've dragged her off the dance floor and sprinkled holy water on her. But then again, Mrs. Apodaca would've sprinkled holy water on everybody in the room. She wouldn't have spared anyone. I pictured her, sprinkling us all and saying prayers. Made me smile. Yeah, I thought, maybe that's what we all needed. Holy water.

I don't know why we decided to go to the river when the party ended. But that's what everyone used to do—either cruise Shirley's hanging out the window looking for trouble, yelling things like "Fuck you and your dog and your turtle!" Fun stuff like that. It was either go to Shirley's or go to the river. Going home wasn't one of the options.

It was two in the morning. I was tired. Angel was staying with Gigi so she didn't care what time she got home. And Gigi's parents kinda let her do whatever she wanted. Sometimes it hurt her feelings, that her parents didn't care more. I could tell. But sometimes, she didn't give a damn. Her idea, that we go to the river. She'd heard about some keg party. So we went.

"You're a bummer, Sammy, you know that?" What was I supposed to say? I'd been working all day. I'd been making ice cream cones, I'd been listening to little kids all damn day long as they changed their minds about everything. I'd been taking crap from angry mothers, crap, crap from everyone. And for what? For pocket money so I wouldn't have to touch my savings. For college. God, sometimes I just hated guys like Adam and Eric Fry and Charlie Gladstein. They'd never had to work at Speed Sweep Janitor Service or Dairy Queen because they needed to. They didn't know what that was like. Never. Nunca. "Yeah, Gigi," I said. "I'm a real bummer." Then I laughed. I don't know why. Maybe I wanted to have fun.

"Give me a cigarette," Gigi said. It wasn't really a request. More like what's mine was hers.

"Give me one, too," Angel said from the front seat.

I smiled at Angel. "Tell your boyfriend to give you one."

Gigi laughed. Good smile. Beautiful. I wondered how come she didn't have a steady. Pain in the ass, that's why. I handed her a cigarette. When she lit it, she blew the smoke out through her nose. Like a real smoker. Like a pro. She'd been practicing. And she seemed older to me right then. Like she'd become a woman. Pifas hadn't looked like that before he left for the Army. He'd looked small. Not like a man. Like a boy. But a boy with big hands. I hoped his hands would help him.

Gigi was staring at me. "What are you thinking?"

"I was thinking about Pifas. I got a letter."

"I got one, too," she said.

"How do you think he sounds?"

Gigi got real quiet. "Well, I don't know. My letter was, well, it was kinda private." She looked out the window.

I nodded.

She turned back to me. "What did yours say?"

"He sounded like he was tired. 'Fuckin' A, Sammy,' he said, 'the Army's kickin' my butt.' He says he doesn't get enough sleep and that most of the guys are okay. Says he gets on with most everybody. Says some of the guys are badasses and he hasn't gotten in any fights. Except once—but that was in a pool hall, and one of his pals named Buddy got him out of there." I shook my head. "He's the same. He says he stays up at night and thinks about us, all of us Hollywood types. Wonders what we're up to." I laughed.

"What? What's so funny, Sammy?"

"Pifas. He said he saved the ¡Viva Gigi! campaign button as good luck."

She started to laugh. But right then, her laugh was sad. I pictured it, that piece of blue construction paper with the words written in black Magic Marker. I pictured Gigi and Angel the night they made them. I pictured me and Jaime handing them out at lunchtime. I pictured Pifas holding it in his big hands. Staring at the words. Maybe he asked himself what he was doing in those Georgia barracks. Maybe he kept whispering Gigi's name over and over.

The radio was playing something by The Turtles, and

Angel was sitting real close to René in the front seat and they didn't seem to know that Gigi and I existed. That's the way these things went.

We didn't say very much else on the way to the river. Gigi smoked her cigarette and let the air through the open window hit her face. I sat there, trying to think of something to say.

When we got to the river, there were cars parked in bunches, here and there. Sometimes, a solitary car off by itself. No keg party. We parked away from the other cars. Soon as René stopped the car, Gigi got out. I thought maybe I'd get out, too. Leave René and Angel some privacy. Yeah, that's the way it was, love was a private thing.

Gigi sat at the edge of the river. I watched her, then sat next to her. She took her shoes off. She stared out into the water. "Did they tell you stories of La Llorona when you were growing up?"

"Yeah. My mom."

"Did you ever wonder if it was true?"

"I believed everything was true."

She laughed. "Tell me the story."

We'd both heard it a million times. Don't know why she wanted to hear it again. But it was night and we were at the river and we were killing time, so I said okay. I'll tell it. "There was this woman. Black hair. Pretty. And she was happy and she had a husband who was pretty good to her and he was good to their three kids. You know, lived in a small house in

188

Hollywood." I could tell she was smiling. "Anyway, they had a happy family. And one day, he doesn't come back. Just doesn't. She goes crazy. Crazy, crazy. She's poor, and she's going up and down the street asking if anybody's seen her husband. And she doesn't have the money to feed her kids, just doesn't. She doesn't know what to do. So one day, someone tells her that her husband's run off with another woman. Mrs. López. He'd run off with Mrs. López." Gigi laughed. Mrs. López liked other women's husbands. "So she really goes crazy. What's she gonna do? Three hungry kids, no husband. So, to make herself feel better, she goes to the river every night. And she cries. To console herself. So, one day, no food in the house, the kids crying for food and for their father, she decides what she has to do. She brings her three kids to the river and drowns them. One at a time, she drowns them. She doesn't have to worry about them anymore. Except that after she does that, she really goes crazy. Crazy, crazy. Totally mad. I mean like one of those women in the Vincent Price movies. Like that. And ever since that day, she's searched the river looking for the bodies of her drowned children screaming, *Mis hijos. Mis hijos.* That was her punishment, to search the river forever until she finds the children she drowned. Wailing and wailing, *Mis hijos, ayyy, mis hijos.*"

Gigi was real quiet. Then she looked at me and shook her head. "You told it too fast. You're supposed to take your time. And you told it like it was a joke. Sammy, it's not a joke. It's not supposed to be funny."

"Sorry," I said.

She shook her head. She could be so ditzy. And then she could turn around and be so serious. "In my version," she said, "the marriage goes bad because he was rich and she was poor. She was an Indian and he was white. And then he got tired of her. Just threw her away—like she was nothing. Just didn't give a damn. He goes back to his kind. Leaves her to her own kind. How come she gets punished and he doesn't? How come that sonofabitch, pinche, baboso, hijo de la chingada doesn't get punished?"

I didn't have an answer. I liked her anger. "I don't know," I said. "The things is—the story's about her. Not him."

"It's not fair."

"It's not a real story, Gigi. It's just a story our parents tell us to keep us from swimming in the river. So we won't drown. That's all. They tell us, 'If you go to the river, La Llorona will get you.' They tell us crap like that so we'll behave, Gigi. Doesn't do a damn bit of good, I guess."

"You're wrong, Sammy. That story's real. It's just the way it is. It's like everything that happens in Hollywood. It's real, Sammy. Saddest love story in the world. A woman loses her husband, drowns her children and searches for them forever. Saddest love story in the world." She looked at me.

I lit a cigarette.

She kept looking at me like she wanted to ask me something. Then finally, she asks, "Anybody ever love you, Sammy?"

"Yeah," I said. "My mom, she loved me. My dad. My sister. They love me. And Juliana, I think she loved me. That makes four people. Guess that's it. Four. Guess that's a lot."

"Five," she said. "Me. Sammy. Me. I love you."

I didn't say anything for a long time. "I guess I knew that," I said. I took a drag off my cigarette.

"But you don't love me back, do you, Sammy?"

I waited. I don't know for what. The answer wasn't going to change. Finally, I said, "No, Gigi, I don't love you." It hurt to say that. It did. "Not like you want me to." Not like I loved Juliana. I wanted to tell her that, but I didn't. It would have made her feel worse, I think, to know I loved a dead girl more than I loved her. I felt sick. Bad. She was gonna start crying. I knew she was. Right then, right there. Nothing I could do about it. I looked at her.

But she wasn't crying.

"I'm sorry, Gigi."

She nodded. "Okay," she whispered. "Guess I already knew that." She kept nodding. "Pifas. Pifas wrote me a letter. He says he loves me. He says he wants to marry me when he comes back. He's crazy, Sammy. I mean I love that guy. I do. But I don't love him like that."

I nodded. She was a smart girl, Gigi. I didn't even know it, but it was me who was crying.

She looked at me. "Ahh, Sammy, you're crying. Why are you crying, Sammy?"

"I don't know, Gigi. You're a good girl. Fine. And I don't love you. And I don't love anybody. Maybe I don't have a heart. Maybe that's why I'm crying."

"Pendejo," she said. "People don't cry if they don't have hearts. Don't be a pendejo."

That made me laugh. That made her laugh, too. So we sat there and laughed. And laughed. And maybe we were both crying, too. Maybe we were both crying for different reasons. Maybe we were crying for the same reasons. And when we stopped laughing, she grabbed my pack of cigarettes from my pocket and lit one.

"I'm not as good a girl as you think, Sammy."

"Don't say that."

"I was with Pifas the night before he left. You know what I'm sayin', Sammy?"

"Yeah. I know."

"You think I'm a puta, don't you?"

"No, Gigi, I don't think that. That's not what I think. I think you gave him something. I think he needed something—and you gave it to him. You made him feel like he was somebody, Gigi. What's so bad about that?"

She was quiet for a long time. Then she started laughing again.

"What?" I said. "What's so funny?"

"You're the only boy in the whole stinking world that would say something like that, Sammy." And then she did start crying. And I held her. Like a brother. Like that. She cried and cried. And when she stopped, she took a breath like she was saying *Okay, it's done*. It's done.

That's when we heard the noise—voices yelling. Like there was a fight. And René gets out of the car and says, "Get in the car, Gigi! Just get in the car! Sammy, did you hear that?" He was wanting some action. I could hear it in his voice. God, that guy always knew what to do at the first sign of trouble. It's like he woke up, sniffed the air and knew exactly what to do. If there was a fight, he wanted to see if there was a way he could join in. He was just that way. "Sammy, let's check it out." Gigi got in the car. I don't know why I was going along. I didn't. Damnit. Then we both listened, "Fucking queers! Fucking queers!" And the sounds of someone or maybe more than one someone getting the holy shit beat out of them by guys who were yelling, "Fucking queers!" René was moving in the direction of the fight. I was right behind him. And then I swear I heard a voice—I knew that voice—I did—and the voice, begging, begging, "Stop, goddamnit, stop—you're killing him! You're killing him. God, stop. God—"

"¡Es Jaime!" René said, "¡Es Jaime! I swear to God that's Jaime. ¡Órale, Sammy, es Jaime!" He took off running toward the voices. I was right after him. I was just running in the dark, trusting René, following him, knowing he had all the right instincts. Like he was leading me into combat. Or something like that. And I didn't have to worry, just follow him, because

193

he'd show me what to do. Up ahead, I could see about four guys kicking two other guys who were on the ground. You could see with the light coming from inside the car—there in the light—both car doors wide open, the light pouring out. Eric, it was Eric's car. "Shit," René yelled. "Hey, damnit to hell! What the shit's going on!" By then we'd reached them. They didn't stop kicking. Just didn't stop. Acted like we weren't even there.

"Relax, we're just beating up a couple a queers," one of the guys said. "Found these two queers kissing each other. Goddamnit makes me fucking sick. What the fuck's it to ya."

René didn't even wait for him to finish. He punched him right in the face. Blood all over the place. I could feel it on my face, on my shirt. The guy fell back yelling, "You fucker, you broke my fucking nose!"

René didn't even hear him. No pity for the enemy. None. "Jaime? That you, Jaime? Jaime?" He knelt on the ground. "Jaime."

"René?"

"You okay, Jaime?"

It was Jaime all right. I could see him, his face all swelled and bloody. And Eric on the ground hardly moving at all.

For a while no one moved—then one of the other guys just kicked René right in the stomach as he was kneeling down over Jaime.

I didn't even think. I was on that guy. He wasn't expecting

me to jump him like that. I don't remember too much. When you're in the middle of a fight, that's all you know, the fight. René wasn't down long. He was up and mad as hell—and all business. Two guys were on me, but they weren't good fighters. They must've caught Jaime and Eric off guard. Jaime was normally a good fighter. I'd seen him in action. No, they weren't good fighters. Not any of them. F.F.A. gringo types who scared people away because they were big and traveled in packs. René could've taken them all. He knew how to fight, liked it, understood it. He was a thinker in a fight. And me, well, I knew how to throw a punch—and how to avoid one. I was good at avoiding punches. Guess that was my talent.

I dodged a fist—then kicked one of the guys right in the balls. He fell. That's the last thing I remember. And then they were running. All four of them. My lip was cut. Not the first time. I could feel blood on my face. Mostly it was other people's blood. All over me. My left cheek was a little sore. Then I saw headlights, heard Gigi's voice. "You guys okay?"

She and Angel got out of the car. She looked down at Jaime and Eric who were barely moving on the ground. "Hey," she whispered. She took Jaime's hand and squeezed it. René was good at fighting, but after the fight was over, he was lost. He and I just stood around, dazed. All we were good for was breathing. So that's what we stood there and did. But Gigi, she knew exactly what to do. She was on her knees, bending over Eric. "God," she said, "God, no, no, we gotta get these guys to the hospital." We just stood there, René and me, looking down at Gigi who was leaning over Jaime and Eric. "Damnit to hell!" She was yelling. "Did you hear me?"

God, they were beat up. I felt sick just looking at them.

I was afraid of hurting them more. But we had to move them. Somehow, we got them into the backseat of René's car. I don't know how we did that. They were really bad off. I thought they might break.

Gigi followed us to the hospital in Eric's car. I think I remember praying on our way to the hospital. I remember watching René as he drove. I kept thinking that maybe this was a dream. It wasn't happening. How could this happen? Were we in a war?

sixteen

"What happened?" The doctor wanted to know.

"What happened?"

"Some guys jumped them," I said. "At the river."

"What were you doing at the river?"

"Saving their asses," René said.

The doctor shook his head. "Crazy kids."

"Yeah," I said. "Stupid crazy kids." Sleep deprivation, I guess. I was feeling punchy. "They gonna be all right?"

He nodded. Not very convincing. Then he looked at me. "I think maybe I should take a look at that lip." He took me in a room, made me sit. He cleaned it up. Hurt. I didn't wince. "I think it'll be all right," he said. "Just don't kiss anyone the next three or four days."

"I'm not planning on it," I said.

We waited for their parents. Eric's parents walked through the doors first. They looked at us sitting there in the emergency waiting room. I pointed in the direction of the doors. They rushed through them, toward Eric. I knew it would hurt, to see him like that. It would've killed my dad if it was me.

Jaime's mom showed up a little later. Not his dad. Guess his dad wasn't too interested. "¿Y mi Jaime? ¿Dónde esta mi Jaime?"

I got up from where I was sitting. "Lo golpearon," I said.

"¿Quién?" She broke down crying. "Es un niño."

I held her. I thought of my mom. Yeah, I thought, we're all babies. I let her go. I wiped her tears. "You're a good boy." So sweet, when she spoke English. I led her through the doors. The nurse, the doctor, they said nothing. I left her there crying. *Jaime, Jaime, hijo de mi vida.*

I called my dad, told him what happened. Left out the queer part. He didn't have to know everything. I told him I was fine. Yeah, sure, fine, told him not to worry. He was mad, but not too mad. Relieved, I think. "Come home," he said. I told him after I found out how they were. We might have to talk to the cops. Maybe, who knows? He said I wasn't excused from going to Mass. I said okay. I'll be home, I said, after I know.

Jaime had two broken ribs. A face so bruised his face swelled like a pumpkin. Eric had a broken jaw. Surgery, his mother said. The cops came. Doctor called them. Had to, he said. We told them what we knew. What we saw. Everything. "And what were they yelling?" they asked again. "Queers.

Found these two guys kissing each other. That's what they said. That's what I heard." René was telling the story. I nodded. The cop wrote on his form.

Eric's parents said nothing. Jaime's mother said nothing.

We sat there.

Eric's father never looked up. Eric's mother hugged us, thanked us, couldn't stop thanking us. *Thank you, thank you, God bless you, God bless you.* Jaime's mother just cried. Mothers broke my heart. Gigi handed the keys to Eric's car to his mother. Hugged her. *God bless you. God bless you.*

We had to drive to the police station. The detective separated us. Each of us had to write down what happened, in a separate room. To make sure we weren't lying. Each of us. We wrote. We gave our essays to the police. They let us go. It was all just a game. They'd never do anything. We knew they wouldn't. "Keep away from the river," that's what one of the cops told us. They never even asked us if we recognized the guys. The guys who did this. Never asked us.

"I'm in deep trouble," Gigi said. Then she laughed. "My parents aren't going to let me go out for the rest of the school year."

Angel shook her head. Her mother was from Mexico. American customs, American kids—none of that meant anything to her. Angel had this look on her face.

"Doesn't matter, anyway," Gigi said. "Big deal." She touched her face. I knew she was thinking of Jaime and Eric.

199

Her face, it was still perfect. She knew that. That's what she was thinking.

René looked like hell. The sun was rising and we were sitting there in the parking lot of the police station. He looked at me and laughed. "You look like shit." He had this look on his face. "They're queers," he said.

We stood there, as if some devil was preventing us from getting into the car. We stood there. Where did you go? Which way did you drive the car when the world had changed?

"I don't care," Gigi said. "Jaime, he's ours."

"Yeah," Angel said.

I didn't know that much about these things. I'd been with Juliana. That was what I knew about love. I didn't know shit about what love was for anybody else.

"It doesn't matter," Gigi said.

"You're full of shit, Gigi," René said. "Just wait till Monday. Just wait till we get to school. The whole damned school's gonna know. The whole damned school. Those guys are gonna make sure everybody knows. And they're gonna make Jaime and Eric pay."

"For what?" Gigi said.

"Wake up, Gigi. No seas tan pendeja. They're doing something wrong. Everyone's gonna know. What's gonna happen to those jotos, huh?"

"Don't talk that way about Jaime."

"He's a pinche joto."

"He's your friend."

"I didn't know—"

"Oh, people are gonna think you're a pinche joto, too, just because you hung out with him since you were five. Take me home."

"We saved their joto asses, Gigi."

"And now you're sorry, huh, René?"

René didn't say anything. He just looked down at the ground.

Gigi looked at me. "¿Y tú? What do you think, Sammy?"

I shrugged.

"Damnit to hell, say something!"

"I don't know."

"We should've let those pinche gringos kill 'em, is that it?"

"No."

"No. That's all you have to say?"

"What do you want me to say, Gigi?"

"Figure it out." She opened the car door. "Take me home."

No one said anything on our way back to Hollywood. When we left Gigi and Angel, Gigi turned around and looked right at me. "You're both thinking you never knew Jaime. You're both thinking you never knew him at all. Well, screw you. Screw both of you. I'm thinking I don't know you, either." She slammed the car door shut. I thought it might stay shut forever.

* * *

Eric and Jaime weren't at school on Monday. They weren't in school all week, but I heard things, heard all kinds of ugly things. I kept my mouth shut. On Thursday, some guy walks up to me at lunch while I'm having a cigarette in the back of the cafeteria—the smoking section—he walks up to me and says, "I hear you're real good at saving queers. Some people save S&H green stamps. Other people save queers."

I grabbed him by the collar. He was with four other guys. I didn't give a damn. "See this fist? I'm saving it for you. You ever come close to me again and you're gonna have this for fucking lunch."

"Let go of me, you fucking spic." That's what he said. That was the first time anybody actually called me a fucking spic. Right then, I was gonna break his face open—except I heard a voice. "That's enough." It was Mrs. Davis, my English teacher. I knew her voice. "Let him go, Sammy." I loosened my grip on the sonofabitch.

"Go on, Danny," she said. "You and your friends, go on." They disappeared. Danny looked back at me, letting me know this wasn't over. Not by a long shot.

I looked at Mrs. Davis. She stood there, looking at me. "After school," she said. "In my room, after school."

So after school, there I was in her room. She was at her desk. She smiled at me as I stood at the door. "Come in," she said. Her voice, it was kind. I knew kindness. I knew what that was. Like Mrs. Apodaca, when she told me my mother was una alma de Dios. Like Eric's mother when she said God bless you. She motioned me to come in. She stopped grading her papers. "You want to sit down?" she said.

"I'll stand," I said. "Are you gonna turn me in?"

"No," she said. "As a matter of fact, I've turned Danny and his friends in to the principal."

"They didn't mean any harm," I said. "Happens all the time."

"I think they did mean harm, Sammy," she said. She bit the tip of her pen. "And if it happens all the time, then we're not making any progress here, are we?"

What did she want me to say? "Turning them into the principal won't change anything," I said.

She didn't skip a beat. Not her style. "Maybe not. Letting them walk around like they own the world won't change anything either." She shrugged. "How's Jaime?" She asked like she cared. I looked at her. She was young. I wanted to ask her how old she was.

"How's Jaime?"

"I don't know. I haven't gone to see him."

"Why not?"

"I don't know."

She looked at me. "I thought he was your friend."

"We live in the same neighborhood," I said.

She nodded. "He's a good student," she said. "I like Jaime." We were dancing around something. We both knew it—

203

except she was the one who'd called me in. What did you want to see me about—that's what I wanted to ask her. But I didn't.

Finally, she looked at me. "People can be very cruel, Sammy," she said.

"I know that," I said. I did know that.

We looked at each other.

"I guess everyone knows about Jaime and Eric—and what happened." I looked at her. I don't know what she expected me to say.

She nodded. "What you and René did—is it true? That you helped them?"

I nodded. But I didn't nod like I was proud of myself. René and I, well, we were just there. I followed. We didn't know—I nodded. "Word gets around."

"Words are like fire."

"Yeah," I said. I think I smiled. "You always say that."

"Because it's true. Words are like fire and they burn."

"Yeah. I know."

"You did a good thing," she said. "They could've been killed." She kept shaking her head. Like all of this made her sad. Then she looked at me. I liked what I saw in her face.

"Not everybody thinks so," I said.

"So what?" she said.

"Yeah," I said. "Well, don't give me too much credit."

"Don't be so hard on yourself, Sammy. You did a good

thing." She stared at the papers sitting on her desk. "You should go see him."

I nodded.

I didn't go.

I never went to see him.

Two weeks later, Jaime showed up at school. His face was still a little bruised. Not a lot. His arm was in a sling. He walked a little stiff. His ribs were wrapped. You could tell. He looked sad. Some people sort of waved at him. Some people just stared at him.

Mrs. Scott—our homeroom Spanish teacher—she'd hated Jaime. Loved Eric. Hated Jaime. But that morning she was nice. To Jaime. She talked to him before class started. But Eric wasn't there. Eric, the guy who always had his hand up. Eric, the guy who spoke the best Spanish. Eric, the gringo who wanted to be Mexican. He was absent.

At lunch, Jaime was sitting alone. He wasn't really eating. René and I looked at each other. Like maybe we should go and sit with him. But then Gigi and Angel went over to him—Gigi and Angel who weren't talking to us, they sat with him. They saved us from having to do anything. That's what we were thinking. They'd saved us.

René and I didn't say anything.

We just sat there in the cafeteria, watching. Some guy

walks by Jaime's table and says loud enough for the whole damn world to hear, "Queer."

Gigi gets up, looks right at him—then slaps the hell out of him. "Say it again," she said, "I didn't hear you." She looked at him until he turned away. Eyes. Bullets. Don't screw with Gigi Carmona.

René and I just sat there, watching, like the rest of them.

After school, René and I walked home. No car that day. We saw Jaime walking ahead of us. By himself. Cars would pass him as he walked. People would yell things. We didn't get too close. He didn't seem to notice. Not us, not anything. Like he was dead.

A car went by real slow. And hit Jaime with a water balloon. It broke against him. He hung his head.

There are times I think, when you know shame. And the shame becomes a part of your knowledge of the world. René and I, we'd helped Jaime and Eric, but it was all instinct. If we'd done something good, then we hadn't done it on purpose. We knew that. And now, we had a choice. René and I, we were better with our fists and our bodies than we were with our hearts. This fight, this fight was harder. We were lost, afraid of the world and its judgments. The world was cruel. And it was crueler to Jaime than to us. We had a choice. Jaime didn't. We knew that, too. He was there, alone, taking all the punches as if the fight belonged only to him. But Jaime was

206

ours. That's what René had known when he'd recognized Jaime's voice that night—that he was in trouble, that he needed help. He hadn't needed to ask questions, hadn't needed to ask why. But, now, the world was telling us something else—that Jaime didn't belong to us after all. An alien. Foreign. I thought of Father Fallon, and how he'd said we were animals. Maybe we thought that's what Jaime was. An animal, not like us, not ours. But we knew that it wasn't true. And so we were ashamed.

I watched Jaime, his head hanging. He dropped his books. He stumbled. He was crying. He was falling to the ground. It was as if he didn't care if they beat him until he disappeared. But he wasn't disappearing, and that made it even worse. I looked at René and I could see tears running down his face, too. "I don't know what to do," he said. "Tell me what to do, Sammy."

I never thought René had tears inside him. I never knew that about him. That night, at the river, he'd been the perfect warrior. Relentless and graceful, afraid of nothing. But now, he was standing still, awkward, waiting for me to say something. I did my Aztec chin thing. Pointing toward Jaime. He nodded.

We walked slowly toward our friend. That's what he was. "Hey," I said. I helped him get to his feet. René picked up his books. "Let's go to the Pic Quick and get a Pepsi. My treat."

Jaime tried to stop crying. He took a breath. Then another. "Okay," he said. "I drink Coke."

"Okay. Coke." We walked slow. Real slow. We weren't in a hurry.

"I'm all wet," Jaime said. "I hate water balloons. I fucking hate them."

"Remember that time we got Pifas when we were kids?"

Jaime nodded. He almost smiled.

We kept walking.

When we got to the Pic Quick, we got our sodas. We drank, lit up cigarettes.

"Gigi was really great at lunch today," I said.

"Yeah," he said. "Gigi's the best," and I knew he was going to cry again.

"You know something, I think girls are braver than guys. Don't you think so?"

He nodded. He looked at René and me. I mean, he really looked at us. His eyes were so black. "Thanks," he said. "I owe you."

"No, you don't." That's what I said. "How's Eric?" Maybe it was wrong to ask.

I didn't think Jaime was going to answer the question. I could see his hands were trembling. "They're gonna have to fix his jaw. It's gonna take some time. His parents sent him back to Pennsylvania—to live with his aunt. Better doctors there. That's what his mom said. She didn't let me talk to him." He nodded. God, his hands trembling like leaves in a storm. "He's going back to Pennsylvania—where no one knows." He took a drink from his Coke. "Me, too," he said. "My dad, he's sending me to live with my uncle. In California." Then he smiled. Like a little kid.

"Maybe that's better," René said. "California. People won't hurt you there."

That's not what I was thinking. I was thinking that people hurt you no matter where you lived. No matter where you went. They'd find you. And then they'd hurt you.

Jaime and René hung out on my porch that whole week. It was safe there. We never said anything else about that night. Maybe we didn't know how to talk about it. Maybe we didn't need to. One night, they stayed for dinner. I cooked, because that's what I did. I was the cook in our house. That's how it was when you didn't have a mom. My dad and Jaime and René and me and my little sister, Elena, we talked and laughed. "It's good," René said. "Yeah, it is," Jaime said. I felt safe. We all felt safe.

The Friday night before Jaime left, we all went out—René and Angel and Gigi and me and Jaime. Gigi and Angel were talking to us again. We were all on the same side.

We rode around. We talked. We laughed. We all told Pifas stories. Everyone had a good story about Pifas. Gigi passed around a picture of him in a uniform. His hair was short. He looked good, he did, took a good picture. The uniform almost made him look like a man. He was waiting for his orders, Gigi said. Maybe they would send him to Germany instead of

Nam. That's what I thought.

We all knew Jaime would never come back. We couldn't face that. We knew the score. We understood. But we didn't. We really didn't. So all night we talked about Pifas. We had a few beers. Not many. Smoked too many cigarettes. We saw the sun rise. "I love the desert." That's what Jaime said. I'd never heard anybody say that.

The next morning, we went to the bus station. We said good-bye to Jaime. Angel and Gigi were full of kisses. They cried. Of course, they did. *We love you. We love you. You'll always be ours.* When Pifas had left, I hadn't hugged him. So this time, I hugged Jaime. I'd never really liked him. We'd never gotten along. But now, I think, we were friends. Friends who lived in different countries. That's what we were. But René and him—René and him had always been friends. Since they were kids. René looked at Jaime. "Did you love him?" His voice was cracking. Gigi leaned into me and I felt her sobbing. I never knew René had it in him—to ask a question like that.

"Yeah," Jaime whispered. "Not that it matters."

"It matters," René said, "it always matters. When you love someone."

They nodded at each other. Gigi was bawling her eyes out. So was Angel. But René and Jaime, they weren't crying.

Jaime got on the bus. And waved good-bye.

We stood there until the bus disappeared. "I'm never gonna love anybody ever again," Gigi said. We all broke out laughing. And then we all started singing that stupid song Dionne Warwick sang about never falling in love again. Gigi kept us on key. That's what we did—sang and laughed on the day Jaime left us.

That night, I stayed awake. I couldn't sleep. I was listening to K-O-M-A, that radio station that only came to us at night. Like it was only a dream. All the way from Oklahoma City. All the way to where I was lying in my bed. I was hoping to hear a song. A song that would tell me everything I needed to know. About love. If only the right song would come on, then I'd be able to sleep.

I thought about my father, how he said you had to love the world, how you had to find a way to love it. As if that was an easy thing. How did you love a world that didn't love you back? How did you do that?

I thought about how everybody at school was so desperate to find a hand to hold. As if we were all about to die. And we couldn't wait anymore. We'd waited so long already. And they told us that it was coming, at any moment, any moment now, we were going to find it. We were going to turn around and look into the eyes of a girl or a boy and we were going to find everything we had always been looking for.

Love was standing there, waiting for us, for me. For Sammy. For Gigi. For René. For Jaime. We were all going to find the country we lived in. We were all going to belong. We were all going to be free. And then what? And then—?

I thought about Gigi and Pifas. And Eric and Jaime. I thought about me and Juliana.

Love was so public. In 1968, love was everywhere. It was in all the songs, it was on all the posters, it was a flower sprouting in my front yard, waiting for me to pick it. Well, maybe love was supposed to be a public thing, maybe so. But for me it would always be something private. Love was something between me and Juliana—even though she was dead. Love was something between Jaime and Eric. And what we had, if it was love, well, hell, it wasn't supposed to be on a bumper sticker.

It's funny, everyone had always told us love was another word for belonging.

No one, *no one* had ever told me that love was another name for exile.

the citizens of hollywood rise up against the system

"Sometimes dreams come true,
don't they, Sammy?"

I wanted to tell Elena that the bad ones,
they're ones that come true.

But I just said,
"Yeah, sometimes
dreams come true."

seventeen

"Hey! Hey you! Where's your belt?"

I was practically running down the hall, late for second period, hated being late, hated standing there waiting for an unexcused absence, Mr. Romero staring at me like I was a few inches away from landing in prison. Like maybe if it were up to him I would be landing in prison. Such a big deal over unexcused tardies. Tardies lead to chaos, that's what our teachers told us. As if what went on in class wasn't chaos. Tardies, hell, and girls, they got away with everything. Boys, they never got away with anything. All a girl ever had to say was "personal." Personal, that meant it was that time of the month. Lied. Girls were liars. Personal always got them an excused tardy. Guys, what could be personal about guys? Sometimes, when I was staring at the slip of paper that said REASON FOR TARDINESS, I'd get the urge to write: I was zipping up my pants at the urinal and I recircumcised myself.

A tragedy, a personal tragedy. Personal. Excused.

"I said, 'Where's your belt?'" I stopped. I looked around and saw Colonel Wright. Everybody hated Colonel Wright. You didn't have to be in his class to hate him. He was staring at me. I pointed to myself. Like an idiot. Like a complete and total menso. Who me?

"Yeah you. Where's your belt?"

I looked down, shit, no belt. How could I have forgotten my belt?

I shrugged. I must've left it in the bathroom. That's what I was thinking of blurting out. Yeah, yeah, he would've believed that one.

"Who's your homeroom teacher?" He said it like he was about to have her court-martialed.

"Mrs. Scott."

"And she didn't do anything about this situation?"

It was a situation. The Viet Nam war wasn't a war. It was a conflict. My not wearing a belt—that was a situation. And they wanted us to learn English. Yeah, yeah.

"I guess not," I said. It was hard to say who he blamed more—me or Mrs. Scott. But I knew who he was about to come down on.

"What's your name?"

"Sammy."

"You got a last name there, son?"

"Santos."

"Santos, go to the office. Explain your situation to Mr. Romero."

"I have a test," I said.

"Well, that's too bad."

The bell rang. Shit. It's a belt, I wanted to say, just a stupid little piece of leather. Just a belt. I knew he could see the disgust on my face.

"What's that I see on your face?"

"Mustard," I said.

"What?"

"Nothing."

"I don't like back talk, Santos."

I hated the way he said Santos. I nodded.

He pointed toward the office. I walked down the empty hall to handle my situation.

Mr. Romero was in the office. He smiled. But it wasn't a nice smile. Romero didn't have a nice smile. Crooked teeth. Crooked brain, too, I think. Nope. Not nice. "Mr. Santos," he said. "Have you and Mr. Montoya gone on any more river patrols?"

Bastard. "Yeah," I said. "Last night we beat the crap outta La Llorona. That's what she gets for drowning her kids."

"A comedian."

"Yes, sir."

"I've never liked you, Santos."

"I've always felt bad about that, sir." It wasn't the first time we'd had conversations like this. He always looked at me the same way. I always looked at him the same way. I wondered what was wrong with me. I was getting an attitude. I'd always had one. Hid it, though. I guess I just wasn't in the mood for hiding. It's like someone had lit a fuse inside me.

He looked me over. "Where's your belt?"

"That's exactly what Colonel Wright wanted to know."

"What did you tell him?"

"I told him it wore out. I told him I was too poor to buy another. I'm from Hollywood."

"I hate smart mouths, Mr. Santos."

"Yes, sir."

"How many days of detention do you think I should give you?"

"Should I pick a number between one and ten?"

"That's it. That's it. Eight days. Eight days of detention." When he got mad, he always repeated himself. If he said it more than once, then maybe he was communicating more effectively. I knew about that. Eight days. That was the maximum. He tore out a tardy slip, stamped unexcused on it—handed it to me. "I feel better," he said.

"Me, too," I said. "I feel real good."

He just stared at me. "Get outta here before I throw your ass out of this school." He kept staring at me. I didn't care. He knew my father. Even my father knew he was a chickenshit. Even my father knew that. And I didn't give a damn what he thought. And sometimes, when I didn't give a damn, I shot my mouth off. And lately I didn't give a damn about what anyone thought. God, who lit the fuse? So, here I was popping off. Not that I was helping myself out here. Eight days of detention. That's what it got me. For having forgotten to wear a belt. For opening my big mouth. I'd have to tell my dad. He'd say, "Sometimes, you should just be quiet, Sammy. You're quiet when you should be talking—and you talk when you should be busy keeping your mouth shut." That's what he'd say. Yeah, yeah.

A belt. A stupid belt. This was January of 1969. America was falling apart. Black Panthers, Brown Berets, farm workers were organizing, every college in the nation was on fire. And what were we worried about at Las Cruces High? Boys' belts. Dress codes. Tucked in shirts. Short hair. Short hair! Not that I wanted to wear my hair long. I didn't like long hair—and I didn't like bell bottoms. Me and ten other people in the world didn't wear them. So what? Guys wanted long hair. So what? Girls wanted short dresses. So what?

Tardy. I hated that word. I handed Mr. Barnes my note. He looked at it. Unexcused. Shook his head. Handed me my test. I sat down, looked at it, multiple choice, wasn't worried, stuff not worth knowing. Dates. That was history? Dates. I was going to remember them after the test? Yeah, yeah. This wasn't learning. I knew that. I did know that. Hated history, hated Barnes who could quote Robert E. Lee and every other general who ever took a breath. Hated Barnes, hated Romero, hated Colonel Wright. Hated Birdwail, though at least I didn't have to spend any more time in his goddamned classroom. Hated my Civics teacher, Mrs. Jackson, who seemed to be only slightly better than Colonel Wright. Got up there and told us things like the S.D.S. was pinko. Pinko. Didn't even know what that was. She'd make anybody want to be a pinko. Told us too many people were tearing down what we'd built up. Tearing everything down and paving the road for the Chinese or the Russians to come on in. Told us our fathers didn't fight wars to hand the country over to hippies and other assorted peaceniks and cowards and other disrespectful vermin. Told us about the domino effect. And we just might be next to fall if we didn't do our job in Viet Nam. That's what she got up and told us. This was Civics—these are things we needed to know. And then she told us how the blacks were ungrateful. "After all we've done. For them." I'm sure all of the citizens of Hollywood were supposed to be grateful, too. And she didn't think much of César Chávez, either. Those people got jobs and no one else would hire them. Where exactly do they think they're going to get a job? She took out pictures of D-Day, showed them to us. Your fathers fought hard for what we have. And what the hell did she know about why our fathers had fought? She didn't know my father. She wouldn't have been caught dead talking to him either. I knew that.

"My uncle died in Korea," I said one day. I was mad. I was

really mad. "He was a patriot," she said. "Brave." Maybe he was. Maybe he wasn't. What the hell did she know? He was dead. And I still didn't understand why he had to die. And my father, the veteran, was heartbroken. I hated this stupid, worthless, good-for-nothing school. Right then, right there, all I felt was rage. Five more months. It didn't matter one damn to me what life would be after this. I wanted out. Out! That's what I wanted.

I turned in my test. Barnes smiled. I was the last to start. The first to finish.

Tomorrow, I would get it back. It would say: "A. Nice work, Sammy." That's what my papers always said.

I hated myself. Sometimes, I did. Because I took the crap they gave me and pretended like it was real food. I took it. I ate it. And I knew what it was—it was all crap. Anything I knew about America, I learned from my father. And from living in Hollywood. And from watching the news. And from reading books. I hated myself because they owned me. Because I let them own me. I knew that. I did know that. And I wasn't gonna do a damn thing about it.

Hey! Hey, you! Where's your belt?

On the fifth day of detention, a Monday, it started to snow. I sat in the back of the classroom—next to René. He'd forgotten to tuck his shirt back in after he'd gone to the bathroom. Lots of guys got caught that way. Colonel Wright had caught up with him in the hall. Colonel Wright, he could spot a guy with an untucked shirt fifty yards away.

I looked over to see what René was doing. Writing a letter to Pifas—he was in Nam now. No Germany for him. I looked out the window and watched the snow fall. It was beautiful, really beautiful. I thought I'd like walking home in it. That's what I was thinking.

Colonel Wright was today's monitor. "No looking out the window," he said. Everyone looked up.

"It's snowing," I said.

"You've never seen snow before, Santos?"

"Not lately," I said.

"I don't like you, Santos."

"Yes, sir. I can't say that I blame you, sir."

Made him mad. He was about to say something else when Gigi walks in. Gigi was always saving my ass. He looked at her. "Well, if it isn't Miss Free Speech." He looked at all of us. "We have a celebrity among us. You want to give that speech for us one more time? We sure enjoyed it."

God, Gigi could give a look. She hated him. More than me, I think.

"And she's late. Late to detention. What do you think about that? And she wanted to be President of the Senior Class. Do you think we should ask her if she has an excuse?"

"It was personal," she said.

He just stared at her. They stayed that way for a while. Then she opened her purse and showed him her feminine hygiene products. Then found a seat.

"I didn't say you could sit down, young lady."

"I'm not in the Army, sir."

"What?"

"Tomorrow there's a Mass for the deaf."

We all laughed. Couldn't help it. An old Mexican saying: Mañana hay misa pa' los sordos. I'd never heard it translated into English. Maybe that's why we all laughed, because it was odd to hear it in English. Gigi, she was a helluva translator.

God, the Colonel hated that we were laughing.

"Everybody. Everybody gets an extra day." He looked at Gigi. "You want to do your classmates any more favors?"

Gigi shook her head. Her eyes were on fire. I knew those eyes.

René and Gigi and I had a snowball fight after detention. It was dark, but the cold of the snow was soft and good. And for a moment, the world we lived in was perfect. Just for a second. And then afterward, we drank hot chocolate at Shirley's. "I hate this bullshit detention," René said. "And I hate that Colonel. I hate that pinche."

"He fought for your freedom." Gigi smiled. "Just ask him. He'll tell you." We laughed. We were laughing at him. The only way we knew to fight back.

"We should do something," Gigi said.

"Something," I said. "An undetermined or unspecified thing."

"Librarian," Gigi said.

"I was just wanting to know what you meant by something."

"A student strike."

"Forget about it."

René was all for it. A fight! Hey! A fight! Any kind of fight. His eyes. Sometimes they were like Gigi's. On fire.

"I'm not gonna organize a pinche student strike," I said.

"They're doing it everywhere."

"In colleges. We're not in college."

"Today is the first day of the rest of your fucking life." René grinned.

"Not gonna do it. I'm not."

"Oh, you're such a pinche good boy, ¿sabes, Sammy?"

"Culo," I said.

"You're the culo," Gigi said.

"I don't know the first thing about organizing a student strike. I'm out. I'm all the way out."

"What are you afraid of? Chicken, big gallina."

"I'm going to college," I said. "You and René can go to hell. In five months, I'm getting the hell out of Cruces High. And then, I'm going to college. And then my life is going to start. And I'm not gonna screw that up just because we're all pissed off. You think you're the only ones pissed off at how things are run at that two bit 7-11 pop stand they call Cruces High? Why don't you get all those gringos to help you out? See if they'll organize a student strike. Let's see how many of them are going to put their asses on the line."

Gigi didn't say anything. She wasn't happy. She'd talked me into a hundred things since I'd known her—ever since second grade when she made me give my last nickel to some little guy she'd owed. Always got her way. Nope. Not this time.

"We can't do it without you, Sammy," she said.

"Forget it, Gigi. NO LO VOY A HACER, RAMONA." She hated it when I called her by her real name.

"Okay," she said. "And if you ever call me Ramona again, I'm gonna slap your lips clean off your face, ¿sabes?" She smiled. "Okay then, you won't do it. Okay." When I said okay, it meant okay. When she said okay, it meant she was gonna come back at you when you had your guard down.

"You're a real vendido," René said. "The real thing."

"Yup," I said. I wasn't budging. I'd been their pinche yo-yo one too many times. Not this time. If they wanted to start a revolution, they could start it without me.

René and Gigi didn't talk to me for a week. Didn't care. I finished detention. Every day, before school, I made sure I was wearing my belt. My hair was getting long. I cut it. I thought of Pifas, his military hair cut, the picture he'd sent to Gigi. All American. From Hollywood.

eighteen

Two days later, I came home from school. Last day of detention. I picked Elena up at Mrs. Apodaca's. Dad was at a Knights of Columbus meeting. The Knights of Columbus. What was that? Catholic men getting together without their wives. Why did Dad go? He didn't have a wife, not anymore. Joined them after Mom died. Maybe it was us.

When we walked in the door, Elena looks up at me. "Sammy?"

"Yeah?" She had this look on her face. That look nine-and-a-half-year-olds get when they're about to ask you a question you don't want to answer.

"What's heroin?"

"Little girls don't need to know about heroin." She didn't like my answer. Nine-and-a-half-year-olds don't like a lot of answers. "You wanna help with dinner?"

She nodded. We washed our hands. The rule. Mom was

gone, but we still lived with her rules. Every time I washed my hands, I thought of Mom. The way she kissed me after I washed them. The way she looked at me. "What are you gonna make, Sammy?"

"How about meatloaf?" Meatloaf was easy. We had hamburger meat. It took a while in the oven, but it was easy. Not very Mexican, but easy.

"And french fries?"

"Okay," I said, "meatloaf and french fries. You peel the potatoes."

She nodded. She stood over the sink and peeled. She watched me as I crumbled Saltines into the hamburger meat. "I want to know what heroin is," she said.

This was a father talk. I was the brother. Not the father. I always said that to myself when I knew Elena had me against the ropes. "It's a drug," I said. "And it's bad."

"What does it do? Why is it bad?"

Not that I knew what it did. "It makes you feel good, I guess. But only for a little while. And then it makes you crazy." I made a face. "Loopy, nutso, crazy, crazy."

She laughed. I could always make her laugh. "What's addicted?"

"Why are you asking me all these questions, Elena?" She could peel potatoes and talk at the same time. She was good, my little sister. I kissed her. Maybe if I kissed her, she'd stop asking questions. Didn't work. Never worked. Kisses didn't work on girls. Not really. No.

"Mrs. Apodaca told Mrs. Garcia that she'd seen Reyes and that he was addicted to heroin, and that he looked like death."

"Oh," I said.

"What does death look like, Sammy?"

"Like Halloween," I said.

"You don't want to talk about it, do you?"

God, that kid could read me. "I don't think you should worry about heroin," I said.

"Dad will tell me," she said. Like, who cares about you, Sammy?

"Maybe he will," I said.

"You forgot the onions," she said, as I kneaded the glop of hamburger meat.

But she got me started thinking about Reyes. He'd dropped out of school. Not that I blamed him. But for heroin? It was true about him. I'd seen him around. God, he was skinny. And his breath smelled like hell. I'd given him two dollars. "Go buy a toothbrush." That's what I told him. I could be mean.

And that night, right when my father was eating my meatloaf and watching the evening news, Mrs. Espinoza came to the door. "Have you seen Reyes? Have you seen my Reyes?" And then she breaks down. "No sé qué voy hacer. Me estoy volviendo loca. No ha llegado a la casa por cinco días." Five days without seeing her son. Crazy, crazy. I imagined La Llorona looked like that. Red eyes from crying, from not sleeping. A face that was old, not because of time, but because worry did that, aged you, made you look like you'd never been young. God, she looked awful. And she was shaking and crying. For her son—like La Llorona.

My father made her sit down, made tea for her. She cried, and she kept asking me if I'd seen her Reyes. She kept rubbing her hands on her thin cotton dress, rubbing and rubbing her hands until I thought she'd sand all the skin off her hands. I thought maybe she needed something to calm her down. I kept shaking my head, until she asked me one more time, and then I couldn't take it anymore, seeing her like that. And I said, "René and I— we'll find him." Where the hell was I gonna find him? It was almost eleven o'clock. Where in the hell were we going to look? Where? My dad nodded. "Yes, yes," he said. "Ahorita salen a buscarlo. Va a ver, señora, ahorita se lo traen." Yeah, we would find him. Ahorita. We would find him. My father picked up the phone, called René, talked to him, talked to Mr. Montoya. He hung up the phone. He nodded at me. I put on my coat. I waited for René, so we could go out into the night and find Reyes. René, he might know. He knew things, got around. Maybe he might know. Before I left the house, I looked at Mrs. Espinoza. "We'll find him for you." I didn't think so.

"So where the hell are we gonna look?" I looked at René. I was mad. I didn't know what we were doing. I got mad if I didn't know what to do.

"I know this guy," René said. "His name's Mark. He's a dealer."

I didn't say anything. I didn't want to know how René knew. I nodded.

We went there, an apartment near the university. René got out of the car, talked to him, talked to him for a long time. He knew this guy, I could tell, the way they talked in the light of the doorway. I waited in the car. Smoked.

When René came back to the car, he lit up a cigarette.

"You've been here before," I said.

"¿Y qué? ¿Qué cabrones te importa?"

"You do that crap?"

"Sometimes I sell that crap—if you want to know the pinche truth." He looked at me. He could see what I was holding in my eyes. "Mr. Santito, Mr. Clean," he said. "Librarian. Not everybody's as holy as you. Not everybody has his head up his ass."

I hated the way he said that, hated the way he looked at me. I didn't say anything, nothing. "Let's just find him," I said. "Let's just find Reyes."

He started the car. "If you ever tell anyone we were here, Sammy, I swear I'll kick the crap out of you. ¿Sabes, cabrón? ¿Entiendes Méndez?"

He sold that crap. How come I didn't know? How come I didn't? Because. Because I didn't want to. I didn't say anything. "Let's just find Reyes," I whispered. "Then we can just go home."

We drove to some trailer house in Mesilla Park. René knew where he was going. He parked, got out of the car, knocked at the door to the trailer house. Some girl comes out. Straight long hair. A gringa. René went in. A little while later, he comes out. He gets back in the car.

"Didn't know you had so many friends."

"Screw you. You want to find Reyes or not?"

I lit a cigarette. He drove to another apartment on Locust, cheap cinder-block apartments. Four of them in a row. René stopped the car on the street. "You wanna go in?"

"That where he is?"

René nodded.

"Yeah," I said. "I'll go in." I got out of the car. We walked up to the door. "You been here before?"

René shook his head, knocked, nobody answered. He knocked again. "Open up!" he said. "It's René." No one answered. He pounded on the door, looked at me, then pounded on the door again. "It's me, René. Open the damned door!" I could see his face, the corner streetlight shining on us. He looked older than me. It was like I'd never seen him before, like I was seeing him for the first time. And I didn't like what I saw. Finally, someone comes to the door, opens it. We stared into the face of some guy, long stringy, dirty hair, stoned out of his mind. A gringo. He could hardly talk. And he says, "René. Far-fucking-out! René." Screwed up, all screwed up. I could see that. René pushed him out of the way, and went into the house. I stood there, staring at this guy's eyes. He stared back at me. They almost didn't have a color, his eyes. Like he'd washed all the color out of them. He just stared at me—like he didn't understand. Like his brain was missing. Like he wasn't even alive.

René came back to the door. He just looked at me. "Sammy," he said. Then he stopped. "Sammy," he said. He looked sick. God. He looked sick.

"What?"

"Sammy!"

"What?"

"Reyes."

"What?"

"Reyes—" I knew. By the look on René's face. I guess I just had to see for myself. *I had to see.* I walked into the back bedroom, looked in, Reyes, he was there, just lying on the floor. I didn't feel anything. I looked at him like I was looking at a thing I'd never seen before, like I was looking at something foreign, not a foreign person, but a foreign thing. And I was trying to figure out what it was. The light in the room was bad, bad, but I could see everything. A bed with no sheets. A needle on the bed. Reyes on the floor. It was as if my eyes had become a camera. I was taking pictures. That's all I was, a camera. Cameras don't feel.

I don't know how long I stared down at Reyes. I just knew I'd be coming back to this room for a long time. I closed my eyes. I opened them. I walked out of the room.

René was leaning against the open door. I walked up to him. He had his back to me. "We have to call the cops," I said.

René didn't say anything. Not a damn thing.

"We have to call the cops, René! We have to call the cops!"

I remember looking for a phone. There wasn't one. No damn phone. Nothing in that house except for a couch in the living room. Nothing. René just looked at me. It was like he was asleep. "Stay here," I said. I took his keys. I drove to the Pic Quick around the corner. There was a phone booth there. When I pulled up, I saw a cop car. A policeman was inside— buying coffee. I stared at his car. My heart was pounding. Pounding and pounding. And the wings I had inside me were at it again—beating like hell, stronger than they had ever beat, and the wings were a whole damned bird now—a whole damned bird and he was beating his wings with an anger that was fighting me to let him out, beating the hell out of all my insides. And I knew that the bird was a pigeon—the worst, most common, meanest kind of bird. A pigeon. And I knew that every time something bad happened, that damned pigeon would wake up and begin beating against my insides, and I would never know any peace.

I closed my eyes. I took a breath. When the cop walked outside, I stepped out of René's car. "You have to come," I said.

"What?" He looked at me.

"You have to come. Please. Please." I think I started crying.

Yeah, I was crying. Damn it. What good was crying? I blamed it on the pigeon.

"What's wrong, son?"

"Please." I pointed. "Around the corner. Will you follow me, please? You have to follow me. You have to."

"Son, you have to tell me what the problem is."

"Reyes. Reyes. He's dead. He's dead!" And then I was really crying. God, why was I crying? It was that stupid pigeon. He was hurting me. I hated that pigeon.

"Show me where, son."

The cop followed me. It only took us a minute to drive to that apartment. René was at the door, waiting. The cop went in. René and I waited at the door. When the cop came back to the door, he looked at us. "What's his name?" He looked sad, the cop did. And angry, really angry.

"Reyes," I said. "Reyes Espinosa."

"Wait right here," he said. Then he saw the guy who'd answered the door. He was passed out on the couch.

"Who's he?"

"I don't know." I was doing all the talking. René was saying nothing. Like he'd lost his voice. "Mrs. Espinoza, she came to my house. She asked me if I could help her find Reyes, that he'd been gone for five days. My dad, he said I should go out and find him. That guy—he's the one who answered the door." I'd stopped crying. But it felt like I was gonna start up again. God. The pigeon.

The cop knew that. He nodded. "There a phone in this house?"

"I couldn't find one," I said.

"I'd better call an ambulance," he said. "Wait right here." He walked to his car. He got on his radio. He walked back. He tried to wake the stringy haired gringo who'd answered the door. The guy wouldn't wake up. The cop looked at us. "I want you to go stand by my car. Just wait there."

So that's what we did. I lit a cigarette, gave one to René.

"He's dead," René whispered.

I didn't say anything. Finally, I said, "They're gonna ask us how we found this place. I'm gonna tell him we saw this guy that we knew who hung around Reyes. We're gonna tell him that I asked, that I asked him if he'd seen Reyes. And he told us that he hung around this apartment a lot. So we came here. And if they ask us who the guy was, I'm gonna say he was just this guy that hung around Reyes, and that I didn't know his name. And if they ask us where we saw this guy, we're gonna say, he was walking down Española Street. Are you listening?"

René nodded. "Yeah," he said. "Yeah, I'm listening."

That pigeon was still flying around inside me. Trying to find a way out. But maybe the only way out was to kill me. I lit another cigarette.

Then the ambulance came. More cop cars. The neighbors all came out.

They took Reyes away. His body. Reyes wasn't there

anymore. And the other guy. The gringo whose name we didn't know. He was still alive, at least I think he was.

They took us down to the station. They put us in separate rooms. They asked me to write down what happened. I'd done this before. That night when they'd nearly killed Jaime and Eric. I wrote down what had happened. Just like I'd told René.

When I was finished, I waited.

I don't know how long I was there.

And then they let me and René go. They weren't nice to us. Weren't mean either. The detective tells us, "See what can happen? See. You guys think nothing's ever going to happen to you because you're young. See what happened to your friend? Do you see?" Guess he was a father. Or something like that. René and I nodded. But he wasn't too hard on us. Maybe he could see what we were holding in our eyes.

The cop, the one who'd been there first, he took us back to get René's car. "Did someone call Mrs. Espinoza?"

He nodded. "Yes, son. Someone called her." I wondered how they'd gotten her phone number until I remembered that I'd told them to call my dad, that he'd know how to reach her. I'd forgotten that. I'd already forgotten half the things that happened that night—except staring down at Reyes' body. I'd never forget. Not ever. And then the cop says, "Boys, I'm real sorry about your friend."

We didn't say anything.

When he left us there in front of that apartment, René and I didn't say anything. He drove me home. I opened the car door. I got out. "We found him," I said. I slammed the car door. I didn't want to see what René was holding in his eyes.

René and I were pallbearers at the funeral. Me and René and his four brothers. My pigeon was still there. But words—hell, they'd all flown away. Everybody in Hollywood had so many brothers. Except me. Most of the citizens of Hollywood were there: Mrs. Apodaca, my father, Gigi, Angel, Susie, Frances, some people we knew from school. Mrs. Davis, my English teacher, she was there. I wondered why. Probably knew Reyes from school. And she was Catholic. I knew that. I'd seen her in church.

At the cemetery, Mrs. Espinoza wailed like a coyote. I couldn't take it. I thought that maybe Gigi had been right when she said the story of La Llorona was true. Mrs. Espinoza was La Llorona. She would search the world for an eternity calling out her son's name, hoping to find him, but he was lost. And she'd never hold him again. And she'd blame herself forever. So she was La Llorona now. When they laid Reyes in the ground, all I could hear was Mrs. Espinoza's wails. I had to walk away. I couldn't take it.

I found myself standing in front of Juliana's grave at the cemetery. I stared at her name and the dates, and I started telling her everything that had happened in Hollywood since she'd died, and I told her about my pigeon, and I even told her I loved her—even though she'd told me never to tell her that ever again.

That afternoon, I was sitting on my front porch. It was sunny. Not cold. Februarys could be warm in the desert. And today, it was warm and it was hard to tell that anybody had died.

René came by. He parked his car in front of the house. He waved.

I nodded.

He sat next to me on the steps of my porch. "Hey, Sammy," he said. We hadn't talked. Not since that night. "I'm never gonna deal again," he said.

I nodded.

"I swear I'm not."

"I believe you," I said.

"No, you don't."

"What the shit difference does it make if I believe you or not, René?"

He looked down. "Don't—" He started to cry. His whole body was shaking. He had that pigeon inside him, too. Maybe everyone in Hollywood had a damned pigeon. "Sammy, Sammy—" And he couldn't stop crying. I thought he'd cry forever. "Don't hate me. Don't hate—Sammy, Sammy—" There was nothing to do but let him cry. I couldn't stand it.

But I couldn't say anything. I couldn't. When I reached for his arm, it was too late. He got up from the steps and drove away. I sat there and looked at the spot where his car had been. And then I saw Reyes lying there. Dead. On the street.

nineteen

The day after Reyes' funeral, I went back to school. I handed in my note to one of the teachers behind the absent line. Three long lines that day. I handed my father's note to her. Just my luck, Mrs. Jackson was on duty. "Missed you yesterday, Sammy."

"Sorry," I said.

She read the note. "Oh, yes," she said. I hated the way she said that. "I don't think we should be encouraging you to go to these kinds of funerals, do you?"

I didn't say anything.

"I don't know if I should excuse this. What do you think?"

"My father was in the army. My uncle died in the Korean War. My father took me to that funeral! Would you like to speak to my father? My father, the veteran?"

"Watch yourself, young man. I don't like that tone."

"Yes, ma'am." I let her see that I hated her. I'd hid that

before. Didn't feel like hiding. Not today. She knew I hated her. I just stared at her. She was afraid. That's the first time I'd ever seen that. Almost made me want to smile. She handed me my absence slip. EXCUSED. Good, I thought. I stomped my way to my first period class. I missed half of what Mrs. Scott was saying. Sometimes, when I got mad, I lost my hearing. Or maybe all I could hear was the conversation I was having with myself. I'd been a good boy at school for twelve years. A good boy. A good student. Straight arrow. Librarian. So I got A's. Yeah, so what? Where was I going to school—Harvard? Yale? Berkeley? Nope. Nope. Nope. The local college. The local boy. The local college. Yeah, yeah. I hated myself. I did. I wasn't getting over it. I wasn't. I was addicted to staying the good boy—addicted. The addiction was killing me. Like heroin had killed Reyes.

I hated that they expected us to behave, expected us to buy all their crap, expected us to say yes sir, yes ma'am, yes, yes, yes, yes. Okay, okay, I could mouth off—especially lately. But what was mouthing off? Mouthing off? What was that? Talk, talk, talk.

That same day, the principal called for a special assembly. They gathered us all in the gym. "Why don't they just shoot us?" Charlie Gladstein said. Loud. So everyone would hear. There we were, in the gym. We said the pledge of allegiance. Yeah, yeah.

"Things are getting out of hand," Fitz said. God, he was

white and dull and plastic. Barbie was more real. "Things are getting out of hand," he said again. "There is a dress code. There is a code of conduct. We are teaching you to be future citizens." Yeah, sure. Imagine that beautiful future. That's what I thought. We all knew why this was happening. Four full detention classes. Chaos. It was taking over. Full of students who weren't wearing belts, weren't tucking in their shirts, full of girls who were wearing their dresses too short. "One young man came to school with a beard," he said. I smiled to myself. Like I could grow a beard with all that mestizo blood in me. Oh, God, a beard. Like Jesus. "And some of you think it's okay to wear patches of the flag on your pants. What gives you the right? And in the most inappropriate and disrespectful places . . ." He didn't mention Ginger Ford who'd come to school wearing IUD earrings. Suspended for two days. He didn't mention all the red-eyed wonders who were wandering the halls like zombies because they'd discovered pot, dope, weed, mota. Or heroin. Or LSD. Not that I knew. But I knew enough. I could see. And who wouldn't want to be stoned out of his ever lovin' mind? Who wouldn't? "We are trying to guide you, to help you find your way on this good earth . . ." I couldn't listen. So I didn't. I took out my notebook, started writing a letter to Pifas. Told him that Reyes had died. Heroin overdose. Maybe I shouldn't tell him. He was in Nam. He didn't need to hear about death. He knew all about it by now. Death. Pifas. Mr. Barnes stretched his neck out to see what I was writing. He looked at me. I kept on writing.

When Fitz finished his little speech, no one clapped. Not one mule-faced student. "Thank you for your applause," he said. Someone booed. People clapped. For the boo. "That's enough," he said. On the way out, everyone got a copy of the dress code and our code of conduct—so we'd remember. "Are we gonna have a test?" I said as I took mine.

Mrs. Davis winked. I liked her. She knew the score.

We all marched back to our classes. With our copies of the dress code.

I saw René every day at school. We didn't say much to each other. He just kinda went his own way. Gigi, too. I ran into Angel. I liked her. I really did. "How is it?" I said. She smiled. "Haven't seen you around much. Seen René?"

"My mom doesn't like him. She says I can't go out with him." She shrugged. "I told him we were just friends."

"Seen Gigi?"

She rolled her eyes. "She's seeing this guy. That's all she thinks about. All she does is be with him and talk about him."

I nodded. I knew Gigi. She found guys sometimes, fell in love, spent all her time with them. Then one day, she was back. Like she'd been dead. And then she was back. "Yeah," I said, "that's Gigi."

"You look sad, Sammy." That's what she said.

"Nah," I said. "I'm just tired." I looked at her. I wanted to kiss her. Because she'd noticed. That I was sad. I smiled at her, walked away.

I guess for a couple of weeks, all I did was go to school and work at the Dairy Queen on Saturdays. I felt like something had died. I hated everything, school, the world I lived in. And all my friends were MIA.

One day, guess I just got lonely. It was a Saturday after work. Hadn't seen René in two weeks. I went by his house on my way back from work, had my dad's car. I knocked at the front door. Mrs. Montoya answered it, smiling. That lady was always smiling. René was more like his father. "Sammy," she said. She liked me. She gave me a hug. "Muchachito," she said. "Ya pareces hombre." I didn't feel like a man. That was for sure. "René here?" I said.

She looked at me, her eyes filling with tears. I hated that, to see her cry. "There's something wrong," she said. "Se me hace que anda con las drogas."

I hugged her. "No, no," I said. "René's not into drugs. I swear."

"Lo has visto?"

I lied. "I see him every day. Talk to him every day. No drugs. I swear Mrs. Montoya."

She smiled. She went into the kitchen and brought out a stack of freshly made tortillas. "For you," she said. "Y para tu papá y para Elena."

I kissed her. *Thank you. Gracias, señora.* Mothers broke my heart.

That night, I asked my dad if I could borrow the car. I knew I had to look for him. For René. Damnit! Damnit! I was mad. Now, I was really mad. So what the hell was I gonna do about all this mad stuff? I swear I thought I was going crazy. I mean the kind of crazy where they put you in some place where you can't hurt anybody. I think my pigeon was driving me nuts—the kind of nuts where you can really hurt someone real bad.

So that night, I took my father's car and went looking for René. Cruising, cruising on a Saturday night. I cruised up and down El Paseo. I cruised Shirley's. I heard about some party at some guy's house. I went there, another keg party, saw people I knew—but no René. Asked everyone. "All doped up," Charlie Gladstein said. "That guy's been doing more weed lately than Janis Joplin." Like he knew all about Janis Joplin. Yeah, yeah. That Charlie.

I looked everywhere. I even went to that trailer house in Mesilla Park. I knocked at the door. That same gringa with long hair stood there, looking at me. I asked her if she'd seen René. Told me he'd been there earlier, that he'd scored a nickel bag. Said she didn't know where he'd taken off to. Just didn't know. But she said I was cute if I wanted to hang around for some fun. Yeah, yeah. I wasn't into fun. Not that night. Not most nights, come to think about it.

I'd run out of places to look. Then I thought about one more place. The river. Why not the river? He liked it there. So that's where I drove. I had the radio on. Judy Collins was singing some sad song about not knowing anything about love at all. I liked her voice. I liked the song. I thought maybe that Gigi had a better voice. And more soul. But Gigi would never be on the radio like Judy Collins or Melanie or any of those singers. Born in the wrong neighborhood, I guess. And too much attitude. I wondered who Gigi was going out with. Made me sad when she went after a guy. They always dropped her. But she dropped her share. Desperate. Sometimes, she was desperate to be loved. Maybe I was too. I don't know. I didn't want to think about that. I thought about Angel. Maybe I'd ask her out. But she hadn't said she didn't like René. Only that her mother wouldn't let her go out with him. And René was my friend. Or he had been my friend. And I was making myself crazy thinking about all these things. Crazy. Crazy. And damnit to hell, what if René was all doped up? What if I found him? What exactly was I planning on doing about it?

There was a keg party at the river. A fire going around the keg. I checked it out. Lots of cars. People were laughing. I stood at the edge—looked in. Not my crowd. Some guy was telling stupid jokes *What's brown and is a sex symbol? Marilyn Montoya. What's brown and rides on a horse named Trigger? Roy Rodríguez. What's brown and hops through the forest? Bugs*

Benavídez. What's brown and rides on a chariot? Ben Her-nández. Everyone laughed. Ha. Ha. Funny, funny. I took off.

There were cars here and there. People making out, I guessed. I thought of Jaime and Eric. How they'd been caught. Together. Two guys. I felt bad. They were gone. They'd been sent away. Here, somebody else take them. Shit. I was tired. I wasn't gonna find René. I wasn't. I drove up and down the levy. Then I saw a car. Off by itself. Maybe. Maybe it was René. I drove down the road toward the river. A small road. A tree. A car. René's car. It was! God! René! I'd found him. I thought of how we'd found Reyes. I felt the pigeon again. I stopped the car, got out. "René? René?" I saw him. It had to be him. Sitting on the hood. Smoking a cigarette. "René?"

"¿Qué chingaos quieres?"

"Hey, what is it?"

"¿Que chingaos quieres?"

"What's up?"

"I don't want to talk to you."

I walked up to the car. "Talk to me," I said.

"What for?"

"Just talk to me."

"Just get away. Vete a la fregada."

"Listen to me. People are worried about you."

"People?"

"Your mom."

"What the hell do you care?"

"Listen, René—"

"No, you listen, Sammy. You get in that car, and you drive, just fuckin' drive. Drive yourself to L.A. or San Antonio or El Paso or Juárez. I don't give a damn where you drive yourself. Just get the hell away."

"I don't like that you're scoring nickel bags."

"So, who the hell do you think you are, Mrs. Apodaca?"

"Talk to me."

"If you don't get your pinche ass outta here right now, right now, I'm gonna kick it—I swear."

"C'mon then," I said. "C'mon."

"I swear, Sammy."

"C'mon, go ahead. A ver, cabrón, vente, dejate venir, vente. C'mon mother, kick my ass. C'mon."

He leapt from the car. Tackled me to the ground. We rolled around trying to punch each other. I got away, got up. Waited for him. He threw a punch. I dodged, then I took a swing, caught him right in the side of his head. Hurt like hell, hard head—and then I felt a punch. Right to my lip. I fell. I swear I saw stars. All of them spinning around me. I just let myself lay there. I knew I had a bloody lip. I was always getting hit there. Maybe so I'd learn to keep my mouth shut. I just lay there. I didn't care if I ever got up.

After a while I hear René's voice. "Sammy?"

"What?" I said.

"Are you all right?"

"I hate you." That's what I said. "You're a pinche. You're a pendejo. And you're killing me."

"Just go away, Sammy. Just leave me alone."

I got up. Walked to my car. Wiped my lip, felt it throbbing. I turned the ignition to my dad's car. Then sat there, the engine idling. But I couldn't leave. I couldn't. I couldn't because I just couldn't stand it anymore, couldn't stand it. Because I'd lost my mother to cancer. Because I'd lost Juliana to a bullet and I carried her around with me and she was getting heavier and heavier and it made me tired and sad, but mostly sad. I couldn't stand it anymore because I'd lost Jaime to an exile I hardly understood. Because I'd lost Pifas to the army. Because I was running out of people to lose. Because I just couldn't stand losing one more damn thing. As if I wasn't poor enough already.

I got out of the car. I walked up to him—just walked up to René and took him by the shoulders and shook him. "Listen to me. Just listen. You didn't kill anybody." I was crying. Damnit to hell, I hated that pigeon inside me. "You didn't kill anybody. You gotta believe me. If you don't believe, then you're a dead man. And if you're a dead man, then I'm a dead man, too. You didn't kill anybody." I didn't let go of him. I wasn't going to let go. I wasn't. "Say you believe me." God that pigeon was killing me.

"I believe you," he whispered.

"Say it again." I wasn't letting go of him.

"I believe you." Then he broke down. I could hear his sobs. Hell, the stars could hear his sobs.

"Say it again!" I yelled.

"I believe you!" he yelled. God, he was crying. Me, too. I was crying, too.

And then—finally—I let him go.

I was one angry seventeen-year-old. Reyes was dead. And he died for nothing. Pifas was fighting a war that we didn't even call a war. And those things were changing me. Something broke in me. Something broke. But that something needed to be broken. It did. Sometimes you have to tear something down so you can build something new. It's like, if you know the house you live in needs to be fixed, well, if you really want to fix it so you can live in it, well, sometimes you have to tear down a wall. And school? School was worse than ever. Like it was about to explode. It was like the whole school was having a nervous breakdown. And I don't know why, but I suddenly thought that it was my job to fix it. Maybe it was because Reyes was dead. Maybe I thought I had to fix the house I lived in because a part of me was dead, too. That's how it felt. Maybe that's what I was thinking when I called Gigi the Monday after I'd found René at the river. I'd found René, and now I was determined to find Gigi. I couldn't stand it anymore. That pigeon inside me was pounding away again. And I just had to put him back to sleep. Or set him free.

So I called Gigi. "Gigi," I said. "What is it?"

"What do you want?"

"Nice telephone manners."

"I'm not planning on being a secretary."

She was still mad at me. Gigi could hold a grudge, I'll tell you that. She could punish you. In the sixth grade, she didn't talk to me for a month, because I'd beat her at tether ball. She'd been the champ. Until then. And she didn't forgive me until after I played her again—and let her win. That's when she talked to me again. High maintenance. That was Gigi. "I hear you're seeing someone."

"¿Y qué? What's it to you?"

"Just asking."

"You jealous?"

"Not the jealous type, Gigi."

"I hate you."

"No you don't."

"I hate guys. I hate them."

"Guess you dumped him."

"In the trash."

"Well, some guys, that's where they belong."

She laughed. I liked it when she laughed. She had a good laugh, Gigi. Maybe I hadn't lost her. Maybe I hadn't lost René either. Maybe we were all still alive. "Hey, why don't we get some people together, hold a meeting, you know, pass out flyers. Have a sit-down strike or something? You know, change the dress code, blow up the school, hang our teachers."

"Serious?"

"I'm a very serious guy, Gigi."

"Don't play with me, Sammy. Don't be that way."

"I'm not playing." She knew me. She knew when I was serious. I could almost see her smile over the phone. "Okay," she said. She said okay. "Who told you I was seeing someone?"

"Angel," I said.

"Just wait till I get a hold of her. Just wait."

I laughed. Gigi. She was back. I'd missed her.

twenty

It wasn't hard to come up with a committee. Me, Angel, René, and Gigi. That was four. Charlie Gladstein, who kept saying if he couldn't grow his hair long, he was gonna explode. And then he'd make this exploding sound with his mouth. Susie Hernández was in. Those school-rule hemlines might as well have been prison. Hatty Garrison—she was in. Because she said it was our civic duty. That Hatty, she was a good girl. Always putting a good spin on everything. And Larry Torres, that asshole. He was still being an asshole. But Reyes had always been an asshole, too, and I felt bad because I'd always been so hard on him, and I'd promised myself I was going to be a better person, so I tried to be patient when I approached him. He said he'd join up, but he said we were all fucked. "Aaaaaahhhhhl fucked up." He said he'd do it, but only because he hated this fucking school and he was so bored that he thought he was gonna die, and that he wanted a little trouble.

And this was the car he could hitch a ride on. But boy, we were fucked up, and it was a miracle we didn't get into another fist-fight. I hated that guy. But he was gonna be on our side. So, I said okay. I put my fists back in my pocket.

We had a plan. We met at Pioneer Park. After school. Twenty of us. Give or take. Charlie. That Charlie Gladstein was one mad bastard. Man, that guy, sometimes he acted like he was born in Hollywood. He'd collected copies of the dress code from everybody. He had hundreds of copies. "We're going to burn these," he said, "just like they burn draft cards." Serious. He was serious. We nodded.

"Okay," I said. "Sit-down strike during lunch. We get flyers. We pass them out. Some people pass out flyers. Some people will just sit down on the lawn in front of the cafeteria. We don't do anything. We don't say anything. Peace, baby." I laughed. We all laughed. "That's all. We just pass out flyers. And we sit. We just send a message. They can't kick us out if all we're doing is having our say."

"That's all? What the fuck is that?" Larry. Larry Torres.

Gigi gave him her look. "You got a better suggestion?"

"Let's storm the principal's office."

René shook his head. "You're full of crap. That'll get us thrown out. Then what? We don't graduate. Then what?"

Gigi nodded. "Look. They think we're stupid. They think we can't think. Sammy's right. This is smart. We pass out flyers. We sit down. We behave ourselves. They won't like it.

254

But if we behave—if we show them we're just having our say—what can they do?"

"But we have to burn these," Charlie said. "As long as we burn these, then I'm in."

"Yeah," Larry said, "at least we have to burn the fucking dress code."

I didn't like it. "Okay," I said. I said okay.

There were three lunch periods. Gigi and René and Angel and Charlie, we all had first lunch. We broke up into groups. Every group had at least four people—to pass out flyers. And we had an assignment. Find twenty people to sit down at each lunch period. To sit down in a circle. That was all. "Hell," Charlie said, "the whole damn school's gonna sit down."

Two days later, everything was set. Gigi and René and Charlie had signed up forty-three people to sit down during first lunch. Second lunch, Hatty and Frances and Pauline had signed up thirty-seven. Third lunch, only twelve people. But Sandra and her boyfriend, Ricardo, said there'd be more. Okay. Okay. We were set. But there were certain things we hadn't counted on. We didn't know about organizing. We thought we knew—but we didn't know crap. Not crap. But, God, we were excited. We were gonna take Las Cruces High by the throat and choke it till it spit out our names.

The night before our strike, Gigi and Angel came over just to hang out. René showed up a little later. Then, Charlie

Gladstein showed up. "Didn't know you knew where I lived," I said. I'd been to his house. I guess I was embarrassed, I mean, this wasn't what he was used to. He didn't seem to notice, though, didn't care. I liked that about him, the way he just got out of his car, waved like he'd been coming over here all his life.

We were scared. But we weren't gonna back down. No way. That didn't make us any less scared. Pigeons. Sure as shit, we all had a pigeon inside us. Except maybe Gigi had a Quetzal. Gigi wouldn't have had a common pigeon. No way, not Gigi. A Quetzal. The Mayans loved that bird because their feathers were like fire—yeah, Gigi had a Quetzal.

My dad came out, said hi to everyone. He was friendly, my dad, liked my friends. Liked everyone, my dad. I'd told him what we were planning to do. "I guess this is your way of loving the world." That's what he said. Then he kissed me. He always did that, kissed me. He looked at all my friends, my dad. He nodded. He was smiling. I was afraid he was going to kiss everyone.

Elena came out, couldn't help herself. "It's late," I told her. "Better go to sleep."

"Aw, Sammy."

"Go on." She kissed me.

"You're not gonna read to me, are you?"

"I'll read to you," Dad said. Elena got this look on her face. I kissed her. "Tomorrow," I said. "Tomorrow I'll read to you."

When they went back inside, Gigi smiled at me. "You're a good brother," she said. "That kid's crazy about you."

"I'm crazy about her, too." Then I laughed. "And when she's old enough to go to Cruces High, there's gonna be a different dress code."

We all clapped. Clapped. Yeah, yeah. God, we were scared.

That night, I had a dream about Juliana. And in the dream, she was running for president, and I remembered how she'd stared down old Birdwail. And when I woke up, I thought that maybe Juliana was alive. And I was half hoping I would see her at school. But I knew she wouldn't be there.

That pigeon was pounding away all morning at school. I thought lunch would never come. Didn't hear a damn thing any of my teachers said. And finally, finally first lunch arrived. We met in the front of the cafeteria. Charlie had printed the flyers, and Gigi had our packet. Me and Gigi and René, we started passing out the flyers. "Change the dress code!" René shouted it like he was selling hot dogs at a ball game. He put a flyer in someone's hand. We spread out. "Change the dress code!" The flyers were going like hot cakes. No one was going into the cafeteria. Charlie was sitting down with a group of about forty people. Just like we planned. They were all sitting in a circle. And they were all holding up sheets of paper that read: CHANGE THE DRESS CODE! But they didn't say a word. Just like we planned.

That's when I noticed a group of F.F.A. types, all in their blue corduroy jackets with their yellow and blue Future Farmer badges. They were standing not too far from where the strikers were sitting. They were talking. I didn't like the look of it. They were trouble. Then I saw a group of pachucos from Chiva Town. They were talking, too. Shit, I thought, trouble. I gave René a look. I pointed with my chin. He saw what I saw. We both had a bad feeling. I handed Gigi my flyers. "Keep passing them out," I said. Just then Fitz and his sidekick, Mr. Romero, walked up to Gigi and me. "What's going on here?"

"We're passing out flyers," Gigi said. She smiled, handed him one.

"You don't have permission."

"It's a free country, Mr. Fitz."

"I want you to stop. Right now! I want you to stop."

René was watching us. "Change the dress code!" he yelled—and kept passing out flyers. I could tell he was watching the two groups, the F.F.A. jackets, the pachucos from Chiva Town. By then, it seemed, the whole school had gathered. I didn't know it then, but Charlie had told everyone to skip their classes and come to first lunch. And they had. They had. But I didn't know that, then. God, it seemed like people were everywhere. All of a sudden. The whole school. Where had they come from? Fitz reached for the flyers Gigi was holding. She was smart. She let them drop to the ground.

She smiled. That's when I looked up and saw the group of F.F.A. types pouring milk on the group of people sitting down. They were pouring milk all over them. Fitz saw them, too. "You gonna let that happen?" I said.

"You made your bed—"

Right then, right there, all hell broke loose. Charlie Gladstein didn't have a pacifist bone in his body. He got up and started a fistfight with one of the guys pouring milk over Jeannete Franco. "You sonofabitch." That was the cue for the Chiva Town pachucos to move in. Those guys from Chiva Town were on those F.F.A. corduroy jackets—all over them. And they were going at it. They didn't give a damn about a dress code. What they knew is that they hated each other and this was as good a time as any to beat the holy crap out of each other. That's when the whole school exploded. Everybody just moved in. Punches everywhere. For once, René and I weren't throwing fists. We were just watching. Gigi and I just looked at each other. Fitz and Romero had disappeared.

I kept watching as students poured out of the building. People were shouting and yelling. But where were our teachers? Where was Mr. Fitz? Where was Mr. Romero? Then Mrs. Davis walks up to me and says. "Sammy, Sammy, my god, make them stop. Look at them. Make them stop." It was a riot, chaos, what everybody was afraid of. All that anger, crawling all over the place with no direction. "Change the dress code! Change the dress code!" That's what I started yelling. Mrs.

Davis caught on. So did René. So did Gigi. "Change the dress code! Change the dress code! Change the dress code!" And then, more voices. And then more, our voices like a steady beating of a drum. "Change the dress code! Change the dress code!" René ran over to the Chiva Town pachucos and made them stop. None of those guys wanted to fuck with René, they didn't, and the chicken shit F.F.A. guys—they were all for stopping the fight. They weren't winning. God, it was all happening so fast. And everybody was chanting, "CHANGE THE DRESS CODE! CHANGE THE DRESS CODE!" Mrs. Davis looked at me and smiled. "You done good, Sammy," she whispered.

I could barely hear her above the chants. "That's not good English," I said.

That's when all the cops came. Every cop in the damn city—they were there.

They stood in a line about twenty feet away from us. There were more of us than them. Not that it mattered. They scared us. All we had on our side was our stupid pigeons.

"Go back to your classes." We heard the voice over the bullhorn. "Go back to your classes or you will be arrested."

The chanting stopped.

"Go back to your classes! Or you will be arrested!"

Gigi moved to the front. I followed her. Couldn't leave her there by herself. René was right behind me. There we were, the three of us, between the cops and the whole school. It was so quiet. God, all of a sudden, the world was so quiet. Gigi turned around and faced the students. "Everybody sit down!" she said. "Everybody sit down!"

And they did. They did just like she said.

That's when Fitz and Romero and all our teachers came out of the school building and walked straight behind the line of cops. The students booed. "BOOOOOOOOO! BOOOOOOOO!" Right then, I hated them all. They were afraid of us. They were afraid. Of us. It made me mad, that they thought we'd hurt them. Hiding behind the cops. I hated them like I'd never hated anyone. And then I noticed that Mrs. Davis was standing right next to me.

"Go back to your classrooms! Or you will be arrested!"

"Come and get us!" I knew that voice. It was Charlie. And then he got up in front of everybody with his stack of papers—the dress code. He held up the stack of papers. "This is the dress code," he said. Then he lit the pages on fire. A few pages at a time. God. The fire, it was so peaceful. Just for a few seconds. And no one said a word. No one moved.

"I'm warning you—you will be arrested!"

"Come and get us," Charlie said. And they did.

Most of us went along quietly. A few of us mouthed off. Our big chance. They took our names. They didn't technically arrest us—or at least, not the whole school. They took our names and our phone numbers, then sent us back to our classrooms. Except Gigi and René and me and Charlie and

Angel, we were taken down to the station. I was getting tired of that police station.

Fitz said he was pressing charges. Instigating a riot. There were others involved. There would be a full investigation. There we were at the police station. Guess maybe I wouldn't be graduating. But I wasn't sorry. I wasn't. Gigi was crying. René, hell, he just looked sad—like he was tired of losing. Charlie kept ranting, "It wasn't our fault! How come they're not arresting those bastards who started the riot? Those F.F.A. shitkickers. Why aren't they arrested?" I finally told him just to sit down. We had it all planned. Shit. We couldn't plan a camping trip to the backyard. I was numb. That's what I was. At least the pigeon was taking a nap.

I don't know what was taking so long. We were in a room. They'd already taken our statements. They'd done that. Now what?

"Jail," René said. "They're gonna put us in fucking jail."

Angel didn't say anything. "My mother's going to kill me." She was more afraid of her mother than she was of jail.

"What about your dad?" René was looking right at Charlie. I knew what he was asking. Our parents didn't know doctors or lawyers or accountants or teachers. Our parents didn't know anybody. But Charlie's dad, he knew some. He knew people. Maybe—

"When my dad finds out about this, he's gonna kick my ass from here to Jerusalem."

That's when we laughed. Because he made a joke. About his own kind. And that's what we did. That's how we'd survived. So we laughed.

And then, the pigeon came back. I knew then that the pigeon wasn't all bad. He wasn't beating me up. He was just there, waiting with me.

We paced. They wouldn't let us smoke. Not in that stupid waiting room. Or whatever it was. I don't know how long we were in there. I kept looking at the door. When it opened—I didn't want to think about it.

"My dad always said I'd wind up en la pinta." René said that. "Maybe he was right."

We all looked at each other.

"What's la pinta?" Charlie asked.

"Jail," Gigi said.

And then, then the door opened. And we all looked at each other. I saw Gigi and Angel squeezing each other's hands. And then this man in a suit walks in, young guy. Younger than thirty. He was all smiles. "You can go," he said.

Charlie's jaw drops open. "Who the hell are you?"

"Your lawyer."

"What?" I kept looking around the room. "We don't have a lawyer. We're from Hollywood. We don't know shit about lawyers."

"Oh, yes, you do," he said. And he smiled. He stuck his hand out and shook my hand. "You must be Sammy. My wife talks a lot about you, says you're really something. I'm Paul. Paul Davis."

I nodded. He shook everyone's hand, had good manners. "She's married to a lawyer?" I said. "Mrs. Davis is married to a lawyer?"

He smiled. "Yup. She sure is."

"What are they gonna do to us?"

"Nothing. Oh, I think your principal wants to throw you out of school, but I don't think that's going to happen. The school board meets on Monday—I've scheduled you and your friends to speak on behalf of the students. If they don't consider changing the dress code, I told them I'd sue them on your behalf. And I will, too. If I were you, I'd just show up to school tomorrow like nothing happened. And maybe by Monday evening, when you talk to the school board, maybe you should bring along a petition. With names on it. And maybe you want to bring some students along." He smiled. We all looked at each other. He laughed. "My wife tells me you put on a helluva good show at school today." He searched our faces. I wonder if he found what he was looking for.

We all went back to school the next day—and nothing happened. Our teachers didn't say a word. Not one word. Everything was the same. Except for Colonel Wright who growled something at me when he saw me walking down the hall. And Mrs. Jackson who said it hurt her to teach students like us. Deeply.

We took up a petition. People stood in line to sign it. Ninety percent of the school signed it. "Ninety percent," Charlie said. He was the one who did the math. A real numbers guy, I was finding out.

René said that he hated the thought that a gringo had saved our asses. I told him to re-laaaaaax. "Look," I said, "how many Mexican lawyers do you think there are in this town? Re-laaaax. They're not all bad." I thought of Mrs. Davis. How she'd stood with us.

I read a statement at the school board meeting. I wore a tie. My dad made me. I told him it didn't make sense for me to wear a tie when I was trying to get them to loosen up. "I don't care," my father said. "You're going to speak to the school board, and you're going to wear a tie." And so I did. Five hundred kids showed up at the meeting. Parents, too. I made my presentation. I introduced myself. "My name is Sammy Santos," I said. "This is my father," I said. He stood. He was proud. Please, Dad. Don't cry. He did that, sometimes. I handed them the petitions. I told them that the citizens of Las Cruces High had spoken. I told them that we did not feel respected. I told them that when you did not respect someone, that you shouldn't be too surprised to find out they hated you. I said that. I'd read it somewhere. Or something like that. I was trembling. And Mr. Davis, well, he stood right next to me.

The school board nodded. I asked them if they had any questions. One man, a guy named Mr. Stafford who had eyebrows that looked like mustaches asked me about the riot. "Some kids from F.F.A. poured milk on the strikers," I said. "Mr. Fitz saw what happened. Ask him. The strikers didn't do anything. Ask Mr. Fitz."

Mr. Fitz admitted that the strikers hadn't been violent. Except for Charlie, and he admitted that even Charlie was only fighting back. "But they provided an opportunity for the riot to occur. They created an environment for chaos to flourish. They threatened the safety of the entire student body." All by ourselves. That's what he said. Yeah, yeah. He spoke against allowing the dress code to be changed. When they asked him if his teachers were for or against the measure, he said his teachers were solidly against the measure. "Solidly."

Mr. Davis produced a petition of his own. Sixty-four percent of the teachers had signed a petition in favor of the student's request to change the dress code. Sixty-four percent, Mr. Davis said. He handed the petition to the school board's president. Mrs. Davis, she'd been working after hours.

There was some discussion. Was it legal to vote in private? They conferred. No, no, they would vote publicly. Why not?

The measure passed unanimously. Not because they agreed with us. I knew that. But because they were afraid. Of us. Their children. I knew that. But right then, I didn't care. We'd done something.

After the vote, the room went crazy. Crazy, crazy. God. Crazy.

We were a fire, and we were blazing, alive, blazing. And we thought, just for a moment, that we were the heart of America.

If you asked me what I remembered most about that strike, if you asked me, I'd have to tell you it was the look on René's face when the board voted to change the dress code. When they all said, "Aye," in unison, with one voice. The look on René's face. He'd looked broken and tired the day when we'd buried Reyes. And old. And he was too young to look so old. But that's how he'd looked. And sometimes, when people got that look, they never looked young again no matter how old they really were. I'd seen it happen.

But that day, after the vote, René wore this look, like it meant something to be René Montoya. We looked at each other. In all that commotion, we searched for each other. I think sometimes, people look holy, they do, that's how he looked. He waved from where he was standing. And I waved back. Hello, René. Hello, Sammy. I remembered the night I'd seen him in the light of the streetlamp outside that apartment where we found Reyes. I'd told myself he was a stranger, that I didn't know him. But there he was, René Montoya. I swear he was holy. Maybe the pigeon inside him had found a way out. Flown away. Gone. Maybe.

And one more thing I remember—Gigi's arms around me

and she kept kissing me on the cheek. "We won! We won! Sammy, we won! God, Sammy, can you believe it?"

Yeah, Gigi, I can believe it. We won. We won.

When I went home that night, I sat on the front porch. Mrs. Apodaca came over and told me I smoked too much. I nodded. Then she shook her head and said that she didn't agree with what we'd done. "You think you've done something? Dressing disrespectfully? You think that's a good thing?" She started to walk away, and then she turned around. And she had a huge grin on her face. "It feels good to win, doesn't it?" Before I could say anything, she'd disappeared across the street.

I found myself talking to Juliana. *You should've seen it, Juliana. It was all so beautiful.*

twenty-one

I had this dream, clean, soft, like dew in the morning light. In the dream, I was sitting on my porch, and everybody I knew was walking by, everybody, and there wasn't any difference between the living and the dead. That was the good thing about dreams. So, everyone is passing by, waving, Hi, Sammy, Hi and the sun is soft and I'm happy just to sit there and watch. God, I'm happy. But there aren't any sounds, no sounds at all. It was like I was deaf. Maybe I was dead. Maybe that's when you're really happy—when you're dead. And the people passing in front of me, they were the ones who were alive. My mom, she passed by and waved. And she was walking toward my dad, who was up the road. She looked so beautiful, my mom, the same way she looked before she got sick. Mrs. Apodaca, she passed by, and she was wearing a hat like she was going to church. Juliana passed by, too. And she was happy, and when she waved at me, it was like there wasn't any more

269

sadness in her. I thought she was as pure as anything I'd ever seen—but just when I was about to reach out and take her hand, she disappeared. And then Elena and Gabriela, those two little girls, they came wandering by, and they were holding hands, and when they saw me, they waved. Hi, Sammy. I could see their lips moving.

And the last one to march by was Pifas. He looked the same, his fine black hair falling into his eyes, the way it always did. He wasn't wearing a uniform, just a pair of jeans and a white shirt. God, his shirt was white. White. And when he waved, his smile disappeared, and then he had this look, this awful look, and then he looked at his hands.

Pifas, he looked at his hands—and they were gone. And there was blood everywhere. Blood.

I woke up sweating. Staring at my hands. In the dark.

In the morning, when I woke, I forgot about my dream.

I'd never left home before. Not ever. Staying out of the house all day—that didn't count. Watching the sun rise over the Organ Mountains from the river after having stayed out all night—that didn't count as leaving home. Didn't count. I knew that. I remember that afternoon—clear as an empty bottle of Pepsi. Clear as Mrs. Apodaca's voice praying a novena. Clear as the look on my father's face when he looked at me.

I sat there, thinking about home. Hollywood, that was

home. Las Cruces, this house I'd lived in all my life. My room no bigger than a monk's. Home was everything that could fit in my room. A bed, a desk, that's all that fit. More like a big closet, really. But it was all I'd ever known. Part of me wanted more. But part of me could have stayed in this house forever. I could still smell my mom in this house. I swear I could. My dad, he'd saved some of her clothes in his closet. Maybe that's why her smell was still in our house. My dad didn't know— that I knew about my mom's clothes.

This was home.

I wondered what it would be like to leave, what it would be like to be homesick. Maybe I was thinking about home and about leaving because I was holding a letter of acceptance in my hand. A letter from a university, a real American university. Not that it mattered. I wasn't going. I knew that, but damnit it felt good to get accepted. But it felt bad, too. I don't even know why I'd applied, a waste of time. Maybe I sometimes had these demons of optimism that just took over my body. But then, life, well, life just sort of exorcised those demons. And I was back to my serious, get-real-you're-just-a-guy-from-Hollywood attitude. That's what you needed to survive. Otherwise you'd break. Like Reyes. Maybe that's why he did heroin—because his dreams were too big. And the only way he could get at those dreams was through shooting some stuff up his veins.

I put the acceptance letter away. Before my father saw it.

He'd just get upset. Get mad at himself for not making more money. I didn't want that. He had enough to worry about. And he hadn't been feeling well. Not that he said anything. I knew him. Just like he knew me. I knew him.

There were two other pieces of mail I got that day.

I was sitting there studying the other two pieces of mail. Mail for Sammy. Sammy Santos. That's what it said on both of the envelopes. A letter from Jaime, and a letter from Pifas. They, they knew what it was like to leave home. Not that I was envious. Not really. I mean, I didn't want to be in Nam and I didn't want to be in Jaime's shoes. I mean, both of those guys had bigger troubles than I did. I mean, Jaime had been sent away because of what he held inside. "To protect him," that's what my father said. I thought maybe it was the other way around. Maybe it was us who needed protecting. From people like him. That's how people acted anyway. And Pifas, Pifas was fighting a war. Getting shot at. God, I thought of him every day. My Dad and I, we watched the news every day—and the war didn't look good. Made me want to cry. And who in the hell would want to go? And who could blame all those guys for burning their draft cards? And me? Hell, I wouldn't be eighteen until September. By then I'd be in college. At the local college. Oh yeah, poor Sammy, disappointed because he didn't have enough fucking money to go to Princeton or Stanford— B.F.D. Big Fucking Deal. No, I didn't have troubles, I didn't. Didn't stop me from feeling sorry for myself.

My only real problem. Which letter to open first. Which one? Not that it mattered that much. I guess I just wanted to enjoy the moment. Hell, I never got letters. Never. I poured myself a Pepsi over ice. I lit a cigarette. I stared at the two letters on the kitchen table. Two letters. Both of them for Sammy Santos. I closed my eyes. I opened them. So finally I decide to read Jaime's letter first. Because it was from California. Because Jaime's handwriting was neater. Because, hell, I don't know why.

Dear Sammy—

 Sorry I haven't written. I'm not much of a writer, guess that's more your bag. Anyway, my mom gave me your address so I thought I'd drop you a line just to let you know I'm doing okay. Not great, Sammy, but okay. I live with my uncle. His house isn't all that big here in East L.A. And I have to share a room with two of my cousins. I get along with them all right. They're a little younger than me. They keep asking why I came to live with them. My uncle tells them that I got into a little bit of trouble. He makes them think I'm running from the law or something. Makes me look like a tough guy. Not that I haven't gotten into my share of fistfights. And my uncle's just trying to help. I guess that's okay. He's cool, my uncle. He told me not to say anything. He said just keep my mouth shut about everything. He says no one can tell the way I am by the way I act. He says that's good. He's real nice to me. Real nice to his kids, too. Lot nicer than my old man, that's for fuckin' sure.

But I miss my mom. She's a good lady, and I think, well, hell, I don't know what I think. I miss her, that's all. I'm going to school and working part-time at a taco/burrito place. Don't laugh. I mean, it's a job and I'm saving money, and school's okay. Not too hard. I have to go to summer school and then go to school next year—at least through the fall semester if I want to graduate. That's cool. I don't really care. I just want to finish. Save money. Get my own place. I mean, what else is there for me to do? My uncle says I can stay here until I graduate. He promised my mom. But after that, I'm on my own. It's hard for him, I know. Small house. An extra kid. And I'm queer. Yeah, well, it's true. You probably don't want to hear it. That's cool. And maybe my uncle just doesn't want me around after I graduate. He's doing this for my mom. I know that. Not that he's not nice to me. He is.

It's real different here than Las Cruces and Hollywood. I guess I never really realized what a small town Las Cruces was. And hell, Hollywood is so small it wouldn't even qualify as a neighborhood here. But I miss it, Sammy. It was home. And I can't go back there, I know. Not ever. I guess after I graduate sometime next December or whenever, I guess maybe I'll move out, maybe go to college. My grades are pretty good and I always wanted to go to U.C.L.A. So who knows? The world's a big place. Just find your place in it. That's what my mom said.

So how's it going in Hollywood? When I tell people that the barrio I grew up in is called Hollywood, everyone here laughs their ass off. I guess I don't think it's so funny. But they do. Listen, I guess I don't have all that much to say. I've written to René but he hasn't written back. Written him twice. Gigi wrote. God, she's really great, huh? If you hear from Pifas, tell him I said hi. Tell him I moved to California, but don't tell him why. He doesn't need to know. No one needs to know.

I haven't heard from Eric. I've written to him a bunch of times. Maybe his aunt is intercepting his mail. I don't know. Maybe I'll never hear from him again. I guess I should just forget about him. I think probably that's a smart thing to do.

Listen, take care of yourself, Sammy. Not that I need to tell you that. If anyone's ever going to make it—it's going to be you. Everybody's always known that.

Your friend,
Jaime

No, not a long two pages but a sad two pages, I think. I read the letter three or four times. Yeah, it was sad. But I thought maybe he was going to be all right in the end. So, he had some problems. Leaving Hollywood didn't make your problems disappear. And that part about me making it. Well, that was funny. That was real funny.

I finished my Pepsi, then got myself another. Man, I loved drinking Pepsi. Everyone in Hollywood drank Coke, but not me, I drank Pepsi. I lit a cigarette. Then I opened Pifas' letter. His handwriting wasn't nearly as neat as Jaime's but there was something about it—I liked it. There was a raised fist at the top of the letter—hand drawn. And under it, he'd written, "Fuckin' A, Sammy." Crazy. The guy was nuts. What in the hell was he doing fighting a war?

Ese Sammy—

Today I was todo agüitado. I mean, I was down. Down, down, baby. I mean, bummed out. Bummed outta my fuckin skull and shit. Maybe it's because my patrol leader es bien gacho. Sammy, I mean gacho. A gacho gabacho. He's from Maine. Fuckin Maine—you should hear him talk. Baby, that's some shit he talks, but it ain't fuckin English. What an asshole! ¡Híjole! If I get my ass shot, he's not fuckin gonna cry. Nope. Just one less pfc to take care of. Not that he takes care of me, just fuckin yells at me that Charlie's gonna shoot all our asses cuz someone like me's not paying attention. He fuckin laughs. Thinks it's funny that a Mexican like me comes from a barrio called Hollywood. Fuck him. See what I mean. Today, I'm one pissed off mother. I am, Sammy. It's just that I'm tired. Damn, I'm tired.

It stopped raining today. Rains all the damned time, Sammy. People in New Mexico don't know shit about hot. Not till they've been to Nam. So it's not raining today and I have two days R&R unless something happens. Something always happens. And it'll rain again. God, Sammy, I just wanna sleep. So that's what I'm gonna do. I'm gonna sleep. I'm gonna get loaded, and then I'm gonna sleep. Look, I'm not fuckin gonna talk about what's happening here. I figure you know as much as I do. No T.V.s here, Sammy. All I know is what I'm told to do. And damnit, I do it. Just one thing, Sammy. You go to college, and you fuckin stay there. I don't want you dreamin blood the way I fuckin dream blood. Maybe someday, you'll tell yourself, God, I could fuckin kill that sonofabitch. Killin him ain't gonna do shit but give you dreams. Some guys here, they dream bad. You ever seen a dog dream? They whine, and they whine, and they tremble like they're gonna fuckin fall apart. That's how it is with some of the guys here. They dream like that.

Gigi writes. Man, Sammy, I love that girl. I do. I

asked her, I asked her if I made it home, would she
marry me. She said she'd think about it. That she'd
really think about it. I think that's a good sign. I mean,
if Gigi wanted to, she'd tell me just to go fuck myself. So,
I figure that if she's thinking about it, that's a good sign.

Don't you think so, Sammy?

Listen, sometimes I tell myself I'm gonna make it,
and go back home, and kiss the fuckin ground. And
kiss Gigi and marry her. I love Hollywood, Sammy. I
love that place. I never knew I could love a place like
that.

Look, if you go out with René and Reyes or Jaime,
have a beer for me. And if you run into any of those
chucos from Chiva Town, kick their asses for me.

Da le gas. Da le mucho gas, baby.

Pifas

I put out my cigarette. Pifas hadn't heard about Reyes. That he
was dead. He didn't know about Jaime either. Hell, I wasn't
gonna tell him. Not me. The hell with it. Let him think that
everything was just the way he left it. That's what he needed to
think. Why the hell not? A place always stays just the way you
left it. Yeah.

I finished my Pepsi.

I tried to picture Pifas in Viet Nam. I tried to picture what
he looked like. All I could see was a boy on a bus who looked

fifteen. With big hands. Pifas at the bus station. But I couldn't picture him in a uniform. Okay, I'd seen that picture he'd sent Gigi but it was like he was just playing. It was just a game. But it wasn't. I watched the evening news with my father. That's what we did, my dad and me, watched the evening news. And Walter Cronkite, with that kind voice of his, he would tell us how many soldiers had died. But he never told us why. And anyway, they weren't soldiers, not to me. They were just guys like Pifas. They weren't all that different from me. Or maybe I was just kidding myself. What the hell did a guy who'd never left Las Cruces, New Mexico, know? I didn't know jack shit. I kept staring at Pifas' letter. It's like I just couldn't stop staring at his words. It was like I was in love with his words. I was in love with them. And then, I see my little sister standing next to me.

"What are you doing, Sammy?"

I was in love with her voice. That was another thing I was in love with. "I was reading a letter from Pifas."

She nodded. "I like him," she said. She liked everybody. She was like my father.

"Yeah," I said, "he's something, that Pifas."

"When is he coming home?"

I didn't say anything. "Read me a story," I said. That was our new thing. I'd stopped reading to her. Now, she'd started reading to me.

"Okay," she said. "I'll read to you." She knew I was sad.

* * *

279

After the riot. After the school board changed the dress code. After all that, things seemed calmer at Las Cruces High. Calmer didn't actually mean calm—it just meant that things didn't feel like they were going to explode anymore. And we didn't have to wear belts, and every day I wore a T-shirt because the weather had already turned, and now I could wear T-shirts to school. I could actually do that. But I still tucked them in and I still wore a belt. But mostly everybody else just went crazy with the things they wore. Dresses got short. Jesus. God. They got real short. If they were too short, girls were still sent home. But, God, they were shorter now. Gigi had given me a tie-dyed T-shirt—to celebrate the new dress code. I didn't get her anything. She wasn't my girlfriend. But I should've gotten her something. But I didn't. I wore my tie-dyed T-shirt once a week. One day I even wore tennis shoes without socks. But when I came home, my dad kind of went mental. He said people were going to think I was too poor to buy socks. He said only gringos did that sort of thing, anyway. "A Mexican man," he said, "wears socks." Yeah, yeah, Dad. Okay, so I never did that again. But you shoulda seen the things people wore. Sandals—never could wear those before—and beads—on ankles, on wrists, around necks, beads everywhere. So now, at Las Cruces High we looked exactly like everybody else in America. This was why we'd fought to change the dress code— for the freedom to look like everybody else.

Colonel Wright, man, he's freaking, he's fucking freaking,

especially because all the guys are growing their hair long. Except for me. Well, mine was getting a little long, not too long. I was experimenting. "It's getting in your eyes," my dad said. I'd push it back. It would fall back down into my eyes. "Maybe you should get a haircut," he said. "Maybe you should get a haircut," Mrs. Apodaca said. "Maybe you should get a haircut," my boss at the Dairy Queen said. Jesus, I only worked there once a week. God. So, maybe I was growing it long. Maybe I was. Even though I didn't really like it that much, but it didn't look bad. Gigi said it looked good. If it would've looked bad, Gigi would've told me. She shot straight, Gigi did. Colonel Wright just shook his head. He really hated me now. He blamed me for the whole thing. "The Ringleader"—that's what he called me. Blamed me for everything. "You and Miss Freedom of Speech" (that would be Gigi). Yeah, he decided he hated us. The demise of western culture. That's what he was saying in his classes. Boys with long hair, girls wearing pants. To school! God! Yeah, yeah. He and Mrs. Jackson said crap like that. As if Colonel Wright and Mrs. Jackson weren't prime examples of the demise of western culture. They hated our clothes. They hated our music. They hated the way we talked. They didn't like the way gringos talked any better than they liked the way Mexicans talked. They hated everything about us. And we knew it—then they wondered why we hated them back. Them and their clothes. And their music. Yeah, I think I was gonna let my hair grow. But not too long. No. Just a little.

twenty-two

So one day, right after I get those letters from Pifas and Jaime, maybe a few days later, Charlie Gladstein comes up to me, and he says, "Hey, Sammy, you gotta get yourself one of these." And he's grinning and showing off the beard he's starting to grow. He could do that. Grow a beard. No mestizo in him. Nope. Hairy that guy. Fuzzy. That guy was real fuzzy. And he was taking full advantage of the new rules. God, he looked happy. He always looked like he was half stoned, but he wasn't. He just always looked like that. "You gotta start wearing one of these." One of these happened to be a black armband to protest the war. I wondered what Colonel Wright would do when he set his eyes on Charlie Gladstein's arm. We were standing in the smoking section behind the cafeteria. He lights up and I light up and he starts telling me that we gotta organize against the war. "We gotta, Sammy. It's our moral duty."

Maybe it was. And then I thought to myself, *I'm gonna get a lecture from Charlie Gladstein, from a gringo.* Still, it wasn't clear to me whether you really qualified as a gringo if you were Jewish. Maybe Jews weren't gringos. I didn't know about that. I didn't. That's when Gigi shows up and stands right next to Charlie. And then they start holding hands.

"So you guys goin' out?" I said.

"Yeah," Gigi says.

You're not supposed to hold hands. That's what I wanted to say. That rule hadn't changed. Nope. Not that one. He's not from Hollywood. That's what I wanted to say. Look what happened to Jaime, I wanted to say. But I knew what happened to Jaime was completely different. Still, Eric hadn't been from Hollywood. He hadn't been. I wasn't being logical. Gigi and Charlie? He'd always liked her. Hell, I knew that. She'd hurt him. She would. Then she'd drop him. That's the way it worked.

But today, they were standing in front of me holding hands. Charlie and Gigi.

"So," I said, "how long's this been going on?" Shit. I sounded like Mrs. Apodaca.

"A couple of weeks," Charlie said.

Gigi smiled. That killer smile of hers.

I smiled back. "That's cool." That's what I said. Then I see René walking toward us, and he's giving me the Aztec greeting with his chin. And I give it back to him. Those chins of ours, they saw a lot of action. And René, he's wearing a black arm-band and a grin. Lately, he was smiling a lot, was getting into fewer fights. And I didn't know about that. Why he was chang-ing. Not that the changes were bad. I mean, not that I cared. I liked René. I'd always liked him. And he was about the only friend I had left. Not that I'd had hundreds of friends. I wasn't like that. Gigi, well, she was my friend, too. But it was hard to have a girl as your friend. You know. It was hard.

I didn't say anything about René's armband.

"Gimme a smoke," he says. And I do, and he stands there next to me and Gigi and Charlie Gladstein. And when he lights up, he looks at Charlie and says, "Are Jews gringos?"

And Charlie laughs and says, "Hell no. You have to be a Protestant to be a gringo."

And then I said, "That's not right. Lots of Catholics are gringos."

And then he nods. "Well, yeah." And then he laughs. "Well, some Jews are gringos. And some aren't." And we all nodded like he'd really said something. But he didn't tell us which Jews were gringos and which Jews weren't. But we just nodded. And I'm thinking this is the dumbest conversation I've ever had. And what in the hell got into René that he asked that ques-tion? I mean, I'd had the question, too, but I wasn't stupid enough to ask it. Not out loud. God.

Then, after school, Gigi asked René for a ride home, right there in the parking lot.

"Where's Charlie?" I asked.

"His mom's in the hospital. He went to go see her." That made me feel bad. My mom, she'd been in the hospital. In the end, before she'd died.

"She gonna be okay?" I asked.

"Gallstones. Whatever those are."

"Oh," I said. Like I knew about gallstones.

And when we get in the car, Gigi says, "Pifas wants me to marry him."

"Yeah," René said, "you told us that before." And he started up the car. And he's driving out of the parking lot.

"Yeah, well, he wrote again," Gigi said, "and he says he wants to know. I'd already told him that we had enough time to decide when he got back. But now, now he wants to know. He says he just can't live without knowing. He says he can't take it."

"Pifas is nuts," I said. "He doesn't know what he wants. He's just a kid."

"He's fighting a war," René said. "That makes him a man."

Yeah, yeah. René thought he was a man, too. René had thought he was a man since he was in the seventh grade. Because he had sex with some tenth-grade girl. Funny, how we all saw ourselves. I didn't think of myself as a man—not a boy, not that, but not a man. "He just turned nineteen," I said.

"A nineteen-year-old man," René said. "He's fighting a fucking war."

"Okay," I said.

Then René stops the car, parks it right there on the side of the road and turns around and looks at Gigi who's looking like she desperately wants a cigarette. Sitting in that backseat. Desperate. And René turns around and asks, "You love him?" That René, he could ask such innocent questions. For a guy who had a fuse as short as a Black Cat firecracker, for a guy who thought he'd been a man since the seventh grade, he sure asked innocent questions. Like a kid. Not like a man. Like a little kid.

"No," she said. Then she looked in her purse for a cigarette. I don't know why she bothered looking. She never had any. "Sammy?"

I tossed her a cigarette. Well, she had a lighter. At least she had a lighter.

"Well, I do love him. But, you know, I love you guys, too. And am I gonna marry you? Hell no, I'm not. I'd kill you."

"Maybe I'd kill you first," René says. Then he laughs.

Gigi bopped him on the head. "Drive."

"Let's get a Pepsi," I said.

And then René and Gigi both laugh and say, "At the Pic Quick." Guess they were on to me. Not that I was so hard to figure out. I wasn't hard—nope, an easy read. They're both laughing and laughing. Like it was so funny—that I liked going to the Pic Quick to buy a bottle of Pepsi.

And just when René's gonna start up the car, he yells,

"There goes Angel." She was walking with this guy just ahead of us. And just when I'm about to yell, "Hey Angel!" just when I'm about to yell that, I see the guy she's with, and he's trying to put his arm around her. And she pushes him away. I look at René and he looks at me. And Gigi isn't saying anything. And we're just sitting there—on the side of the road—watching Angel and this guy. Watching. And then she's telling him to get lost and he's pushing himself closer to her, and I recognize the guy as one of Huicho's brothers. I hated those guys. I had my reasons. I hated them. And then he tries to kiss her, and Angel's trying to push him away, and all her books go flying, and then I yell, "That's enough, cabrón." And we're out of the car, and we're there, we're right there, standing in front of Angel and that bastard, Celso, Huicho's little brother. And René starts to say something, but then decides he doesn't want to say anything at all. I mean René could take or leave words— he could. So he just punches the guy. And Celso falls to the ground. And Angel runs to the car to where Gigi is and René just stands there looking down at Celso.

"Levantate, cabrón. Haber, cabrón, levantate. Te voy a dar en la madre." That's the thing about René, sometimes, when he got pissed off, his English went out the window. But Celso wasn't gonna screw with René. He shook his head. He wasn't gonna get up, nope, he wasn't. "If you ever come close to Angel again, your pinche head's gonna be part of the pinche pavement. ¿Entiendes, Méndez?" Then René just walks away.

And I'm standing there, just looking down at Celso. He and his brother, they'd jumped me before. I just looked at him. I didn't feel bad. I hated him. I wanted to kick him. I wanted to kick and kick and kick him.

I walked back to the car—and I wondered why sometimes, there was so much hate, and not just in the world, but in my heart. And I felt sad. So many things made me feel sad. Gigi holding hands with Charlie, that had made me sad, and I didn't even know why. It wasn't that I loved Gigi. I didn't, not like that. It wasn't like that. Jaime's letter, shit that made me sad. Pifas' letter. Shit, that really made me sad. I didn't want to be sad, I didn't. I was a senior. Less than six weeks away from graduation. It was spring. It was a nice day. Perfect. What did I want? What the hell did I want? But really, I knew what I wanted. I wanted Juliana. I wanted to hold her hand like Charlie held Gigi's. That's the only thing that I really wanted. That was the only thing I was never going to have.

I walked back to the car. My fists in my pocket.

We drove to Shirley's—the drive-in part. Gigi ordered a Cherry Coke. Angel ordered a swamp water—part Seven-up, part Dr Pepper. I got a Pepsi. And René was drinking a root beer. Everybody had their own drink. That's the way it was. Gigi and I were in the backseat. Angel and René were in the front. I couldn't figure those two out. Maybe they liked each other. Maybe they didn't. I wasn't sure. René was always talking about the girls he laid. Big talker that way. Maybe it was all true. And maybe it wasn't. Who knew? Guys were such liars. When it came to girls, guys lied. They lied when they were sixteen, seventeen, eighteen. And they would lie when they got to be thirty. That's the way it was.

But René, he didn't talk that way about Angel, he didn't, not that she was the kind of girl that was about to give him any. Nope. Angel just wasn't like that. Not her style. And she knew about René. So maybe she liked him anyway.

So Gigi's drinking her Coke and kind of watching how Angel and René are eyeing each other. Gigi always knew the score about things. Because she watched. She looked over at me and says, "So what should I do?"

"About what?" I said.

"About Pifas."

"Tell him the truth," I said.

"Don't fucking tell him the truth," René says. "No, no, no. ¿Qué tienes, Sammy? What the hell's wrong with you? He's in Nam. He doesn't need more fucking reality."

"Viet Nam or no Viet Nam—honesty's the best policy."

"Shit. That's a gringo thing."

"Honesty's not a gringo thing." That was Angel. That was her voice. "You're full of it. You think gringos are honest. You're full of it, René."

"Ooouuuuhhh, Angel!" That would be Gigi's voice. "Da le gas, baby!"

I was laughing. Yeah, yeah. I could laugh. Not a lot. But I could laugh.

"You have a nice laugh, Sammy." Angel was looking at me. I looked away. I don't know. I just looked away.

"So what the hell am I supposed to do?"

"Give it a rest, Gigi. Who knows? Who the hell knows? You think I know, Gigi? I don't. You think René knows?"

"Tell him you love him, Gigi."

"You're full of shit, René. You can't lie to a guy like that. It's Pifas."

"You think women don't lie to guys? Sammy, you really have your head up your ass."

Gigi took the cigarettes out of my shirt pocket.

"Help yourself," I said.

She broke out laughing. She had a killer laugh. I could see why Charlie was crazy for her. I could see that. She lit a cigarette. "What would it hurt, if I lied to him?"

"So he comes home from Nam and he expects to marry you, right? And you tell him, *Oh, I forgot to tell you, I'm dating Charlie Gladstien, that gringo.*"

"It's not settled whether he's a gringo or not," Gigi said.

"Yeah, yeah." That's what I said. Yeah, yeah.

"So I break his heart when he comes home."

When he comes home. "Look," I said. "René's right. Just lie to him. Tell him you love him. He's fighting a war. He's going through all kinds of shit. Hell, lie to him. Make a mess now. Clean it up later. Like cooking dinner."

"Right," René said. Not that he knew anything about cooking dinner. He knew about eating. He knew about that. Cleaning up? I don't know.

Gigi looked over at Angel. "Why not?" she said. "What could it hurt?"

"And besides," Gigi said, "he's just lonely. When he gets back, he won't even want me. He'll go back to being Pifas. I mean, can you see that guy working steady. Being a father? Can anybody picture that?" She took a drag from her cigarette. "I'll tell him I'll marry him. That's what I'll tell him."

That was the thing. She didn't want to hurt Pifas. Nobody wanted to hurt him. Pifas was a funny guy, screwy, I mean that guy wasn't marriage material. No way in hell. But he got his feelings hurt kind of easy. It was like a part of him was made of glass. I never understood that about Pifas. He was a year and half older than me, but he was always following me around. Like a kid. I never really understood that. He was always a little lost, never quite found himself. One minute he was wanting to kick your ass and the next minute he was giving you the shirt off his back. I don't know. Maybe you just can't know anyone. Maybe that's not possible. One thing I did know—it would've killed him, if he'd have known that we were all sitting in a car at Shirley's talking about him. It would've killed him to hear us.

"I'll write the letter," Gigi said. "Tonight. I'll write it—and I'll mail it." She had this serious look on her face. I knew that look. I wore it all the time.

twenty-three

So the next day, I go to school. Like every day. René picked me up. It was kind of a routine now. René would pick me up. Except when his car was having problems—then we'd walk. So that day, he picked me up. And there, in the parking lot of Las Cruces High School, Joaquín Mesa and Charlie Gladstein and Ginger Ford are passing out black armbands. "Make peace, not war." They kept saying that to everybody as they handed out black armbands. René was already wearing his. I stared at it. Sitting there in René's car. Stared at his black armband and at him and at Charlie who was handing out armbands. I guess he was an activist now. I wondered what that felt like. To be an activist. "Make peace, not war," I told René. I kind of smiled.

"That's right," René said.

"You solve everything with a fist, René."

"Look. I don't go looking for fights."

"They just find you."

"I don't back down, Sammy."

"You sure as hell don't. Chingazos—that's what you know, René."

"You're all pissed off, ese. And fuck you, Sammy. I know more than chingazos. Why are you all pissed off all of a sudden?"

"I don't know," I said. And I didn't.

I just sat there. The first bell rang. Five minutes to get to class. We both just got out of the car, then walked inside. We were both in the same homeroom class. Spanish IV-S with Mrs. Scott. Jaime and Eric, they'd been in that class too. But they were gone now, like they'd never been there. It was at the other end of the school, our class. And god, the hallways were crowded. I was tired of pushing my way through. Tired, and as we're making our way through the halls, René says, "I don't understand you, Sammy. Something's eating you."

"A pigeon," I said.

"What?"

"Nothing."

I don't know why—but all that day I had a bad feeling. The pigeon inside was making noises. Charlie walked up to me at lunch and I felt bad because I wasn't wearing an arm-band. I thought maybe I should be wearing one. I mean, my dad and me, we talked about the war all the time. He didn't like it. I didn't like it. What was there to like about the war?

Guys like Pifas were getting killed. Shit. But I wanted to run, I think. It was too hard. Everything was too hard. I don't know why I was thinking those things. But that's what I was thinking that day. I just wanted to go home and sleep—and maybe when I woke up, the world would be fine, the world would be good, the world wouldn't be at war. I would be able to go to college anywhere I wanted to go. And it wouldn't matter whether I had money or not. Pifas would be home— saying stupid things, making me laugh. Because there wasn't a war. Jaime and Eric, what they felt about each other, well, it wouldn't matter to anybody. Nobody would care. Beause they weren't hurting anybody. And heroin would still be around, but nobody would be using it—because they didn't need it. They didn't need it to feel good. They didn't need it to help them get through the day.

Mrs. Davis wanted to know what was wrong with me. She said I looked distant. "Yeah," I said. "I'm a little distant." She wanted to see me after school. So, I went to her classroom after school.

"Your paper," she said. "Sammy, you're going to college, aren't you?"

I nodded. Pinche Harvard. Yeah, yeah. I started to cry. So I just left. I didn't know what was wrong with me.

I walked home. I stopped at the Pic Quick, bought a Pepsi and a pack of cigarettes. I was looking at the sky. And I felt small. And I remembered looking at the stars one night when

I'd been with Juliana. And I had felt as large as that sky. I had. That night. And now, now I felt small when I looked at the sky.

When I got home that day, there was a note on the table from my dad:

> Sammy—
> Power went out at work today. Came home early.
> Elena needs some new shoes so that's where we are.
> Don't cook tonight. I'll bring home some hamburgers.
> Oyes, you left the iron on this morning. You could've
> burned the house. Be careful. Where are you? Come
> home.

Come home. That's what he said. As if I were gone.

God. I was restless. Usually, I'd just pick up a book and read. And read. And nothing existed. Just the words on the page and me, and the whole world disappeared. But the whole world didn't feel like disappearing. Not that day. It wanted to stay close. Right by my side. The world. And it didn't feel good. It didn't.

So I went outside and sat on the porch. I looked across the street and saw Mrs. Apodaca working on her yard. He'd been dead for a while, Mr. Apodaca. But she was still keeping up the yard. And maybe her heart had healed. Maybe it had. Enough to care about a garden.

Sometimes, I helped her out, mowed her lawn. But only when she asked. She was proud as hell. And a pain in the ass. She just couldn't let things alone, couldn't give the citizens of Hollywood a break, just didn't have it in her. Her and her novenas and her holy water and her prayers, her and her hats, her and her strict ways. Nobody was ever good enough. But we'd made a kind of peace, she and I. We had.

I saw her take off her straw hat. She wiped the sweat from her brow. Then she saw me. She waved. I waved back. We were friends now. "You shouldn't smoke." That's what she yelled.

That made me smile.

She shook her head and kept working.

I took a drag off my cigarette. I looked up at the sky. I felt a little better. I wondered why I'd started crying in front of Mrs. Davis. What the hell happened there? I didn't know. Shit. Then, I see René's car pull up in front of my house. And Gigi gets out. She gets out—and I wave but I can see that something's wrong, something's really wrong. I can see that. I can see it on her face. And René, he gets out of the car, and he has this look on his face. And then Gigi, she looks at me, and she drops to her knees, and she starts crying and screaming like a crazy woman. "Sammy!" And I couldn't stand it. "Sammy!" And she cries and she cries and she can't stop because she doesn't even own her body anymore. And I walk toward her as she's kneeling there, and I pull her up, and I'm holding a question in my eyes, but I know I'm holding the answer too. And

297

my heart is breaking, seeing Gigi that way, and I want to tell her to stop, to please stop, and I know I had hate in my heart, I hated again, only I didn't know exactly who I hated, maybe my country, maybe Pifas for going off to Viet Nam, maybe myself for being all screwed up, maybe all the adults in the world who let bad things happen to hurt girls like Gigi.

And then, finally, Gigi, she stops crying long enough to tell me, to tell me, even though I already knew. "Sammy! Sammy! Our Pifas. Our Pifas is gone. He's gone, Sammy." And she looked at me, like maybe I might say something, maybe I could do something to change what couldn't be changed. "Sammy, God, Sammy, our Pifas is coming home." I knew what that meant. In a coffin. In a body bag. Pifas was coming home. Maybe that's what I had been feeling all day. Maybe that was it. Maybe my pigeon had known. But on the day Pifas left, even then I'd known he would never be coming back. Because even he knew it. "Sammy," she cried, "Pifas—"

I just held her. "He never got my letter, Sammy. He never got my letter."

"Doesn't matter, Gigi. It doesn't matter anymore." That's what I whispered. I kept holding her. That's all I could do. Just keep holding her. If I'd known all along that Pifas would never be coming home, then how come it still hurt? How come it felt like someone was taking a sledgehammer to my heart? "No," that's what I kept saying over and over. "No." What good did it do—to keep whispering no.

I remembered that night at the river when Gigi had sang for us, for me and René and Pifas and Angel. Mostly, I think she'd sang for Pifas. God, I'd never heard anything that pure. And I'd thought that the world should end like that—with a woman singing a song. But that's not the way the world ended. The world ended with a boy. Killed at war. That's how the world ended.

I don't remember how long Mrs. Apodaca had been there, standing beside us. With her arms around me and Gigi. I just remember hearing her voice. Soft. "Shhhhh," she kept whispering. And her voice was like a wind, the softest wind in the world. "Shhhhh," she said. And she smelled of lilac and mint. Like a garden. "Shhh," she whispered. And I just let her hold me and Gigi. I just let myself sob into her shoulder.

Gigi sang at the funeral. The Ave Maria. Didn't know she knew Latin. "I don't," she said. "But, well, I guess I just liked that song. So l learned it."

We hung out on my front porch after we laid Pifas in the ground. "Well, I guess I don't have to marry him," Gigi said. She didn't laugh at her own joke. We didn't either.

We didn't talk much. Mostly, we just sat there and smoked. And smoked. We didn't bother going back to school that day.

I told René what I'd thought the day we took Pifas to the bus station. "I thought maybe we should've taken him to Canada."

"What's in Canada?"

"Trees," I said. "A sky."

We went to the river.

We drank a beer.

Angel and Gigi and René and me. We sat there and looked at the river. It wasn't carrying much water. Not this year.

The day after Pifas' funeral, we went back to school. Charlie and his friends were still passing out black armbands in the parking lot. Gigi said she was gonna call off the thing they had. That's what she'd told us at the river. "What was the use?" she said. I looked at Charlie, and wondered if he loved Gigi. Hell, what did I know about love?

I took an armband from Charlie.

"Peace," he said. "Peace, Sammy."

Yeah, yeah. I didn't know anything about peace either. I looked at René. "Tie this thing on me, will you?"

René looked at me. "I thought you didn't want to wear one of these things."

"I didn't want to wake up this morning either. So what?"

"Don't talk like that, Sammy."

"Like what, René?"

"Like you've given up."

He tied the armband on me.

"Give up? Then why the hell am I wearing this?"

* * *

300

We walked through the hallway. Five more weeks, I thought. Five more weeks and I would be gone. I would be a ghost. I wouldn't matter a damn to these halls. They weren't built for me, not for Sammy Santos. That's what I was thinking when Colonel Wright walks up to René and me—right there, right in the hallway. Right there, in the crowded hallway. "What's this?" he says. And he reached for René's armband. Like he was gonna rip it right off.

René didn't say anything.

"I asked you a question, son."

René pulled away from Colonel Wright's grasp.

But the Colonel was mad. He was really mad. And he moved right up to René, right in his face. And he looked right at René and he says, "You're a coward, son. That's what you are." And he said it so loud that everyone around stopped, just stopped. And the hallway got real quiet. And then he pointed at René and he looked at all the kids and he said, "This here is what a coward looks like." And I thought René was going to explode, but my pigeon came awake right then, and I couldn't figure out why I'd hated that pigeon because I understood then that he always came around exactly at the right time, and so, me and my pigeon, we knew we had to get to work and do something. I kept thinking that if René lost it, he would take a swing. And he'd been arrested before, and if he took a swing, maybe his life would be over, and I couldn't let that happen. When the Colonel grabbed René's arm and tried to rip his armband clean off his arm, that's when I pushed him. That's when I pushed the Colonel away.

And the Colonel just stared at me. And I could see what he was holding in his eyes. Fucking good-for-nothing little son-ofabitch, ungrateful cockroach who doesn't know crap, who'll never understand anything about the business of living. God, I could see everything he was holding there. And it was a kind of freedom to see it. To see all his hate written there, in his eyes, on his face. It was so clear.

"Santos," he said. "I'll meet you and your friend here in the principal's office."

"No sir," I said. "I won't be at that particular meeting."

"What? Santos? You plan on graduating?"

"That's exactly what I'm planning." That's what I said. There were so many things I wanted to say to him, a thousand things—and then suddenly I didn't want to say anything at all. I was tired. Damnit to hell, I was tired. It had been such a long year. And I wondered when I would get to rest. God, I was so tired. And I hadn't even turned eighteen yet. I wanted to look that sonofabitch right in the face and spit at him—spit—just spit and keep on spitting.

He grabbed my arm. I hated the warmth of his hand. "Pifas is dead," I said. And he let go of me. He knew who I was talking about. He'd read it in the newspaper, he'd seen a picture of Pifas' mother kissing his coffin, clutching a flag—clutching a flag instead of clutching a son. God. "Epifánio Jose

Espinosa was killed in action. In Viet Nam. Epifánio. They brought him home. Not all of him, Colonel. They couldn't find his hands. Blown clean off. His hands, Colonel, they stayed in Nam. His hands stayed there, Colonel, but the rest of him, the rest of him, they buried yesterday. Say his name for me, Colonel. Say it. Goddamnit! Say his name for me." He grabbed my arm again and started dragging me toward the office. But I wasn't going to let him. I pulled away from him. I was stronger. He knew I was stronger. "Epifánio," I said. "His name meant epiphany. It's what happens at the end of a story or a poem when something is revealed. It means we've learned something."

He let go of my arm. He stood there looking at me.

"It means we've learned something, Colonel."

He stood there. Lost. He looked defeated, the Colonel. That's how he looked. But he was standing, and he was alive. And, Pifas, hell, he was dead.

René and I, we just kept walking down the hall.

I hadn't remembered my dream about Pifas, about all the people who were passing by in front of my house—waving at me. The living and the dead. Waving at me. I hadn't remembered. But that day, after the incident with Colonel Wright, I remembered. I'd dreamed Pifas' hands.

That night, before I went to sleep, René called. He just wanted to talk. I lay in bed talking to him. I told him about the dream I had. He said, "Sammy, soon you'll have better dreams." René, he'd changed. He was different now. He could have gone either way I think. He was going to live. I knew that now.

When I fell asleep, I had another dream. Juliana was walking down the street—and she had someone with her. It was Pifas. And she left him standing there in front of me. He walked up to me on the front porch. And I could see he didn't have any hands. And he was sad. And I was sad, watching him. And I couldn't do anything about his sadness. His sadness or mine. Couldn't do anything about it. And then as he raised his arms—his hands, his big beautiful hands, they were there. God, they were there. And he was waving. "Hey, Sammy! Hey, Sammy!" He wasn't waving good-bye. He was saying hello. Pifas, he'd come home.

welcome
to hollywood

"It's better just to forget
everything that's happened."

"Why is that, Sammy?"

"You can't change the past, Elena."

"I don't want to forget, Sammy."

"Well, I guess I don't either."

twenty-four

Things never end the way you expect them to.

We start off down one road—toward a place we've picked out on a map. A place we've spent years imagining. Then something happens. And everything changes. Maybe the problem is that we expect too much. I mean, what did I think was going to happen to me after high school was over? Did I think I was going to wind up in Hollywood—the one in California?

I don't know why I'd bothered to make so many plans. Eight schools—that's how many universities I applied to. I planned it all out, all by myself. And I never told anyone. But after the letters started coming in, I told my dad. Well, really, he's the one that always got the mail—so he figured it out soon enough. Eight schools. And that's just how many acceptances I got. Well, they didn't really know me, anyway. If they would have known who I was, they wouldn't have accepted me. All they saw were my grades and those stupid essays I wrote. So I told myself that really those schools accepted an idea of me.

Berkeley. That was the place on the map that I'd picked. And that school had said yes. And my dad had saved money, and he said yes too. Berkeley became a secret my dad and I shared for a few brief months. For a while, I really started believing that it was really going to happen. Me, Sammy Santos from Hollywood was going to Berkeley.

When my dad gave me the letter, my whole body shook. And when I opened it, I said, "They took me! They took me!"

My dad cried and said, "Of course they did, hijo de mi vida."

I didn't know I had that kind of happiness inside me. I thought all I had was that damned pigeon. Anyway, like I said, we spend years imagining and making plans. And then something happens. Something always happens.

Things never end the way you expect them to.

There were lots of parties the night we graduated. That was the plan—go to lots of loud parties. We were the generation of loud. Rock wasn't rock unless it was loud. What was Jimi Hendrix if he wasn't loud? What was Three Dog Night? What was Grand Funk Railroad? Loud, baby, that's what we liked. Except me. I hated loud. Hated loud and hated beads and hated bell-bottoms. I never liked slogans and that's what everything was. Sometimes, I wonder if I was ever really a part of my own generation. If I wasn't a part of my generation and if I wasn't a real Mexican and if I wasn't a real American, what the hell was I? I was my pigeon. That's what Elena had decided. I was Al, my pigeon. I'd given him a name. If the pigeon was gonna stick around, he might as well have a name.

Graduation was pretty damned dull for the most part. That was the school administration's plan. Dull. They loved their plans more than they loved the kids they taught. More than they loved us. They'd warned us about demonstrations. Graduation wasn't political. That's what they told us at practice. And it was also no place to demonstrate your egos, your originality, or your sense of humor. "Make your jokes somewhere else." Yeah, yeah. When Susie Hernández got her diploma, she raised her gown and showed the world her latest short dress. Here. Here's my sense of humor. She didn't care. Her father was in some bar getting drunk. Again. And Gigi? Gigi threw kisses. Like an opera star taking a bow after the opera was over. Kisses. Kisses for everyone. We all reached out to catch them. Some guy named Brian took out a big sign from under his gown that said, "Love and Grass." And Charlie Gladstein—not to be outdone—had a sign too, "Peace is a state of mind." René was sitting in the row in front of me. When Charlie whipped out his sign and showed it to the audience, René whispered, "Yeah, sure, it's right next to the state of Chihuahua."

And when it was all over, diplomas in hand, we marched

out. And the Class of 1969 was history. Our parting gift to Las Cruces High: a new dress code and a bronze plaque that read: "Love is the Answer. Peace is the Way." Oh, we were so fucking cool. Only we didn't know what love was. Peace either. Peace was not something the world taught us about. The only redeeming thing about that plaque was that Colonel Wright and Mrs. Jackson would hate it.

But now the plan was to do some serious partying. Some of us in our class had been born to do just that. And only that.

Me and my friends, we started out at my house—not exactly a center for wild blowouts. Dad had put up Christmas lights all over the porch. Red and blue, our school colors. Dad, he was so straight. And predictable. And steady. I laughed when I saw the lights. Funny. René thought it was really cool. Pifas would've said "Fuckin' A, Mr. Santos, Fuckin' A." It was really Hollywood, those lights. Some little kids came by and looked at the house. They laughed. But they liked it. I liked it too. And all the little kids, they brought other little kids. And they pointed. "¡Mira! ¡Mira! And it's not even Christmas."

And me, I was all dressed up for the occasion. I was wearing a new shirt. Green. The color of olives. It was the only shirt I'd ever picked out myself. Pure silk. Soft. Like my mom. Like Juliana's skin. Soft. My dad, he'd bought me everything I had. I'd never really cared. He'd just pick clothes out for me, bring them home, and he'd say, "¿Te gustan?" And I'd say, "They're great, Dad." He knew I didn't care. But this shirt, I'd picked it out myself. Cost me fifteen dollars. A fortune. And for the first time in my life, I went into a men's store and gave myself a good look in the mirror. Nice shirt. Fifteen dollars.

Gigi wore a dress the color of the sun. I swear that yellow dress glowed. That dress made you want to touch her dark skin. That was the point, I think. Gigi, she was something. She always had been, always would be, and I hoped one day she'd look at herself in the mirror and say it: "I'm something. I'm really something." Her and Charlie had broken up, gotten back together, broken up, and graduation night, they were back together. He was crazy about her. I mean, loco, baby. I mean that guy had it bad for Gigi. Gigi liked him too. But really, I think Gigi liked the idea of someone worshipping her. That's why she got mad at me—because I wouldn't always go along with her bullshit schemes. Because I didn't worship her. At least not in the way she wanted me to. Not that she wasn't great, Gigi. She was. Yup, she was something. But she was also hell.

But graduation night wasn't about love and dating—it was a group thing. We'd survived something together. A place called Las Cruces High. We were done with it. And it was done with us. So me and René and Susie and Angel and Gigi and Charlie and Frances and her new boyfriend, Larry Torres, who could still piss me off in ten seconds flat, we all went out together. No fights, I told myself. Keep your fists in your pockets.

We got in two cars. Angel and I wound up in the backseat

of René's car, and Susie and René looked like maybe they had a thing for each other. Bad idea, I thought. Susie didn't put up with much. Spoke her mind. René didn't like that. He said he did. But he didn't like that at all. No, they didn't go together any more than Gigi and Charlie. Already, Susie and René were in the front seat arguing about how many beers a girl should drink. "One. Maybe two," René said. "That's it."

"And a guy?" Susie wanted to know.

"Many as he wants. As many as he can handle."

Angel rolled her eyes at me. I laughed.

I lit a cigarette.

"Gimme one of those," Angel said.

"You don't smoke."

"Sometimes I do."

"Your mother's going to kill you."

She shrugged. "Just give me one," she said. So I did. She didn't even cough when she lit it. She was a natural. Maybe that wasn't such a good thing, taking to a bad habit like that.

She looked at me. "How come you never talk to me, Sammy?"

"I don't?"

"No. You don't. You talk to everybody. Except me."

"Is that true?" I felt stupid. Maybe it was true. Well, it was true. I never knew what to say to her. She was always so quiet. It seemed like so much work to talk to her. Even though I liked her. How could you not like Angel?

"Yeah, Sammy, it's true. You just see me as Gigi's friend—someone who follows her around. A cat she carries around. Or a dog she walks around the block."

"Where do you get that? People don't do that crap in Hollywood. Dogs. Cats. That's crap."

"You know what I mean. You think I'm just her little friend."

"That's not true." It was. It was true. Shit. I wasn't doing well here. She knew I was lying. Girls, they always knew. They had a little compass inside them.

She nodded. "You're in love with her, aren't you?"

"With who?"

"Gigi."

René and Susie had stopped arguing, and they decided to join our conversation. That was the problem with traveling in cars—no privacy.

"Hell no," René said. "He's not in love with her. You think he's fucking nuts? Are you in love with me, Angel? Are you?"

Angel looked at René like she'd look at a brother who was always being stupid in front of the whole world. "Who can love you, René? There's only one thing you want from a girl, and you want it when you want it. And if you don't get it, you move on. And if you do get it, you still move on."

Susie laughed. "The whole world knows about you, René."

"You and me don't have anything to do with what Sammy feels for Gigi."

"You're the one who brought up the subject, René," Angel said. Something was happening to her. She was busting out of herself.

René wasn't keeping his eyes on the road. He kept trying to turn around as he talked. That made me nervous. Angel was a better driver. "Well, I say Sammy doesn't love her."

"Drive," I said, "you're gonna kill us. I don't want to die. And I can talk, you know?" I looked at Angel. "I've never loved Gigi. I haven't. Not ever." I felt like I traitor. I was betraying her. Like there was something wrong with being in love with her. Like she wasn't worth anything. That's not what I meant. I felt like she was a part of me. What I felt for Gigi wasn't nice and neat. Not everything fit into neat little categories. Especially not Gigi. I've never loved her. I felt like I was slapping her in the face.

"So how come you and Gigi are always talking?"

"She's like my sister. She calls me. ¿Qué quieres que haga? You want me to hang up on her?"

"Admit it. You like talking to her."

"Sure I do. Who doesn't? So what? Who doesn't like talking to Gigi? She's like a sister."

"You have a sister."

"She's ten, Angel. Damn. Can't guys be friends with girls?"

"René can't." That was Susie. Then she and Angel started laughing. They were having a good time, laughing at René.

That was kind of a hobby for them—laughing at guys. Especially at guys like René.

"Tengo muchas amigas. Girls like my ass." René at least knew enough not to believe his own bullshit. His words were as empty as his wallet.

"Your ass is the only part of you they like," Susie said. She could be like Gigi sometimes.

"Name one," Angel said. "Name one girl who's your friend."

René was thinking. "Hatty Garrison. Hatty Garrison. She's my friend."

"You never see Hatty Garrison. Never. And besides, you asked her out, and she turned you down flat."

"You did? You asked her out?" I said. "You did?"

"That's a damned lie. I didn't. No way in hell."

"Yes, you did," Susie said. "The whole school knew. Hatty told Pauline. And Pauline told the whole school. Ya sabes como es la Pauline. She told the whole world."

René didn't say anything. "Why are we talking about shit like this? Chingao. Who cares?" He lit a cigarette as he drove. He looked at Angel. "Angel, you're my friend."

"Being friends was my idea. Not yours."

"Who cares whose idea it was? We're friends, aren't we?"

I watched Angel puff on her cigarette. "Yeah," she said, "we're friends."

"Not by choice," Susie said. "Guys. Guys are all the same. They don't know how to be friends with a girl. Not one damn guy."

"Gigi and I are friends," I said. I looked at Angel. "Angel and I are friends." I looked at Susie. "You and me, we could be friends. Only you're not interested in having guys be your friends, are you?—So what are you screaming at guys for? Hell, you're just as bad."

René laughed at that one. And then we were all laughing. At each other. At our dumb conversation. Who knew why we were laughing? Who cared? We just wanted to laugh. We'd known each other all our lives. We'd graduated from high school together. We were scared of what was going to happen tomorrow. Sure we were. Everything we knew was gone now. We were scared. Why not laugh? At the stupid things we said.

René parked the car in front of the abandoned farmhouse right behind Cruces High. Site of a hundred fights. That's where everyone went to have it out. That's where everyone went when they needed to explode—take out their rage on some other's guys face. I'd been there a few times myself. Against my will. And when it wasn't against my will, it was always against my better judgment. I hated to fight. But you'd never know it. Too many fights. That was the thing about high school. Too many fights. I was glad it was over.

That farmhouse, it made me think of Pifas. Pifas was always getting cars to follow him here. He could come to blows with someone he'd be hanging out with a week later. That Pifas. I missed him. "What are we doing here?" I said.

"Right this way," René said as he got out of the car. "Órale! We're gonna have some fun. Baby, baby, fun." Fun was his favorite word. Maybe that's why his mom called him Chiste. René was yelling and laughing like a crazy man. So we piled out of both cars and followed René into the old farmhouse, which wasn't anything but a small four-room adobe place with dirt floors and busted-out windows.

Once we were in the front room, René started lighting candles. And as he lit the candles, we could all see there was a table there, and on the table there were some bottles of wine and some plastic glasses, and there was some ice in an ice chest with beer in it, and there was Bacardi rum and Coke and lime to make cuba libres. And there was even some Fritos and potato chips and stuff. And after René finished lighting the candles, he screams out like he was James Brown or some- thing like that, "Yeeeooooow! ¡Órale, let's party! Let's swing some nalga, baby!" And then he let out another scream and took a swig from a bottle of Bacardi and then he yelled out, "Listen, everyone. Welcome! Welcome to Hollywood!" And then he just laughed like a pendejo. Like he was drunk. But he wasn't. He was just letting go. But, God, he made me smile, that guy. He could be so many different things, René. I was beginning to understand that he was a lot of different people. And that was the good thing about him, that he could be so many people, all in one body. And maybe all those people inside him were all fighting for control. I wondered how he was gonna turn out. "Welcome to Hollywood!" he screamed. "Where the girls tease you more than please you . . ." God, sometimes he was as good a performer as Gigi. He went on for a while, making us laugh. That's what he wanted to do, make us laugh. Because that had been Pifas' job. And Pifas was gone. So now René was taking his place. This party, I guess it was his gift to us. And he'd planned it and paid for it. All by himself.

It was fun, hanging out in that farmhouse. René must've worked hard to clean it up because the last time I was there, it was full of junk and all kinds of crap. He'd cleaned it up. In some places, there was the faint smell of urine. But not too bad. Who cared about a little urine?

It was fun. God, I hadn't had enough of that in my years at Cruces High. I hadn't. Too serious. I needed to change. Already, I was making other plans. To change myself. I was addicted to making plans.

We were drinking and smoking. But we weren't drinking too much. René and Charlie—they were the biggest drinkers. Angel, she was drinking more than usual. I noticed that.

After a while, a few more cars showed up. I guess René invited some other people. And after a while, there were maybe forty people there, and the radio was going, and people would dance when there was a good song, and everyone was laughing about the stupid things we did. And I could smell pot which was better than smelling urine. And this one girl did this great impersonation of Gigi's speech when she ran for president of the senior class, and we all clapped and laughed our asses off and Gigi said, "Not bad—but you didn't move your hips right." And then René starts reenacting that time when we were passing out flyers to change the dress code. "Change the dress code! Change the dress code!" he yelled. Just like he'd yelled it that day. Like he was selling peanuts at a ball game.

I remember sneaking out of the farmhouse to get some air. I looked up at the stars. There were millions. And from Las Cruces, New Mexico, in 1969, you could see them all. I swear. You could see every damn beautiful star in the sky.

And then I heard this voice, "Someday, Sammy, you're gonna be up there."

I knew that voice. It was a voice I'd keep with me forever. I didn't even turn around. "I don't think so, Gigi. But I like it here. On the ground. It's a good place. Maybe I'll be a farmer."

"Yeah," Gigi said, "maybe I'll be a nun."

We both laughed.

"You think in another life we were brother and sister?"

That made me smile. When she said that. "Maybe. Maybe we were."

"We had this huge hacienda in Mexico before the Revolution. And our father was this big badass patrón."

"We were probably twins," I said. "And our dad was a peón who worked for that badass patrón."

She laughed. It was a soft laugh. "I got you something," she said.

"What?"

"It's not much," she said. She looked in her purse and handed me her lighter. "Here," she said, "so you can see."

I flicked the lighter. In her hand she was holding a small pin of the Mexican eagle. The farm worker eagle. "It's for people who fight for good things, Sammy." She kissed me on the cheek, and pressed the farm worker eagle into my hand. When I clutched it tight, I thought of Juliana's fist.

"Gigi," I said. "Do you like my shirt?"

"That's a funny question."

"I'm a funny guy."

"Yeah. Yeah, Sammy, I like your shirt. It's a beautiful shirt. The most beautiful shirt you've ever worn."

"I want to give it to you."

"Really?"

"It's the only shirt I've ever bought."

"Really?" She laughed. "Estás loco, ¿sabes? You're one crazy Hollywood guy, Sammy."

"Yeah. I guess I am."

"You'd give me your shirt?"

"Yeah."

"When?"

"Now," I said. And so I took off my shirt. Not that I felt too naked. I mean, I've always worn T-shirts. My mom, she said a man should always wear a T-shirt. She took the shirt and stared at it. Then she put it on over her beautiful yellow dress.

And then she started to cry. "Shhhh," I said. "It's okay."

"I'm scared," she said. "What's gonna happen, now, Sammy?"

We never left the old farmhouse that night. All those plans we had about going to all those parties. Up in smoke, those plans. About three o'clock in the morning, people started wandering off. They played my song on the radio. Frankie Valli singing *You're just too good* and Angel came up to me and said, "Sammy, you want to dance?"

And I said, "Angel, I think I would."

And it scared me, the way she fit in my arms. It really scared me. And the way she smelled made me tremble. And I wanted to kiss her. And that scared me too. Because I didn't really know Angel. I knew Gigi. I'd known Juliana—at least as much as anybody had known her. But, Angel, I didn't know her. So why did I want to kiss her?

Because she fit in my arms.

When the song was over, we looked at each other. And then I felt stupid. She felt stupid too. So that made me feel better. Not much. But some.

And then we went outside and looked up at the stars. On

the radio, Janis Joplin was asking the Lord to buy her a
Mercedes Benz. In 1969, she was still alive. And so were we.
Angel and I, we listened to her sing. And we didn't say a word.
And I think we were kissing each other in our heads.

twenty-five

A couple of weeks after I started my job at Safeway, I got trained as a checker. I liked it, punching in all those prices. You had to think, concentrate, and you had to memorize all the prices. It wasn't bad. I could do this. For a summer. It was only for a summer. René got a job roofing houses. Shit. Hard work. "I like it," he said. "When I get home, I'm good and tired." Gigi, she was working at the Rexall Drug Store. "You should see who goes in there to buy rubbers," she said. Like I wanted to have a copy of the list.

We hung out. Some. Not a lot. But some. It seemed like it was gonna be a normal, quiet summer. That's how it started out.

And then one day, everything changed.

I woke up that morning. It was raining. And the breeze was cool. Not such a normal day. Not for the desert. I went into work, and half the checkers were out. Everybody had some lame excuse and the manager, Mr. Moya, he said, "Listen, you're on your own. No more training. That's over now. Can you handle it?" He'd stop by and watch me, and by the end of the morning he said, "You're a checker. You're a real checker." He said it like I'd done something, like I'd reached this goal, like I had a career. "You're from Hollywood, right?"

I nodded.

"I grew up in Chiva Town." I knew what he was saying *And here I am—the manager of Safeway.* That was a good thing. It was good. But I had other plans. What I didn't have planned was the phone call I got at about two o'clock that afternoon. Mr. Moya called me back to his small office. He had this serious look on his face. I knew something was wrong. He handed me the telephone. I didn't know the voice on the other end. No reason I should have known it.

"This Mr. Sammy Santos?"

"Yes sir."

"Look, son, your dad's been in an accident." Then he waited. The pause was too long. That scared me.

I could feel Al, my pigeon inside me, and Al was clawing at my heart. I couldn't say anything. And finally I heard myself say, "Is he dead?"

"No, son." And the pigeon settled down a little and got quieter. But my heart, God, I swear my heart—

"It's bad, son. It looks real bad." Then Al got up again and was flapping his wings and he was really beating the crap out of me.

The hospital wasn't far. Not far at all. Took me a couple minutes to get there. It had stopped raining.

God, the breeze was cool. Almost cold. For a June day. God, I was shivering.

They didn't let me see him before they took him into surgery.

"He's not conscious, son."

"Is he—?" I couldn't finish my question.

The doctor was nice. I didn't know anything about doctors. I'd never been to one. He was what I thought doctors would look like—looked just like the doctor who'd talked to us when they had taken Jaime in that night. That awful night. He was a gringo, had soft blue eyes. He was maybe fifty— about my dad's age. He was deciding what to say to me. "I don't know about internal injuries. Maybe some head injuries. The injuries on his head, they look pretty superficial. It's hard to tell right now. But his right leg, it's really bad. Don't know if we can save it."

"The leg doesn't matter. I want my dad."

The doctor nodded. "We'll do our best, son."

"If he dies, Elena and I, we won't have anyone. Do you understand?"

He nodded.

I reached for a cigarette, then realized I was sitting in an emergency waiting room.

"Aren't you a little young to smoke?"

I shook my head. "Mexicans from Hollywood start smoking when they're twelve." I smiled. I don't know why I said that.

He nodded. "Hollywood?" Then he smiled. "Oh, you mean the barrio on the east side?"

What other Hollywood would I mean? "Yeah," I said.

"How old are you, son?"

"Seventeen. Eighteen, September first."

"Going into the army, are you?"

He was trying to be nice. I knew that. He didn't have to be sitting there talking to me. But he pissed me off. He did. "You have a son?" I said.

"Yeah. He's nineteen."

"He in the army?"

"No. He's in college."

"Oh," I said.

I think he understood what I was saying. "Look," he said—and then a nurse came out and pulled him to the side. I thought for sure he was going to tell me that Dad was dead, that he'd died, that I'd lost him. And that Elena and I were orphans. Orphans in the world. America was the worst place to be an orphan. That's what I thought. What was I gonna do? Without him. What were me and Elena gonna do? Without a mother. Without a father. "We're going in now, son. It'll take some time. Maybe a long time. If you need to leave, that's okay. Or you can wait."

"Will he die?"

"I don't know, son. He looks pretty bad. Is he a fighter?"

"Yeah," I said. My bottom lip was trembling. It did that sometimes. I hated when it did that. Like my lip didn't give a damn what the rest of my body thought. My lip and Al, my pigeon who was doing some kind of wild, unstoppable dance inside me.

I watched the doctor walk through the doors. I walked outside. God, it was cold. For June. June was supposed to be hot. That was the plan. It was supposed to be hot. I lit a cigarette. As I stood there, I realized I hadn't asked anyone about the accident, about what had happened. He was hurt at work. That's all I knew. What the hell difference did it make, anyway. His leg? Fuck his leg. I didn't care about that.

I didn't know what to do.

I wanted to just sit there and cry. But I knew I had to keep it together for Elena.

I stood and smoked my cigarette.

Then I went home. And waited. I didn't think anything. It's like I'd turned myself off. I didn't want to think anything. Feel anything. I wasn't going to think of all the possibilities. Was death a possibility? I was just going to wait.

I don't remember what I told Elena. That Dad got hurt. I

don't remember. She wanted to come with me, to see Dad. I remember that. But I didn't let her. And she got real mad. Maybe I was wrong to leave her with Mrs. Apodaca. But what if something went wrong in the operating room? I didn't know. I didn't want to feel. That's what I really remember. It's hard not to feel. Try it sometime.

I remember sitting in the waiting room. Waiting and waiting. I'd go outside and smoke. Then come back in. I don't know how long I'd been waiting. Hours. And then finally, the doctor came out, and he said, "Your dad's in recovery." He shrugged. "His leg, well, we couldn't save it."

I nodded. Screw his leg. I didn't care about his leg.

I wouldn't leave the hospital until they let me see him.

And finally, they did. Dad was still groggy. Confused, I think. About everything. And his face, it looked beat up, and he had bruises everywhere. "Superficial," the doctor had said. "They'll heal in no time. They're just regular bruises." How could bruises be regular? Like gasoline.

I didn't know what to say, so I just took his hand. "Dad," I whispered.

"Sammy?" His voice sounded so tired. God.

"You're gonna be okay, Dad." I don't know why I was whispering. I just was. Then I thought, "He doesn't know about his leg."

"Sammy, I'm sorry. I'm sorry, I'm sorry."

"Shhhh," I said, "it's okay, Dad."

I stayed there until he fell asleep. He was sad. But even after he fell asleep, he was whispering my name.

I kissed him on the forehead before I left. That's what he always did. Kissed me on the forehead.

He smelled like blood. And like some kind of medicine.

It was night when I walked out of that hospital. The rain had washed the sky and the air was clean. It was like the windows had been dirty and now they sparkled. Now, we could start over again. But how many times in a lifetime did you have to start over? Dad. Dad knew how many times. But it was a question I would never ask him. I wouldn't like the answer.

I knew Elena was waiting, so I went home to her. She read me a story. That's how we did things now. She woke me up in the middle of the night, screaming. She was having a nightmare. She was a dreamer, Elena, always had been. Had good dreams. Had bad dreams. Always dreaming. I got up and held her. "Don't leave me," she said.

"I won't," I said. So I stayed there with her. So she wouldn't dream anymore.

The next day, my dad had to have another operation. There were some internal injuries, internal bleeding. They had to remove a kidney. I wasn't exactly sure why. But I took their word for it. What choice did I have?

I stayed all day. He didn't wake. I thought he'd never wake again.

I called Mrs. Apodaca, told her to keep Elena. I stayed the night, fell asleep, and when I woke, Dad was alive, his eyes wide open. "Talk to me," he whispered.

The doctor told me he wasn't sure if my dad knew what had happened to him. "You're tired, Dad, you should just sleep."

"Talk to me," he said. He wanted me to tell him.

I didn't know how. I didn't. But he was waiting, and I knew I had to tell him. "What's worse, Dad, losing a leg or losing a son?"

"Losing a son," he said.

"You still have a son, Dad." That's what I said. I waited, watched him nod, and then I said, "What's worse, Dad, losing a kidney or losing a daughter?"

"Losing a daughter."

"You still have a daughter, Dad." That's what I said.

I took a pizza home. I didn't have the heart to cook. Elena loved pizza. We ate on the porch, and she asked me a hundred questions about what had happened to Dad and what had happened at the hospital, and I answered them as best I could. Not that she was satisfied with my answers. She never was. She said Dad answered her questions better than I did. "That's because dads are smarter than brothers," I said. She shook her head. She knew bullshit when she heard it.

After we finished our pizza, I gave her a dollar and she and

Gabriela went in search of the ice cream truck. I was worried about Elena. She seemed happy enough as I watched her skipping down the street. But she'd had another nightmare. Mrs. Apodaca told me she'd screamed and screamed in the night. That scared me. She was scaring me. And Dad, I didn't know if he'd make it. He was scaring me too. I wonder if everybody knew that I was scared. I didn't want them to know. Not anybody.

Just then, as I was thinking all these bad things, René's car parked in front of the house. Him and Angel got out. God, his hair was getting long. And his skin was dark from working in the sun. And he'd lost some weight. He was wearing sunglasses and a black T-shirt and I could tell he was trying to be cool. And he was. René was always cool. "Pareces vieja, cortate la greña," I said. And we all laughed. My hair, it wasn't so short anymore, but it wasn't long. Not like René's.

"You're lookin' like a fuckin' Republican," René said. He took his glasses off. He'd been practicing. I swear that René. He cracked me up, that guy. "¿Y tú jefito? How's he doin'?"

"He's okay." Now I understood why people said thanks for asking. Now, I understood. "They're gonna give him a prosthetic leg."

Angel nodded. "I'm really sorry, Sammy." She was sweet. Her voice. Really sweet. "I'm leaving tomorrow," she said, "moving to Tucson." It just came out. Just like that. I'm leaving.

"Oh," I nodded. I wanted to tell her I'd miss her. But it

sounded stupid and awkward and dull. But it wasn't as if I was so damned creative with the words I used—even on a good day. I spoke like everyone else. I kind of stood there, and wound up saying nothing but, "Oh." What a fucking pendejo.

"We're going out. We're gonna meet Gigi and Charlie. We thought maybe—"

"I can't," I said. I thought I saw something in Angel's face. Like she was hurt. I stood there. I smiled at her. "I have something for you," I said.

I walked in the house and wrote something in a book I'd special ordered. Leather cover, the works. It was a beautiful book. I'd wanted it so bad. But it was just a book. It wasn't a kidney or a leg. And I wrote, "Be something, Angel. Be something for all of us. Love, Sammy."

I walked outside and handed it to her. She looked at the book and smiled. *"Great Expectations,"* she said.

"Yeah, *Great Expectations.*"

She kissed me on the cheek, and then she pointed softly at my chest, at the place where I had my heart. "Keep that, will you?"

A few days later, my dad was looking better. I didn't lose him, my dad. That was what mattered. He'd thought about a lot of things, I could tell. He was looking less tired, but he didn't look like the dad I knew. He would never look that way again. He aged after that. He'd always looked young. But not after that. "There was a truck full of lumber," he said. "And all of a sudden, it was raining two-by-fours on your old man." He tried to laugh. He never said another word about that accident. Later on, he'd sometimes talk about his leg, not the accident, but his leg. Talk about it like it was a friend he'd lost. Me and my leg, we used to do this. Me and my leg, we used to do that. He was consistent, my father. He didn't spend a lot of time licking his wounds.

I spent that day with him. He slept a lot. He was still tired.

I watched him sleep. And thought about things. Him and me.

Before I left, he said, "Go back to work." I knew what he was saying. Go back to your life. But he was my life. He and Elena. He kissed my hand. "You have your mother's hands," he said. Maybe another guy would've been pissed off to hear their father say that. But not me. I was happy to have anything that had belonged to my mother.

I'd had plans. Plans change. The summer was slow. I read a lot. René met some girl roofing a house. She'd given him a glass of cold water. He'd taken the water and her phone number. Her name was Dolores and she was one of those Mexicans who didn't speak any Spanish. God. With a name like Dolores. Okay. No Spanish. That was cool. This was America. Except she couldn't talk to her grandmother. All she said was, "Well, she's old, anyway." I didn't like her. Not because she didn't speak Spanish, but because of what she'd said about her grandmother—like an old lady didn't matter. But René liked looking at her. Who wouldn't? Take a picture. Lasts longer. Yeah, yeah. Gigi rolled her eyes when she met her. Right in front of her.

"That was so fucking rude," René told her afterward. We were sitting on my porch.

"Taking a girl out just cuz you want to get laid—that's what's fucking rude, René. So don't talk to me about rude. ¿Qué me crees? ¿Pendeja?" Gigi, now she knew Spanish.

"Lay off, Gigi, why can't you be nice to her?"

"What for? Like I should make nice to that pendeja when I won't ever see her again once you get finished screwing her?"

"Shut up, Gigi."

"No," she said. "I don't like her. And you don't like her either, René."

"You can be such a bitch, ¿sabes, Gigi?"

"Why? Because I don't put up with your babosadas? Look, just keep me away from your girlfriends, okay. I don't wanna know, René. Okay?"

"What about you?"

"What about me?"

"You and Charlie are acting like Mr. and Mrs. Gladstein." He lit a cigarette, blew out the smoke through his nose. "Screwing like rabbits."

Gigi crossed her arms. She was pissed. I thought she was

gonna slap the hell out of René. She reached in her purse. It was a suede leather bag, really, like all the hippies had. Charlie had given it to her. She rummaged through it, looking for cigarettes. "Here," I said. And I handed her one. I gave her a light.

She raised her head and blew out the smoke toward God. "René," she said. "Everyone knows I'm still a virgin." And then she laughed.

And then, René and I, we laughed.

God, we laughed. And after we stopped laughing, she slapped the side of my head. "You didn't have to laugh so hard, cabrón," she said.

I brought my dad home on a Sunday. Elena looked up the word "prosthetic" in the dictionary. "Plastic," my dad said, and then he knocked on it. "Better than wood."

I thought of the lumber that fell on him.

"Same shoe size," my dad said. Smiling. Sometimes, he was like a little boy, my father.

I cooked his favorite meal. Mine, too. A roast with potatoes and carrots and onions and gravy, an American meal. We sat down to eat. It was good. "I got my deposit back," I said. Dad looked at me. He knew what that meant. That plan, about going away to school, that plan, it had been changed.

"No," he said.

I looked at him. I wanted him to know that there was no way in hell I was leaving, not now. Couldn't leave. Wasn't possible. Wasn't possible for me to think of leaving him and Elena. And the money we'd saved, we were going to need it for other things now. I knew that. He knew that, too. And California, well, it wasn't a real place, anyway. Our Hollywood was better than their Hollywood. Yeah, yeah. "And I registered at State," I said. I let that statement hang in the air. Waited for him to grab it as it hung there.

He looked at me. "¿Cuándo?" He was sad, my dad. He looked at me. I knew what he was holding in his eyes: my Sammy, my Sammy, you worked so hard.

Don't be sad, I wanted to tell him. "Two days ago. I got off early from work. I went and registered."

He nodded. "I'm sorry," he whispered. He kept nodding. Then he looked down at his plate. He always did that.

"I don't care about going to college at a fancy school, Dad."

"Sammy—" I don't know what he was going to say next because he just stopped. He kept staring at his plate, then tasted the roast. "It's good," he said.

I looked at him. And we nodded at each other.

So that was that.

In August, I bought an old beat-up '55 Chevy truck that needed a paint job. All I needed was something to get me to school and to work—I wasn't planning on taking any road trips. The engine was good and the price was right. Smelled like an old truck. You know that smell. Like the sun had burned the insides out over the years. Like the sweat of all the owners. That was the smell. But I liked it. I'd never owned anything, not like that. I thought the whole world was watching. Not that the world cared. The world didn't give a damn about a seventeen-year-old punk from Hollywood buying a beat-up truck and driving it around town like it was a Mercedes. But I couldn't help but grin. I was grinning my ass off.

Mrs. Apodaca said I needed to paint it. She liked things nice and neat. Like that green lawn of hers. Like that sidewalk of hers that you could eat enchiladas off of. "Red," she said, "paint it red."

I drove to Gigi's house and honked. She came out. "Sammy! You got a truck! It's great! What a great truck! My brother knows someone who'll paint it for you, cheap. You should paint it yellow." She jumped in the truck. I laughed. At least she didn't have a purse so she wouldn't have to go through the charade of looking for her non-existent cigarettes. "You want a cigarette?" I said.

We drove to René's house around the block. We honked. His little sister came out and said he was still asleep. Ten o'clock and he was still asleep. But it was a Saturday. A good day for sleeping in. Not that I'd ever done things like sleep in. "Wake him up," Gigi said. "Tell him there's a girl out here who thinks he's cooler than Ringo Starr." Ringo Starr, that was Gigi's favorite Beatle.

René showed up at the door a few minutes later, barefoot and shirt unbuttoned.

"Vámonos, huevón!" Gigi yelled.

He shook his head. "¡Ay voy! ¡Ay voy!" He disappeared into the house and was out a few minutes later. Wearing his shades and a bandana.

"You look like a badass pachuco," I said.

"Like the look?" He was even wearing khakis.

"Yeah," I said. "You gonna wear that when you go before the draft board?"

"Hell no! Screw those guys. Let 'em try and take me. I'm not fucking going."

I was sorry I'd brought it up. Shit. "I can drive you to Canada now," I said.

He laughed. "Yeah, this thing wouldn't make it to Juárez."

"Hey, hey, don't talk like that about my new truck."

"New?" Gigi said. "Yeah, well, I have an aunt who thinks she's still in her twenties."

"Hey," I said. "I love this truck."

"It's okay," René said. "All you have to do is paint it black. Jet black." Great. Everybody wanted to change my truck to make it more acceptable. Red. Yellow. Black. Right then, right there, I decided not to paint my truck. People didn't like it— hell, they could walk.

We went riding around, the three of us. Me and Gigi and René. I drove down to the levee and parked the truck. As I was driving, I was listening to Gigi and René talking. Arguing, really, but that's how they talked. "You dumped her, didn't you?"

"I didn't dump her."

"You're a puto, you know that? A big puto."

"What's that supposed to mean?"

"If girls can be whores, then guys can be whores too. And you're a really big whore, René. You'll lie down and sleep with anyone. Puto. That's what you are."

He rolled his eyes and lit a cigarette. He looked around as I parked. Then he looked at Gigi and me. "This is the place," he said. "That night, this is right where Jaime and Eric were parked."

Gigi took René's cigarette out of his mouth—then took a drag—then gave it back to him. "Those cops, they didn't even try to find those bastards. What if they would've killed them? Jaime would be dead. Eric would be dead. And nobody would've cared."

She put her head on René's shoulder. "You saved them. Best thing you ever did in your whole damned life."

"I didn't save anyone."

"Yeah, you did. You saved them. They would've killed them."

"Yeah, yeah, I saved them. Now there are two homos wandering around in the world—free to be homos." Then he laughed.

"Don't be mean," Gigi said.

"I can't help it. I'm one mean sonofabitch. Every time I try and be nice, it doesn't work. Last night…," he shook his head. "Last night, I broke up with Dolores, then went out and picked a fight. I kicked some guy's ass. I did. Shit. I coulda killed that guy. With my fists. And you know something? I wasn't even hitting him. I was hitting—shit—I don't know who the hell I was hitting. Not him. Some guys had to pull me off. It's like I just wanted to hit and hit and keep on hitting."

René, I didn't know him. Just when I thought he was changing, he'd change back to what he was, to who he'd been. Like he was afraid to become someone better.

He laughed. But not a real laugh. "Someday, I'm gonna kill someone. And then what?"

"No," I said. "You're not."

"Why, Sammy? Because you said?"

"That's right. Because I said."

I didn't know it, but that was the last time I would see René. At least for a long time. Just like Pifas, he'd been drafted. He didn't tell us. I knew why he'd broken up with Dolores. I knew why he'd picked a fight and wanted to kill someone. I knew why. Maybe René knew why too. Such a smart guy. Such a waste. A week later, I went by his house, and his mom gave me a letter. "Te dejó ésta carta, mi'jo." I guess he wasn't the good-bye type. He just left. Maybe that's what he did to all the girls he went out with. One day, he was there—and the next day, he was gone. The letter was addressed to me and Gigi. So I called Gigi on the phone that evening, and I said, "René's gone. I went by his house. He left us a letter—you wanna hear it?"

"Yeah," she whispered. I could hear the hurt. I knew Gigi. I knew that thing in her voice. I knew exactly what it was. So I read it:

Sammy and Gigi,

Look, I just didn't know how to say it. Uncle Sam owns me now. Look, I could've done something about this, but I didn't. And now it's too late. Look, you're the best friends I've ever had. That's the fucking truth. Even you, Gigi. I'm not gonna write—I'm not into that. Jaime, he finally gave up writing to me. I never wrote back. I just don't do that. Maybe to my mom. Probably, I'll write to her. So, if you ever want to know how I'm doing, check with her. Listen, I know Pifas didn't make it back, but I'm not gonna get myself killed. I promise you. Make peace.

René Montoya from Hollywood.

Gigi was crying. She wouldn't stop. God, I felt like I'd spent half a lifetime listening to Gigi Carmona cry.

The other half, I'd spent listening to her laugh.

When I hung up the phone, I cried too. I cried for René

and for Pifas. I cried for my dad's leg. I cried for never having gotten to go to a school I worked my damned Mexican ass off to get into. I cried for my mother. I cried for Juliana.

I didn't see Gigi too often after that. I ran into Susie Hernández and she told me that Gigi and Charlie had formed some kind of rock band. Gigi was the singer, and Charlie was the lead guitarist, and Larry Torres' older brother Ronnie and one of the Díaz brothers, they were all in the band. But Susie didn't know the name of the band. "She's gone way hippie, that girl," Susie said. "Who ever heard of a Mexican hippie?"

"Chicana," I said. "Gigi's a Chicana."

"Oh, yeah. I forgot. Me, I'm just a Mexican." She laughed.

That night I called Gigi. But she wasn't home. I told her mom to have her call me. But she never did. I kept calling, but she wasn't home. "Nunca está aquí," her mother said. Never home. Nunca.

I started college a few days before my eighteenth birthday. It was okay. Better than Cruces High. That was for damn sure. I was taking fifteen hours. And I worked as a part-time checker at Safeway. I didn't care if I had to work hard. So what?

Sometimes I looked at my dad's leg. I wondered where legs went, the ones you lost. I wondered if they were like dreams. Once you lost them, they never came back. I wondered about that.

I was in search of another plan. In the meantime, I thought it would be good to keep myself busy. And so I did. One Friday afternoon, I got a phone call. It was Gigi. "We're playing on the grounds of the student union tomorrow at noon—Sammy, me and Charlie, we have a band. Something Cool—that's the name of our band. Will you come, Sammy?"

"Sure," I said.

The band wasn't so great. They hadn't decided who they were. Cheap imitations of a lot of other bands. I mean, really cheap. Tried to make up for everything by being loud. A lot of bands did that. And everybody was starting up a rock band after what happened at Woodstock. Concerts were happening everywhere. Nobody talked about money back then. But that's what it was about. Money. Only they all said it was about making music. Yeah. Sure. Anyway, what the hell did I know? I wasn't a big rock guy. I didn't know shit about music.

But Gigi, she had a voice. People stayed and listened to Gigi. She was wearing a long white cotton dress with yellow daisies all over it like she was a garden. And she sang that song, *Beautiful People,* and I swear I never wanted the song to end. She was better than Melanie or Joan Baez. God. I wanted to stay there. Stay right there and listen to Gigi singing forever.

I remember clapping and clapping and clapping. Pifas would have loved her even more—if he'd seen her, if he'd have been alive. And then another group came on, and they played real hard rock, and they looked like they were stoned. Looked like they didn't like taking baths. That was the new look. That was it.

I went to look for Gigi and Charlie. We talked a little bit. And I could see that Charlie and Gigi, they were really together now. And I was glad. Because Charlie, he was a good guy. I remember what I'd thought when I first met him. I'd thought he was like the notes I took on the margins of my books. Yeah, that was Charlie. That wasn't such a bad thing. And he loved Gigi. She needed that. If ever I met a girl who needed to be loved—it was Gigi Carmona.

"We're leaving," she said. "Me and Charlie, we're going to California."

"That's where everybody's going," I said.

"I'll write," she said.

But I knew she wouldn't. She was like René. She would be too busy living.

I nodded.

"I'm glad you came, Sammy. To hear me sing."

I nodded.

"You ever gonna leave Hollywood, Sammy?"

"I don't know. I don't think about it much." I wondered if she knew I was lying.

She rummaged through her purse and took out a black rag. She tied the rag around my arm. Gentle. Like she was afraid of breaking me. "For Pifas," she said.

I nodded. "For Pifas."

I don't know what she saw in my eyes. But she took my face and held it between her hands and held my face for a long time. As if she were memorizing me.

Her hands were as warm as the morning.

Then she let go.

I stood there, and watched her and Charlie walk away. Then Charlie turned around, "Hey, Sammy!" he yelled. "Next year in Jerusalem!"

I waved and yelled back, "Is that near Hollywood?"

Gigi turned around. I could see she was crying.

Don't cry, Gigi. Don't cry. I don't want to remember you that way.

That was the last time I saw Gigi.

I went to the river that night. By myself. I smoked a few cigarettes and listened to the radio. There was a keg party in the distance. I could see the small fire they'd built. I could hear laughter. Someone was laughing. That was a good sign.

I wandered around my entire first semester like a lost boy, didn't have friends, didn't want any. I'd lost them. My friends. They were gone. When I got too sad, I'd tell myself that I only lost my friends. My father, my father had lost a leg and a kidney. No tears on his face. What had I lost, anyway? But I couldn't help missing them. Pifas and Jaime and Angel and

René. And Juliana and Gigi. My heart hurt. So, I tried to stop thinking about them. I kept busy. I made other plans.

That spring, there was a girl wearing a yellow dress at the student union. Yellow as the sun. The girl smiled at me. And I smiled back. But I wasn't smiling at her. I was smiling at Gigi.

twenty-six

Sick. That was a word I'd grown up with. Enferma. In two languages. Sick meant death—at least in the logic of my boyhood. Because of my mom. In Spanish, that word was a woman. And now, Mrs. Apodaca, she was sick. Enferma. That word was becoming her first name.

On good days, Mrs. Apodaca still managed to step out into her garden. She'd give her roses a good, hard look, as if she was willing them to behave, to stay orderly, the way she'd trained them. But she no longer touched them, as if she was learning to let go of the things she loved. Letting go was not a virtue she'd ever practiced.

On bad days, Mrs. Apodaca stood at the door and looked out. On those days I don't think she even saw her garden. She was looking out to see something much bigger than what she'd planted in her small yard. She looked like she was looking out toward a swallowing sea. And what she saw in those

347

waters was not death nor the future, but the past. Her husband. Her daughter sleeping in her arms, newly born, resting in the open air for the first time. The streets of Hollywood. The food she'd loved to cook, the taste of it in her mouth. The simple houses of a village in Mexico. The sound of her mother singing a song in a voice as familiar as the lines of her working hands. It was as if she was trying to memorize the entire world she'd known—in case she might need a fragment of it after she died. That fragment might be her salvation.

I studied her like I'd always studied her. Like I studied a good book. Good books taught you what you needed to know.

My dad and I, we kept up her yard. We weren't as meticulous as she had been—but she didn't seem to mind. Or notice. That was the sad part. She wasn't out there telling us how to do it right. I missed her finger pointing at something in the garden—something only she saw. I missed that finger. I missed her disapproving voice. "No seas tan inútil." To be useless. That was on her list of sins.

I missed her sturdy body that dared anyone brave enough to try and break her.

I missed her disciplined eyes.

I was working in her garden one day, talking to myself. I do that. I still do that. I looked up and she was standing on the porch. "Who do you talk to?"

"No one," I said. I was still lying to her. I never learned.

"When I talk, I talk to God. Or Octavio. But you—you don't talk to God."

"Sometimes I do."

"Mostly you don't." There was still a remnant of disapproval in her tired voice.

"No. I just talk to myself, I think."

"I think you talk to Juliana."

I didn't say anything.

"Do you still miss your Juliana?"

I looked down at the ground and pulled a weed from her lawn. I hated this. Me and Juliana, we were a private thing. But Mrs. Apodaca was determined to get an answer. Even then, as her body was dissolving. Even then, she was stronger than me.

"Sometimes," I finally whispered. "Sometimes I still miss Juliana."

"You think of her too often," she said.

"Not too often."

"It's been a long time."

"No."

"Yes."

"I like thinking about her."

"Why?"

"I just do."

She shook her head. "She was young. And her father killed her. And you loved her." She looked at me.

"That's not a sin," I said, "to love someone."

"No," she said. "And it's not even a sin to love the dead."

"So there's no sin. So there's no problem."

She shook her head. "But what about the living?"

"The living know how to take care of themselves."

"No. That's not right, hijo. Óyeme, Samuel. The dead. It's the dead who know how to take care of themselves." She kept looking at me. "Let her go, mi'jito."

I nodded. But I didn't know how. To let go. I was like her. Refusing to let go of things. And she knew. And she couldn't teach me to unclench my fist. She couldn't. She knew that, too. I pulled out another weed.

"See," she said. "Only the living care about pulling weeds."

One afternoon, I dropped by her house. She wanted to go outside. I helped her to the porch. She sat there, looking out, saying nothing. And I knew she was already leaving. "¿Qué va a pasar con mis rosales?" She looked at me.

"I'll take care of them," I said. I remembered that summer when she'd shown me everything about caring for roses—about which parts of the bush were dying and which parts were being born.

We sat there for a long time. "Todo lo que nace tiene que morir."

I nodded. Mothers and girls and boys who went to war. And women who loved God. And roses. They all had to die.

* * *

I went to church and lit a candle for her. I whispered her name. All my life, people had been dying. And I wondered if it would ever stop. I knew it wouldn't. But I hoped anyway. "Don't take her." That was my prayer. What did God want with a strict woman who liked to lecture people and keep a neat lawn? What did God want with a woman like that?

A few weeks later, I came home after studying at the library. It was after midnight. Dad was waiting up for me. He never did that. He'd done it a little when I was in high school, but not a lot. "Mrs. Apodaca's in the hospital," he said. I saw what he was holding in his eyes. I hated to see that look.

"What about Gabriela?" I said.

"She's here. She and Elena are asleep."

I nodded.

"If Gabriela comes to live here—" He looked at me. "Is that okay with you?" He didn't have to ask. But he did. He was like that, my father.

That was the first time in a long time that I wanted to kiss him.

"Seguro," I said. "A man can't have too many sisters."

My dad nodded. "You're a good boy."

"I'm not a boy anymore, Dad." That's what I said.

"No," he said. "You're not." He looked sad, like he couldn't even talk. So he just whispered. "Mrs. Apodaca wants to see you."

He looked at me, tired, my dad. Weary—that was the

word. Mostly he tried to hide those things from me—but not tonight.

"She's been good to us," I said.

"You didn't always think that."

"She was hard."

"And now?"

"She's softer now."

"She was never as hard as you thought."

"I was a boy. I didn't know."

My dad put his hand on my face, then pulled it away. "Maybe it's you who's softer now?" It wasn't really a question. "It's not a bad thing to be soft," he said. He reached down and scratched his prosthetic leg. A nervous habit. Reaching for something that was gone.

Mrs. Apodaca was praying her rosary when I walked into her room. She placed her finger on her lips. I could see the outline of her bones. Her flesh was abandoning her, like leaves abandoning a tree in November. She looked so thin. And her skin was gray, like a spent and poisoned soil. I bowed my head and let her finish. I knew how she felt about her prayers. I wondered what she was praying for. I had always wondered that.

When she was done, she gathered the rosary and placed it on her lap. She looked at me. "Why haven't you painted your truck?" she said. Her voice was dry and old. But she wasn't that old, Mrs. Apodaca—in her fifties. It made me happy to see that look of disapproval on her face. "Tres años andas en esa troca."

"Sí, Señora, almost three years." I smiled. "I guess if I don't paint that truck, people are going to think I'm poor." I handed her a glass of water.

She half smiled at my joke—then drank the water slowly, her hands shaking. "People already know you're poor," she said. "And they also know that you take no pride in the things you own."

Still lecturing— that was okay. I'd fallen in love with her lectures. "Sí, Señora," I said.

"Estoy muy enferma," she whispered.

I nodded. It sounded like defeat. Back then I didn't know the difference between acceptance and defeat.

"Y cansada. Hijo, estoy tan cansada." She took a deep breath and closed her eyes. "I had a dream about your mother. She was beautiful, tú mama." That was the only time she sounded soft, Mrs. Apodaca, when she talked about my mother. "You were so strong when she died."

I didn't remember it that way at all. I shook my head.

She pointed to the chair. "Siéntate. I want to tell you something."

I sat and moved my chair right next to her bed.

"My mother and father, they gave me to God."

"I know," I said. "When our parents baptize us, they give us to God."

"That's not what I mean. My parents, they took me to a convent." She looked at me. "That's how it was done, sometimes. When your family was rich and you had too many daughters. They would give a daughter to the church." She smiled. "Maybe—," she shook her head. "Al cabo no importa. That's where I learned English, in the convent. Those were my assigned subjects—English and Spanish. That's what I would be teaching in the school we had." She looked at me. I knew she wanted me to ask her something. But I didn't know what to ask.

"You didn't want to be a nun?" Maybe that wasn't the right question.

"Seguro que sí. To be a nun is a holy thing. I wanted to be a nun. Yes. But I didn't want to teach the daughters of the rich. Anyone could do that. I wanted to work with the poor. Like Catherine of Sienna."

I didn't know anything about Catherine of Sienna. "And they wouldn't let you?"

"No."

"And so you left?"

"I wasn't obedient."

"I know," I whispered.

She laughed. Me too. Then we just looked at each other. Like we were friends. "But my family," she said, "they'd given me to the Church. I shamed them. I broke a promise."

"It was your father's promise."

"A good daughter keeps a father's promise."

"I don't think so."

"You're like me. Too ready to disobey."

"There are things we have to fight."

"You like to fight, don't you?"

"I've had to learn."

"Is it such a good thing to learn?"

"Yes."

"Why?"

"Because I want to live."

"To spend your days fighting? That's no way to live."

"You did," I said. I shouldn't have said that.

She didn't smile. She didn't get angry. She didn't say anything. She looked at me. And I wondered what her eyes had been like when she was a girl. "There was a gardener." She shook her head. "He brought me here, ese jardinero."

"Mr. Apodaca?" I said.

She nodded. "Octavio."

I understood now. Why she never spoke of Mexico. And why she carried herself the way she did.

"Was it hard?"

"I hated it here," she said. And then she squeezed my hand. "It was just a place to run to. Because I could never go back. I had to choose. Octavio or Mexico. And here—," and then she smiled. "Oh, but I had Octavio." For a moment, I could imagine her as a girl, running away from the convent with a young man named Octavio Apodaca. A young girl like Gigi. Like Angel. Like Juliana.

"I've written everything down," she said. She took out an envelope, the pages bursting out from it. "I want you to give this to Gabriela—when she's old enough." She pushed the envelope into my hands then looked away. "Will you?" she whispered. "No tengo a nadie." I remembered the day I'd caught her crying in the church. "I lost three in the womb before Gabriela. God never let me see—" She stopped. I hated to see her cry, to see her so weak. I hated that. Sometimes, when I was growing up, I hated her for being strong. I'd wanted to see her just like this. Weak. I'd sometimes prayed for her to break.

I was ashamed.

She tried to keep speaking, but her lips were trembling.

"I'll be a good brother," I said. "I promise."

She fell back on the bed and nodded. I wanted to wipe her tears. But I wasn't sure if it was the right thing to do. She closed her eyes and nodded. "I ran," she said. "But from God? You can't run from God."

We all belong to God. That's what she'd told me once. So that's what I whispered, "We all belong to God."

She nodded, and kept nodding until she fell asleep. I sat there, staring at the envelope with the story of how she'd come to the United States. The story for Gabriela, so she'd know.

I sat there for a long time. When I got up to leave, she

opened her eyes and smiled at me. "There's a picture," she said, "of me and your mother before you were born. It's in my house. I want you to have it." She closed her eyes again. "If you see anything else," she whispered, "just ask Gabriela."

"No," I said. "That's enough."

I don't know why, but I kissed her hand. I thought of Pifas, his hands, how they'd stayed in another country. Maybe something was growing there, in that piece of ground where Pifas' hands lay buried. I wondered if roses grew in Viet Nam.

I kissed her hand.

I came home. I tried to study. I went to bed. I woke up in the middle of the night. I was dreaming of my mother. She was wearing a white dress. She was young and she was calling my name.

I got up, put on my pants and walked across the street, shirtless and barefoot. I walked into Mrs. Apodaca's house and looked for the picture of her and my mother. It was on Mrs. Apodaca's dresser. They were so young, my mother and Mrs. Apodaca. They looked like girls, like sisters. I never thought of Mrs. Apodaca as being beautiful. But in that picture, she was as perfect as a new moon. I took the picture and held it. I sat in that room for a long time. In the morning, when I woke, I was lying on Mrs. Apodaca's bed, hugging the picture of her and my mother.

Two days later, Mrs. Apodaca died.

But she and my mother were alive in that photograph.

The day after Mrs. Apodaca's funeral, I had my truck painted cherry red. I hung up one of Mrs. Apodaca's rosaries on the rearview mirror. It smelled of roses. After a while, I took to talking to Mrs. Apodaca when I drove that truck. Even now, that rosary is hanging from my rearview mirror. When I drive, I still talk to her. Well, I don't really talk to her. I argue with her. She still thinks she has all the answers.

twenty-seven

I still hear from Jaime. After everything that happened, he and Eric finally got together, and then, well, Eric was killed in a car accident. Accidents, they happen. They happen all the time. That's how life is. We have plans. And then something happens. And everything's gone. Like Mrs. Apodaca's garden. Like my father, who got up to get a drink of water in the middle of the night, and had a stroke. He hung on for a while, but he was so sick. And he finally let go. "Voy a ver a mi Soledad." Gone to see my mom. Those were his final words. The day after his funeral, I found a sign he'd painted on a piece of plywood among his things. He'd made the sign a couple of months before his brother was supposed to come home from serving in the Korean War. The sign said: "Welcome to Hollywood. Population 67." Then the 67 was crossed out and said 68.

But his brother never never made it back. He was shot two

days before he was supposed to come home. In Korea. A bullet right through his heart.

Tonight, I'm sitting here, trying to remember the boy I was when I fell in love with a girl named Juliana. We lived in a place called Hollywood. I can still see the streets and the houses—small—all of them. Some of them neat and taken care of, some of them as ragged as the people who lived in them. Some of them, more or less in the same shape as when they were built. Some of them, with rooms added on in every direction, rooms added on with leftover materials. You didn't call a builder. You didn't call an architect. You did it yourself. And it came out like it came out. The one thing you never did was move.

Some of us made it out. Most of us didn't. Not alive, anyway. Not fair. Hell no.

When she was a little girl, Elena used to ask me, "If you could be anybody, Sammy, just for a day, who would you be?" I never had an answer. But now, I have an answer. If I could be anybody just for a day, I'd be Jesus Christ, that's who I'd be. I'd go to all the graves. I would stand there. I would close my eyes and lift my arms. I'd be Jesus Christ—I'd stand in front of the graves of all the people I loved. And I'd raise them back to life.

All of them.

And after they were all alive again, I'd hug them and kiss them and never let them go. And I would be happy. I would be the happiest man in all the world.